The writer was born in]   .. now lives in St Albans with her husband and grown-up son. She was educated at East Barnet Grammar School and then pursued a secretarial career. Her hobbies are gardening, cooking and needlework.

She has had stories published in women's magazines, and 'Nan's Secrets' is her second novel.

She is currently working on 'Nan's Choices' which is the third in this five-part family saga, originally inspired by anecdotes of her grandmother's early life.

NAN'S SECRETS

Stella Cullip

Nan's Secrets

Vanguard Press

VANGUARD PAPERBACK

© Copyright 2001
Stella A Cullip

The right of Stella Ann Cullip to be identified as author of this work has been asserted by her in accordance with the Copyright, Designs and Patents Act 1988

All Rights Reserved

No reproduction, copy or transmission of this publication may be made without written permission.
No paragraph of this publication may be reproduced, copied or transmitted save with the written permission or in accordance
with the provisions of the Copyright Act 1956 (as amended).

Any person who does any unauthorised act in relation to this publication may be liable to criminal prosecution and civil claims for damage.

A CIP catalogue record for this title is available from the British Library
ISBN 1 903489 27 X

*Vanguard Press is an imprint of
Pegasus Elliot MacKenzie Publishers*
www.pegasuspublishers.com

First Published in 2001

**Vanguard Press
Sheraton House Castle Park
Cambridge England**

Printed & Bound in Great Britain

Dedication

With love and gratitude to:

Rob - the long-awaited son, who made my life complete.

Ken - no daughter could have had a more caring father.

The friends who were there when I really needed them:

Anne, Carol, Kim, Linda and Pat.

PART I: 1947 - 1948

"Hello, Mum. It's me, Rita."

Like an uncanny echo from twenty-five years ago, the words sounded in Nan's ears. Silently she stared at the bulky figure hesitating in the shadows of the basement doorway. It was not her daughter's form she saw, but that of her own younger self.

She fleetingly experienced the same churning sensation of fear that had assailed her on that previous occasion. Then she had been the one on the doorstep, a baby in her arms and three small daughters clustered about her, as she had waited for her own mother's response. Having returned from Canada, still recovering from her traumatic experiences there, she had sought out the only refuge she knew, at number thirty Holfield Terrace.

She had been so terrified that Emily Fisher would send her packing, and oh, the relief when she and her children had, albeit grudgingly, been allowed to share her parents' home.

Returned abruptly to the present by the glacial cold of that March night in 1947, already being hailed as one of the most bitter winters ever known, she reached out a hand and drew Rita through the doorway.

"Come in out of the cold then, girl. You're letting all the warmth out - and there's not much of that, goodness knows!"

In the dim light of the basement passage, Rita was a

pathetic sight. Hunched up in a shabby brown coat, head and shoulders swathed in two faded woollen scarves, she was a very different figure from the last time Nan had seen her.

It had been the summer of 1945, when the whole country was still scarcely able to believe that the terrible war years were finally over. Nan had waved her off quite cheerfully as Rita had gone with her boyfriend, Matt, to spend a holiday with his family, who lived and worked on the inland waterways in the Midlands. Just like a kid let out of school, Nan remembered sadly, as she relieved Rita of her battered case and then her other burden, while the girl shed her outer garments.

Looking down into the face of her second grandchild, whose existence until this moment had been unknown to her, Nan's eyes blurred. When Rita had not returned from her holiday, her mother had not really been surprised. Rita had always been the irresponsible, 'flighty' kind. After the war years spent in the munitions factory, it must have seemed like heaven to find herself among Matt's scattered family who led a gypsy-like existence on the canals. Matt himself was still officially in the army, but with the war over, Nan guessed he felt it unnecessary to return from his leave.

Rita had sent the odd, misspelt postcard or note at first, and Nan was sure that her daughter was quite happy. She had inherited the same wanderlust and disinclination for roots and responsibilities that her father had possessed so abundantly.

It had been these very traits that had led to much of the anguish that Charlie Stuart had caused Nan, and brought such a traumatic end to their marriage so long ago in Canada. Gazing down at her sleeping grandson, Nan wondered fleetingly if he stood any chance of a stable future with such a heritage on his maternal side and the affable, feckless Matt as a father.

As usual, Nan's practical common sense quickly dispelled her musings when the baby stirred and Rita held out her arms for him.

"He's been ever so good on the journey, Mum, but I expect he'll want a feed soon. Could you let me have some milk to warm up? I don't think I've got enough to satisfy him."

"You still feeding him yourself? What's he called and how old is he, then?"

"His name's Benjy and he's nine months. He was born last June. But he's not very big and it seemed easier to go on feeding him myself as much as I could. Cheaper too..."

Nan unwound the baby's shawl and was repelled by the sour, unwashed smell that it released. Clearly he needed a change of clothes. A good bath wouldn't go amiss either, thought Nan, as she caught her daughter's anxious eyes.

"Right, my girl. Let's get you both sorted out. Then you can tell me why I've not had a word for over a year to let me know your whereabouts."

"I'm really sorry, Mum, honestly. It was just that Matt's family were always on the move - I was never much of a one for writing, you know that - and when I realised I was expecting..." Her voice tailed off and she twisted together her ringless hands, chapped and reddened from the cold.

"...you thought I'd be angry and really give you what for!" Nan shook her head sadly. "'Course I'd have been upset, Rita. I always tried to bring you up to have some proper standards and to know right from wrong. But since I was pregnant myself when I married your father, as I never kept any secret from you girls, I could hardly be too disapproving, could I?

"Disappointed, yes. After all, it's no start to a marriage, worrying about a little one, especially when you haven't two halfpennies to rub together, but I thought you knew me well enough to realise I'd always stand by you. Same as I would any of my girls".

Rita's face crumpled and she started to sob quietly. "Oh Mum, I'm ever so sorry. I didn't know how you'd take it, especially as me and Matt have never got married. His family aren't like us - they have different ways of going on."

"So I'd imagine!" Nan sniffed, then shook her head as she drew Rita within the comforting circle of her arm. "You are a silly wotsit and no mistake! It upset me far more not hearing from you for all those months. Just a card at Christmas and no address for me to write back. Tell you the truth, love, I'd have been surprised if you hadn't brought me home another grandchild. I half guessed that's why you kept away."

She nodded down at Rita's swollen stomach that threatened to burst open the buttons on her stained and shabby winter dress, partially covered with a moth-eaten grey jumper. "By the looks of that, I'd say it won't be too long before he has a brother or sister. Am I right?"

"Yes, Mum." Rita gazed at her anxiously. "That's why I've come back, really. You see, Matt's got into a bit of trouble - had a row with his dad - and the family threw us out. Matt was desperate trying to look after me and little Benjy, and with the new baby coming, we just didn't know what to do for the best.

"So we thought if I came back and stayed with you for a while, he could try and get some work by himself - labouring or even signing on as a merchant seaman for a few months. Then p'raps we can get on our feet." She looked pleadingly at Nan.

Rita, like her sisters, had an unshakable faith that when they had a serious problem their mother would always provide a solution. No dilemma was so impossible that Nan could not resolve it. They firmly believed this, and, subconsciously aware of their trust, Nan unfailingly rose to the challenge.

Now, in the short term the answers were relatively simple. "Come along into the kitchen, both of you. Billy's the only one home tonight, so we can get you sorted out in peace and quiet." Nan opened the door into the familiar, homely surroundings and spoke cheerfully to the grey-haired figure busy at the table with his woodwork.

"Look who's here, Billy. The wanderer has finally returned!"

Billy Wright smiled delightedly as he got up to welcome the newcomers.

He was very much a patriarchal figure in Nan's family now, although there was no blood tie at all. Ever since he had entered their lives when Nan's brother, Fred, had drowned under the ice at Alexandra Palace back in the twenties, Billy had become an indispensable member of the household and far more than just a lodger.

He and Nan shared a strong and loving companionship which to strangers often made them appear like man and wife. But that had never been an option. Although Billy had long ago confessed to Nan that he loved her very deeply, owing to the injuries he had received in the trenches in the first Great War, he had been physically incapable of any married relationship.

On Nan's side, he had accepted that she would never fully recover from the loss of David Harris, the Canadian doctor whom she had met again in London during the war years and later promised to marry. While escorting evacuee children to Canada, his boat had been torpedoed and all were lost. Nan had got on with her life, and valued enormously the bond that existed with Billy, but he had always known that David would never be replaced as the one true love of her life.

Now Billy gave Rita a cheerful hug, before putting on the kettle for the ever-welcome 'cuppa', their usual panacea in moments of stress or celebration. Nan settled Rita beside the range, where their carefully hoarded fuel ration was burning low, and vigorously attempted to poke some more life into the blaze.

"How we're expected to keep body and soul together in this weather I do not know. The coal ration's a joke and it doesn't seem as though this cold will ever end. I've never known snow like it – well, except in Canada of course - but there folk were prepared for it every winter.

"Now I'll heat up some milk for little Benjy and some soup for you. You look just about fit to drop, my girl. Then we'd better sort out where you're going to sleep. That baby needs his nappy changing, if I'm not mistaken, and I daresay a good wash wouldn't go amiss for either of you!"

Billy smiled, knowing how overjoyed Nan must be at the return of her daughter after so long. He methodically cleared away the mess from the table, where he had been putting the finishing touches to a doll's cradle that he was making for young Miranda's second birthday, next month. No doubt she would be fascinated at the arrival of her new baby cousin.

The effort of finding her way home to that north London suburb in the appalling weather conditions, waiting on draughty stations or at windswept bus stops, before her money ran out and forced her to beg lifts from strangers, seemed now to have caught up with Rita.

Thankfully she relinquished the baby to Nan, sank down into the haven of the old armchair and allowed herself the luxury of abdicating all conscious responsibility to her mother. The latter was in her element. She ransacked the battered case to find some clean baby clothes, heated up a bowlful of water and laid Benjy on a clean towel on the kitchen table before she stripped and bathed him.

Billy made the tea, sliced bread and warmed up some leftover soup from the family supper, which he laid on a tray in front of Rita. By the time she had finished the simple meal, Nan had Benjy dressed in his nightclothes and settled on her lap, as he sucked contentedly at a bottle.

"He's fine, Rita. Although I must say he does seem a bit thin and pale. I think he could do with some fattening up, couldn't you my pet?" She smiled down at the big blue eyes that regarded her solemnly from beneath a downy thatch of wispy fair hair.

"He hasn't been too strong, Mum. Keeps on getting coughs and colds, and can't shake them off in this bitter weather. I've been at my wits' end sometimes." Rita gazed dolefully at Nan, who thought she had really not changed much from the miserable youngster worried about laddering her last pair of stockings just before setting off to a local dance.

"Don't worry, love. Now you're home again, living in a proper house instead of traipsing about those draughty canals, he'll soon be fit and healthy. You look as though you could do with feeding up yourself."

"Well, it's been difficult living with Matt's family on the barge - it was very cramped - and I didn't have an easy time when Benjy was born, or carrying this one, come to that."

"So what was this trouble that Matt got into?" Nan put

the baby on her shoulder to wind him and looked enquiringly at Rita. "How serious was it?"

"It was just the family really. His brothers and dad got drunk one Saturday and he got into an argument with them. One thing led to another - his mum started shouting at me, said I was lazy and good-for-nothing, just because I was tired all the time - and in the end they threw us off the barge.

"Matt sold a few bits and pieces to get some money for my fare home, and put me and Benjy on a train south. He promised me he'll write as soon as he gets a job with some regular money coming in. He was going to walk to the winter quarters of one of the travelling fairs, where a cousin of his was living. Thought he might stay with them for a little while and see if they needed any casual labour, just to earn his keep. When the weather gets better he's going to make his way to the coast and try and sign on with a merchant ship."

Nan nodded. "At least he's trying to support you, love. Shows he's got some sense of responsibility, even if he's showing it a bit late. You know you're welcome to stay here till the baby comes, although things may be a bit tight for space, and that's a fact."

"But I thought it would be just you and Billy here. Haven't Joan and Harry got a place of their own by now?" Rita yawned widely and struggled to keep her eyes open.

"There's nothing they'd like better, but it's this post-war housing shortage. Harry doesn't earn a fortune working in the wireless shop and it seems cheap places to rent are like gold dust nowadays. So many families bombed out and looking for new homes. So for the time being they know they'll have to stay on here.

"I'm only too happy to have them, and little Mandy is a treasure. I'm out quite a bit with my job, so Joan has the place to herself a lot of the time. It's not often a case of two women sharing the same kitchen. Mandy still has her cot in their room to save on heating, so the other bedroom on the top floor is empty. You and Benjy are welcome to have that. Irene certainly won't be wanting it again."

"How is she? I've often wondered if she's still in Cornwall. Has she married that sailor of hers, yet?"

"She's fine. Happy as Larry she is, down on that farm. One of the few good things to come out of the war, that was. Joining the Land Army was the best job she could have found anywhere."

Nan smiled as she thought of her other twin daughter. Rita and Irene were certainly not identical, in looks or temperament. The former was placid and happy to drift through her days, taking the line of least resistance. But Irene was the total opposite.

She was Nan's kindred spirit in many ways, with her practical common sense, her love of the land and growing things, her homemaking skills and her no-nonsense attitude to life.

But she was not completely like her mother. For behind Nan's down-to-earth practicality, there still ran a strong vein of romanticism that all the hardships of her life had never quite erased. Therein lay the similarity with her eldest daughter, Joan. Although Nan would stoutly assert that she loved each of the girls equally, deep down there was a special empathy with her first-born.

This sprang in part from the few happy memories Joan invoked of Nan's life in Canada, and also from the shared secret, which neither had ever divulged to another soul, regarding Nan's first grandchild, Miranda.

It was Joan's voice that now sounded in the passage and she came into the room, followed by the thin, wiry figure of her husband, Harry.

"Brass monkey weather out there, Ma, and no mistake! Reckon there'll be another fall of snow before morning."

"Well, if you will go gadding about to the pictures, when anyone with any sense is sitting at home by the fire, it's your own fault, my lad!" Nan shook her head at him in mock rebuke. As he grinned cheekily back, she thought how dear he had become, this son-in-law she cherished like her own offspring.

Joan was staring wide-eyed at her younger sister. "Rita! Where on earth have you sprung from?" She affectionately embraced her and then registered the presence of the now sleeping baby that Nan had placed in the chair by the fire.

"And who's this? Don't tell me it's yours?" She crouched beside the sleeping bundle and gently brushed a stray tuft of hair from the smooth-skinned forehead.

"His name's Benjy, not 'it', and of course Rita's his mum. What d'you think of your new nephew, then?" Nan bustled about making a fresh pot of tea and Billy winked at Harry as the two men sat down at the table, away from the feminine conclave around the fireplace.

The two sisters eagerly caught up on the main events of the period they had spent apart. Joan, like her mother, had always guessed that Rita was living quite happily in the bosom of Matt's unorthodox family and expected that she would turn up again in Holgate, sooner or later. Her own life had been on a much more conventional course since the end of the war.

She had settled contentedly into the domestic routine, looking after baby Miranda, running the house and devoting herself to the rehabilitation of her husband, Harry, after his traumatic experiences fighting overseas.

For long months she had believed him killed, when he had been left behind on Sicily, wounded and separated from his army unit. Cared for by the local peasants, suffering from amnesia, he had been ill for weeks. It was during that period he had lost his left arm in a primitive amputation, after a bullet wound had become gangrenous. Eventually his memory had gradually returned and he had made his way to Rome, where he had finally been rescued and sent home after the city's liberation.

Poor Joan had been under an enormous emotional strain as a result of her own personal problems during the war, which she was forced to keep secret from her newly returned husband. Instead, she made a supreme effort to restore his self-confidence and help him come to terms with his physical weakness and disability. This process was happily accelerated when they learned that Joan was pregnant. He soon returned to his old cheerful self, with his indefatigable cockney sense of humour.

He quickly learned to cope with only one arm and used the knowledge he had acquired as a radio operator in the Army to secure a job in the local wireless shop. Old Mr Cooper, who owned the business, took a real liking to Harry, and Joan was thankful to realise that he had found a safe niche in life. Miranda's birth seemed to complete the metamorphosis, and she was now the apple of her father's eye.

Nan left them all talking and went upstairs to open the spare room and do her best to warm it up as quickly as possible. She lit a small oil stove, made up the bed with clean sheets, piled on quilts and blankets and tucked two hot water bottles inside. As she went to draw the curtains, she paused for a moment and looked out at the thick flakes whirling past the window. The street, deserted and silent, appeared like an alien landscape in its white mantle.

As always, the sight of snow was a reminder to Nan of her years abroad, so long ago, and the horrific winter when she had been abandoned with three small children in the Canadian backwoods. How near they had all come to dying, but somehow she had ensured their survival. It was her sister, Ruby, who had died in that God-forsaken shack - having given birth to Mavis, her legacy to Nan.

In the next few days Rita and Benjy quickly became a familiar part of the household at number thirty. Rita had never been domesticated by nature and in no way interfered with Joan's normal routine. If asked, she would cheerfully wipe up or peel potatoes, but if left to herself, would drift about the house or curl up by the fire with a film magazine on her lap.

Benjy proved to be a fretful baby at first, and Joan and Nan were concerned to improve his diet and build up his skinny frame. He had a hacking cough and permanent sniffles, which worried them both.

"Once we get some better weather Rita must take him out for long walks to get the sunshine on his poor little body. We'll ask Harry to get the old bassinet up from the cellar again. Mandy's too big for it now, and I think Billy said one of his cronies from the market could lay his hands on a push-chair that Harry could do up for her."

"When the better weather comes!" Joan sighed and looked out at the snow-covered back yard. "I'm beginning to wonder if that will ever happen, Mum." There was a listless, depressed tone in her voice and Nan looked at her thoughtfully. Increasingly over the last weeks she had felt that Joan was becoming very despondent, and Nan was concerned about her eldest daughter.

"Is everything alright, love? Is it just the weather

getting you down, or is there some other worry? I'm not being nosy, but I'm always here if you want to talk about things."

"I know, Mum." Joan smiled gratefully and looked down at the pink jumper she was knitting for Miranda. "I suppose it's just everything getting on top of me, for no real reason. It seems the chances of our finding a place of our own are so small, and although we're grateful to you for having us all here..."

"...it's not the same as your own home. I understand, Joanie, believe me, I do. Of course I'd be sad to see you all go - you know how much I love having little Mandy around - but everyone should have their own place. Besides, you'll need more room if you and Harry decide to have another little'un, won't you?"

Joan flushed and twisted her wedding ring round and round.

"I wouldn't hold your breath waiting for that to happen, Mum. These days Harry is more wrapped up in the shop than anything else. You know he's always putting in overtime and he and Mr Cooper are so full of plans for the future. Another baby is the last thing on his mind at the moment." It was obvious from her tone that this was a sore subject and Nan was thoughtful, picking her next words carefully.

"Everything is alright with you and Harry though, isn't it? I know how difficult it must have been for you to get...close to each other again. You were apart for so long, and so much happened to both of you." There was a long silence as both women remembered that dreadful episode in 1944.

Joan had believed Harry killed and embarked on a love affair with Oliver, one of the fighter pilots at the RAF base in Kent, where she was stationed with the WAAFs. It was the great passion of her life, and when Oliver was killed during the D-day landings she was utterly devastated. Immediately after this she received news that Harry was alive and coming home.

Assailed by an enormous guilt for her unwitting betrayal of her husband, Joan had been further shattered by the realisation that she was pregnant with Oliver's child. It was Nan with her usual common sense, tempered by compassion, who had persuaded Joan to keep the truth from Harry and allow him to believe the baby to be his - conceived in the first few days of reunion with his wife.

The two women had never spoken about Miranda's parentage and they were the only ones who knew the truth. The little girl with dark eyes and straight brown hair was seen to inherit her mother's looks, although Oliver too had been a darkly handsome man.

The silence lengthened and then Joan said quietly, "I know I'm very lucky to have Harry and Mandy. He's devoted to us both and his plans for the future are centred round making a good life for us all. But I'm twenty-eight years old and after coming through the war, I just can't imagine that the rest of my life is going to be spent in some little house in Holgate, cooking and cleaning and looking after Harry and our kids!

"I just feel there must be more to life than that, Mum. I feel so...empty, sometimes. Like all my feelings are withered up inside me. Mandy is the only part of my life that brings me any real sense of purpose or joy."

Her words faded into silence and she buried her face in her hands. Nan knew that her daughter was remembering the passion she had found with Oliver, the plans they had made together for after the war. They had talked of travel, maybe even living abroad. Oliver wanted to write and Joan loved talking to him about books and art, letting him introduce her to a world outside the mean streets of Holgate's grey suburbia.

Quietly Nan held her daughter and swallowed the lump in her own throat. It was odd how history repeated itself within the family, she thought. Her beloved David had talked to her of their future together after the war. He was determined to legally free her from Charlie, her first husband, who had abandoned her with their three children to starve while he ran off with Nan's own sister, Ruby.

In all the years since, she had heard no news of Charlie, and David had been sure that his solicitors would make it possible for Nan to marry again. Then the two of them would return to David's home in Canada, within the sound of Nan's beloved Niagara Falls, and they would be happy for the rest of their lives together!

Only the war had robbed her of David, as it had robbed Joan of Oliver. But Nan at the age of fifty-three was resigned to living out the rest of her days in number thirty . Her fulfillment would come through seeing her girls settled, and enjoying her grandchildren. Billy was a faithful and loving companion and Nan ensured that her own days were too busy to allow brooding over what might have been. The nights, of course, were a different matter.

Now she searched for words of comfort and wisdom to offer Joan. "I understand how hard it must be for you, Joanie, and I've no easy answers. All I can say is, make your happiness where you can. Be glad for the small joys in this world, and above all make sure your days are well occupied. That way you'll have no time to dwell on the past - or dread the future, come to that.

"Concentrate on Mandy while she's still at home. The baby years go fast enough, so make the most of them. Once she starts school you'll have more freedom and then you can think of doing some sort of job outside the house. You could even train for something new. You were always the brainy one of the girls, and women seem to be in demand nowadays. Try and plan a future for yourself, not just as a wife and mother, important though that is."

"Yes, of course you're right, Mum. I must be more positive. Harry's a good husband and he deserves a better wife than I am. I'll try and live each day as it comes and shake myself out of this stupid depression. When I look at poor Rita with no word from Matt and no idea what the future holds for her and Benjy, not to mention the other poor little thing, I ought to be shot for moaning.

"Besides, we've got Irene's wedding on the horizon this summer, and that's something we can all look forward to, can't we?"

"That's it, love, keep smiling, eh?" Nan squeezed Joan's hand encouragingly and reached up to the mantelpiece for Irene's last letter. This was one daughter who was always a source of comfort, even at a distance.

"She says that Robert's ship will be docking at Plymouth later this month, so they'll have some time together and hope to finalise all the plans for the wedding. They want to come up for a long weekend so they can have a chat with the vicar and sort out all the details. Irene's determined to have you as matron of honour and Mandy as a bridesmaid. I wonder if she'll be a bit young, though."

"Oh, she'll love it, Mum. You know how she enjoys dressing up. Besides, I'll be right there to keep an eye on her in the car and at the church. I wonder what colour dresses Irene wants us to have?"

"I daresay it'll be a case of take what you can get! We all took rationing for granted during the war, but nearly two years later and there still seems no end to it. I never thought we'd see the day when bread was on the ration!"

"Well that's one thing Irene won't have to worry about. Living on a farm I expect they make their own and have all the butter and eggs they can eat."

"Still, she's always been good about sending us parcels, hasn't she? No doubt she'll be loaded down when she comes for the weekend with Robert."

"I'm looking forward to meeting him - he sounds a nice chap, doesn't he, Mum?"

Nan nodded. "Yes, I think she's done alright for herself all round. Gets on really well with his parents and they'll have one of the workers' cottages to live in as soon as Robert's demobbed from the Navy. Irene reckons he's longing to get back on the land again. His family have lived at the farm for three generations, so I can't see them moving. I'd dearly love to see it for myself."

"Well you'll be able to go down for a holiday when they're properly settled. Or help out when she has another grandchild for you!"

"There can't be too many for me. Especially when they're as gorgeous as this little madam." She held out her arms to the sleepy-eyed toddler who peered round the door, having finished her afternoon nap.

Miranda was certainly a little charmer. She was a serious looking child with huge brown eyes and matching hair secured in two tiny pigtails. She was interested in everything and always full of questions. Forward for her age, her imagination peopled her world with unseen friends, and when something amused her the small chubby face would split in an enormous smile as the wide eyes beamed trustingly at those around her.

All of the household was enthralled by her winsome

ways: Nan was always ready with a cuddle and bedtime story; Billy delighted in fashioning wooden toys that were so scarce in the shops these days, and Harry would make her shriek with excitement when he tossed her up in the air or gave her rides around the house on his shoulders in what he called a 'flying angel'. Even little Benjy would give her a toothy smile and stop his grizzling when she appeared beside his bassinet to jiggle him about and sing him a nursery rhyme.

Miranda was the epitome of childhood innocence and unquestioning happiness. Looking at her sometimes, Nan would offer a silent prayer that nothing should disrupt this beloved first grandchild's secure home life.

By the end of April the thaw had finally set in and the bulbs in Nan's window boxes were belatedly blooming. The whole house gleamed under the strenuous cleaning onslaughts of Joan and Nan (with a little assistance from the ballooning Rita) as they prepared to welcome home Irene and meet her fiancé for the first time.

Billy had offered to sleep on a camp bed in the basement 'front room' (the sitting room used only on high days and holidays) so that Robert might have Billy's bedroom to himself. Irene would have to sleep on a mattress on the floor in her own old room, as Rita and Benjy now slept in the beds the twin sisters had previously used.

Billy had brought home an armful of flowers when he did the marketing for his little greengrocery shop, so Nan was able to brighten the place with tulips and daffodils, and although the furnishings of number thirty might be showing their years of wear and tear, not a speck of dust could be found anywhere. The air was filled with an appetising aroma from the huge pot of stew simmering on the stove, with its ingredients from carefully spent meat coupons, not to mention the bountiful contributions from Billy's shop.

Nan could scarcely speak when she opened the basement door to Irene, and wordlessly embraced this much-missed daughter. The latter was somewhat taller than her mother and the hours working outside in all weathers had given her cheeks a healthy glow. Her shining fair hair was worn in two braids encircling her head, and her youthful slimness had now filled out a little with the addition of strong muscles built up in the years of labouring on the farm. She and the tall sailor beside her, with his wavy fair hair and twinkling blue eyes set in a tanned face, made a handsome couple.

That first evening the kitchen of number thirty was a cacophony of noise and laughter. They all had so much news to catch up on and everyone seemed to speak at once. Nan and Billy busied themselves unpacking the generous provisions that Irene had brought, which were so welcome in those days of still stringent rationing. A chicken and a duck, both dressed ready for cooking; eggs, carefully wrapped; a home-cured ham; cheese and butter; and pots of home-made jam and jelly. What a treasure trove they unearthed from Robert's kit bag!

Of course the main topic of conversation was the forthcoming wedding and Irene had a list of matters to sort out while she was paying her visit to Holgate. With rationing still such a problem and Robert's relatives all living in Cornwall, it had been decided to keep the numbers quite small. Irene would be married in the local church where Joan, and Nan before her, had both embarked on matrimony. Nan was determined to provide the wedding breakfast, such as it was, herself.

"As the bride's mother, that's my privilege", she told

Robert, when he attempted to protest. But she willingly left to him the responsibility for flowers, cars and the photographer. The couple would have a few days staying in a hotel in London as a short honeymoon, before travelling back to Cornwall.

"Robert's hoping he'll have finished with the Navy for good by then, so we'll be able to move into our own cottage straight away." Irene's eyes glowed with enthusiasm as she described it to Nan.

"It's so lovely, Mum, I wish you could see it. It's about five minutes away from the farmhouse where I live now with Robert's mum and dad. Of course it all needs painting up and Robert wants to modernise it as we go along - maybe even put on an extension when we start a family - but it's right next to the orchard and there's a stream running at the back. I'll have my own little kitchen garden at the side - it's everything I've ever dreamed about, Mum."

"I'm so thrilled for you, love. You deserve to be happy, and I know your Robert will make sure you are. He's obviously a sensible, steady chap, and sharing his love for the farm, you're bound to make a go of it together."

"I'm really glad you like him, Mum. I think you'll get on alright with Mr and Mrs Tregaron as well. They're very quiet, country people, but ever so kind and they've always made me feel part of the family - even before Robert and I got engaged."

"It's nice that they're coming up for the wedding. I know it's a long way to travel for a couple of nights, and it can't be easy for them leaving the farm with all the animals and that."

"Oh, Jem, the stockman, will take care of things, and they'd have hated to miss the big day. With Robert being an only child, he means the world to them."

"I wish we could put them up here. But you can see how it is, now that we've got Rita and Benjy sharing your old room, and by mid-June the new baby as well, perhaps."

"Don't worry. They'll be quite happy staying bed and breakfast at the Railway pub, and you're having them here for the other meals, aren't you?"

"I certainly am, although I reckon it's going to be bedlam on the day. I'll do as much cooking as I can beforehand, but all the sandwiches and such will have to be made in the morning. Reckon Billy and me'll be up at the crack of dawn to get it all done!"

"Same old Billy. I don't know where we'd all have been without him over the years." Irene glanced at her mother fleetingly and thought it a shame that she was still mourning for her beloved David, even though the devoted Billy was living under the same roof. Irene was too down-to-earth to fully comprehend the depth of her mother's feelings for her lost fiancé. She was also, like the rest of the family, unaware of Billy's personal history that precluded the possibility of his ever taking a wife.

The wedding clothes were a paramount problem in view of the ever-present rationing. But Nan had always been adept with her needle, which had helped her daughters enormously through the war years, when she became an expert at 'make do and mend'. Now the 'New Look' was fashionable and Nan scoured the shops and markets to find sufficient material to make herself a smart blue dress that reached to mid-calf, with a basque effect over the hips. Her waist was still small enough to allow for the nipped-in style, and when she examined the fit in the mirror, she had to admit to a modest satisfaction.

She found a small, pre-war hat in a cupboard and

covered it with the lining of an old coat, which she dyed to match her new dress. Adding a wisp of white veiling gave it quite a festive air. In her best peep-toe white court shoes and matching short gloves, she felt she wouldn't let the bride down, which had been her main fear.

For, delighted as she was that Irene had found a husband from a comfortable, farming family where her future security would be assured, Nan was slightly nervous of acquitting herself properly with these new in-laws.

Irene looked a picture in the slim-line dress, with its slightly flared hemline and draped bodice. She insisted on wearing fresh white roses in her head-dress to match those in her bouquet, which were mixed with pink and white carnations. The long veil, which reached to the floor in a train behind her, had been in Robert's family for several generations. It was a delicate mist drifting over her gleaming hair, which for this special day was brushed free from its usual braids.

Joan looked dignified and elegant in a two piece costume of rose pink with a matching veiled, pillbox hat. She carried a small posy of sweet peas and freesias and, with her dark hair swept up away from her face, made the perfect foil for the bride.

Standing quietly between the two sisters as they waited for the hired cars to take them all to the church, Miranda looked quite angelic. Her white short dress with its puffed sleeves and round neckline was decorated by a broad blue satin sash and she wore white socks and ankle strap shoes. Her hair had also been brushed free of its pigtails and hung almost to her shoulders beneath a silk wreath of artificial blue and white flowers. In her hand she carried a tiny basket of mixed rosebuds.

As Billy took a snap of them all for his family album,

Nan swallowed yet another lump in her throat. It had been that sort of day from the start. Mr and Mrs Tregaron (or Isaac and Betty, as they insisted she call them) had arrived first thing to offer help with the food preparations. He promised he was a dab hand at slicing bread and his wife was soon stirring the glacé icing for the butterfly cakes. They both took to Billy straight away, and any awkward feelings Nan had felt about not being good enough, quickly disappeared forever.

The June day was a scorcher, which was wonderful for the wedding, but a trial for Rita, who looked like a ship in full sail in her voluminous pink maternity smock. She drank endless cups of tea and then had to make corresponding trips to the outside lavatory. She thought she was a week overdue, and by the look of her, Nan thought that might be under-estimated.

When the cars arrived to take them to church, Nan turned for one last look at Irene. She was standing beside Billy, who looked as proud as punch to be giving her away. If only this marriage is not beset by the trials and tribulations of poor Joanie's, Nan thought, as she gave her daughter a reassuring smile, telling her, "You look beautiful, love. Your Robert's a lucky chap!"

The service went off without a hitch and everyone said the usual complimentary things about the bride and her attendants. Miranda behaved perfectly and it lightened Nan's worries about them to see Joan and Harry beaming proudly together as their daughter posed for the photographer on the church steps. At least they were united in their love for her, even if their marriage was flawed in other ways.

Back at number thirty, the reception was soon in full swing. The 'front room' had been cleared of most of its furniture to accommodate a trestle table across one end and wooden bench seats down the sides - all borrowed from the local community hall. Nan's food was universally praised and the happy couple cut the single-tiered cake amidst the usual jokes and awkward speeches.

There were several good luck telegrams, including one from America. Nan sighed momentarily as she thought of Mavis, the youngest of her four girls. Her letters were infrequent and usually full of the luxurious lifestyle she enjoyed in her palatial home with its swimming pool, servants and large cars.

After the war, Mavis had wasted no time in following her G.I. fiancé, Irvin, back to America, where they quickly married.

Nan had known that Mavis always intended to find a wealthy husband, and she had done just that. Irvin's father owned his own flourishing business, and since Irvin was an only child, it seemed that Mavis was set for life.

In all the years of Mavis growing up, Nan had made every effort to treat her with the same devotion that she had given the other three girls, but in her heart she knew that she had failed. It would always be a source of regret that she could not honestly believe that she had fulfilled the promise she had made to her sister, Ruby, who was Mavis's natural mother. But the only person privy to that secret was Billy.

Robert's best man, a fellow sailor, told some jokes that broke the ice, and after a few sherries, beers or glasses of port, the company was ready to kick up their heels and enjoy a dance to the strains of the piano accordion, played by Billy's friend from the market.

"You must be very proud of your Irene, Nan my dear. She's a lovely girl and a hard worker too. Isaac and me couldn't wish for a better daughter-in-law, and that's a fact." Betty Tregaron raised her glass of port and lemon in a silent toast to Nan, as they stood by the window getting a breath of air, while the youngsters executed a wild Conga through the basement rooms.

"I'm just so thankful she's found a steady lad like your Robert. I know how much she loves the farm life, and it's what I've always wished for her. She's over the moon about the cottage you're giving them."

"I do hope you'll pay us all a visit soon. We'd make you very welcome, and it's a lovely part of the world, if I do say it myself." Betty gave her comfortable chuckle and surreptitiously eased the band of her corset, which was beginning to give her 'what for' in the heat of the party.

It was only after they had all noisily waved off the young couple in their taxi, and called goodnight to the last revellers at around two a.m., that Nan and Joan suddenly realised they had not set eyes on Rita for a while.

"Perhaps she heard Benjy and went up to see to him. Or maybe she decided to take herself off to bed. She must have been tired out after all the excitement. It's not easy carrying in the summer months, I remember that myself."

Nan smiled reminiscently and then turned abruptly towards the back door as she heard a faint sound from the yard.

Stepping outside she scanned the darkness, and then a faint voice moaned from the shadows, "Mum, Mum, I'm over here. The baby's coming. The pains are ever so bad now. Oooh!!!" Rita's anguish became somewhat noisier and Nan hastened to bend over her daughter. She was hunched in the corner behind the coal shed and one leg was bent awkwardly beneath her bulky figure.

"Rita, girl! Whatever are you doing out here? Why didn't you tell us when you started?"

"It's all happening so quick, Mum. I came out to get some fresh air, 'cos I was feeling a bit faint inside with all the crowd and noise, just before Irene went off. When I got out here I tripped over something - Mandy's spinning top, I think it is and I couldn't get meself up. I reckon I've broken me ankle!

"Then the waters broke and the pains have just got quicker and quicker. I tried to call out, but everyone was making so much row with the music and dancing, nobody heard me." She groaned loudly as another contraction surged through her body, and Nan squeezed her hands whilst Joan stroked the hair back from her damp forehead.

"Joanie, fetch Billy and Harry to help me get her inside. I don't think she'll wait for the midwife. Go and put some water on to boil and then fetch blankets and clean sheets to make up a bed on the kitchen floor. It'll be easier than trying to get her up the stairs in this state. 'Sides, we don't want to wake the little ones - that's the last thing we need! Oh, and fetch some clean towels and baby clothes. Seems to me my new grandchild is very eager to make an entrance!"

The next half-hour passed in frenzied activity. Billy, Harry and Nan carefully supported Rita back indoors, trying to keep her considerable weight off the damaged foot. Joan soon laid out a makeshift but comfortable bed on the floor, filled every available vessel with water to heat on the stove, and then joined Nan in offering what comfort they might to the suffering Rita.

Billy set off to bring the midwife while Harry went to the call box to phone the doctor and tell him about the injured ankle. Nan uttered a silent prayer that Rita's moans would not reach enough of a crescendo to disturb the sleeping children above.

She fleetingly recalled the last baby she had delivered, in such contrasting surroundings. That had been in the bitter cold of the Canadian backwoods, in the primitive shack, where Ruby had come in search of refuge. Her daughter had been Mavis, a tiny, puny object that Nan had feared would never survive. Shortly after the birth, Ruby had died, with her last breath extracting the promise that Nan would bring up Mavis as her own child. It had been the start of many dedicated years that had cost Nan dear, as she strove to overcome her instinctive antipathy towards the child, who was the ever-present reminder of Ruby's betrayal with Nan's own husband, Charlie.

Now Nan was soaked with sweat herself on this hot summer night, as she encouraged Rita to give one last push. "That's it, love. Nearly there, pet, nearly there." Then Joan was weeping unashamedly as she watched Nan lift up the wrinkled red form, squalling into life, as they both said together, "It's a boy, Rita, a lovely little boy!"

They had just finished cleaning up mother and baby between them when Billy arrived with the midwife, and the doctor hot on their heels. Harry had been sitting amid the wreckage of the wedding reception in the 'front room' wishing he hadn't given up smoking when convalescent after the war.

By the time the doctor had bandaged the ankle, which was only twisted, not broken, and the baby had been weighed and pronounced by the midwife 'a handsome young fellow', Nan was practically out on her feet.

The men gave Rita a 'chair lift' upstairs to Nan's room, so that she could sleep undisturbed, and Nan was more than ready to climb wearily into the bed in the room above, beside young Benjy. It was nearly four a.m. and she had been on her feet for twenty-two hours. A wedding and a birth in one day was really a bit much for anybody she thought, as her head touched the pillow and she sank into immediate sleep.

It seemed the next moment that a tiny voice was babbling in her ear as Billy and Miranda appeared in the room - the former to proffer a welcome cup of tea to Nan, and the latter bent on telling the sleepy Benjy about his new baby brother.

"Oh, Billy, you are a star! I really needed that cuppa." Nan smiled fondly at her reliable old friend as he set about changing Benjy's nappy, while Nan gave Miranda her usual morning cuddle.

"Well, I reckon you could do with a longer lie-in, Nan, but I daresay Rita will be needing some help with the little'un. Joan and Harry are already clearing up the muddle left over from the party. I know Harry promised he'd get the borrowed trestles and benches back this morning. They'll need 'em for Sunday school later on."

"I feel fine, thanks, ready to cope with anything. After all, it's something to celebrate - another daughter happily married and a third grandchild safely delivered by me own hands!" They smiled at each other in complete understanding, and Nan thanked providence once again for a life that was now so blessed. After the vicissitudes of her early years and then all the horrors of the war, it seemed that she had finally reached a safe harbour.

She understood that Joan had her marital problems, but sincerely hoped they could be ironed out with time. Irene looked set to have a secure, happy marriage with her new husband and his family. Mavis was safely ensconced in her luxurious lifestyle - well out of range of mischief-making - in America. Best of all, Nan had three healthy grandchildren whom she was thoroughly enjoying.

In the difficult times that lay ahead, she was to remember that moment of mentally counting her blessings, and think ruefully, "You should know at your age, just when life seems on an even keel, some nasty surprise is always waiting round the corner."

The rest of the summer passed relatively peacefully. At least, as peacefully as possible in a household containing a new baby; two small children; a married couple experiencing increasing strains in their marriage; and two people in their fifties, who sometimes wished they might enjoy each other's company without so much intrusion from the younger generations.

One piece of news that surprised them all came from America. Mavis was pregnant. She had never made any secret of her lack of maternal instincts, so Nan presumed that perhaps she was feeling obliged to provide an heir to Irvin's family business. She could not imagine the worldly-wise Mavis being the victim of an 'accident'.

Rita's baby, named Luke Matthew, was a contented, chubby infant with a mass of gingery brown curls, which were a legacy from his father. Little Benjy, by contrast, was a rather solemn, undersized child, which Nan secretly assumed was the result of his unsettled early months spent with 'those gypsies' among his father's family. Rita was very loving towards her children, but in a rather absent-minded way.

"Feckless, that's what she is," Nan would say to Billy disapprovingly, when yet again she had answered the baby's wail for its next bottle, because Rita had wandered off to the shops and forgotten the time, chatting to some of the girlfriends from her years at the munitions factory.

"You do too much for her, Mum. You should make her look after the boys herself. They're her responsibility, after all." Joan pursed her lips and shook her head as she picked up young Benjy, who was yet again anxious to investigate the coal scuttle, much to Miranda's delight.

She adored her young cousins, and although a placid, obedient child herself, was fascinated whenever Benjy misbehaved. She was always immaculate, disliking getting her hands or clothes at all grubby, having been fastidious from an early age. But she found Benjy, smeared in chocolate or coal dust, an hilarious sight.

"Yes, Rita should be a better mother, Joan, and I do tell her so, when I get the chance. But you know what she's like. She's always been a daydreamer, and I'm afraid even motherhood hasn't changed her. She does love the boys, but she's not very organised, that's all."

Nan beamed into the rosy face of baby Luke and put him over her shoulder to wind him. "Besides, I love looking after the babies. It's a treat to have them here, and they grow up so fast. When you girls were all tiny I was so rushed off my feet trying to keep a roof over our heads and food in your mouths, I never had a chance to really enjoy you properly. That's the pleasure of being a grandmother. Isn't it, my pet?" She put out a free hand and stroked back the strands of dark hair that had escaped from Miranda's pigtail and the little girl snuggled close. Joan sighed as she caught sight of her own disapproving countenance in the mirror above the mantelpiece. The forehead already showed a permanent frown line and there was a discontented droop to her mouth. Each morning it was becoming more and more of an effort to get up and face the day ahead.

She and Harry rarely had a proper row. It was more an insidious drifting away from each other, as their relationship was eroded by the pressures of everyday life, with no passion to alleviate their humdrum existence.

Increasingly, Harry immersed himself in the work at the radio shop, battling to overcome the problems of dexterity that were caused by his missing arm. Mr Cooper relied on him more and more, but the old man was rather a stick in the mud where the business was concerned, and Harry was eager to make changes and try to expand.

Money was not plentiful, and though Harry was a good provider, it was a constant struggle for Joan to budget, and the post-war shortages were a continual source of irritation. The economic situation in the country was making life miserable for everyone - rationing was even stricter than during the war - and Joan had little cheer in her life to compensate.

Her early romantic feelings towards Harry - her first boyfriend - now appeared in retrospect as simply a juvenile infatuation. When she had believed him killed and embarked on the wartime affair with her fighter pilot, Oliver, she had then realised what true passion was all about. In the aftermath of Oliver's death and the subsequent unexpected return of Harry, it seemed as though she had been on an emotional roller-coaster. Miranda's birth had been a source of comfort and joy, as well as drawing her closer to Harry, at first. He adored the little girl, believing her to be his, and finally regained the self-confidence that his wartime experiences had shattered. But as time went on, Joan found that the memory of Oliver had increasingly come between her and Harry. Especially in the most intimate side of their relationship.

She had steeled herself to welcome Harry back in her bed, and while hating the need for such hypocrisy, had attempted to return his eager lovemaking. If he had ever suspected it was a sham, he never discussed it. But as time went on, their marital encounters dwindled. Joan of course never initiated them and Harry was so physically worn out after long days absorbed at the shop that any faint hope of regaining a sexual closeness was fast fading.

Joan day dreamed more and more about the idyllic months of her affair with Oliver and her joy in Miranda was bitter-sweet, when the little girl displayed a passing mannerism that recalled her natural father.

Joan's constant depression cast an aura about her that was felt by the rest of the household and Billy knew that Nan was profoundly worried about the future. She felt that living in a home of her own might help Joan, but with the post-war housing shortage and lack of money that seemed an unlikely prospect.

In November the household at number thirty underwent another change. Nan was at home from work, recovering from a heavy cold, listening with Joan to the wireless. They were engrossed in the scene being described outside Westminster Abbey, where Princess Elizabeth was marrying Prince Philip.

"Her frock sounds a real picture, Joanie. Although I bet she's feeling the cold in this weather. Still it's not keeping the crowds away, is it?"

"I wonder if Rita will get a proper sight of her? Can't say I'd want to be up there in all that crush. Still, that's Rita all over. Leave her kids for us to look after and go traipsing up West with her girlfriends to gawp at the royal family!" Joan sniffed derisively, but then smiled in spite of herself as Luke grasped her finger in his chubby hand after she finished changing his nappy.

"Oh, I know, Joanie. But she was so excited to be

going out for the day, and the boys are no real trouble, are they?"

"No, Benjy's fine, so long as he stays inside Mandy's old playpen." She looked at her daughter happily crayoning at the kitchen table, replaced Luke in his Moses basket, then settled down opposite Nan, beside the fire. With their cups of tea in hand, they listened to the commentator's excited description of the newly-weds emerging from the Abbey.

Their pleasant interlude was rudely shattered a few minutes later by a loud knocking at the street door.

"Drat! Who can that be? I should have thought everyone would be listening to the wireless, same as us." Nan stood up reluctantly, and went to answer the summons.

For a moment she did not recognise the awkward figure hunched up in a shabby duffel coat, an old kitbag at his feet. Then as he stepped towards her with a shy smile, she knew him at once. "Matt! Why this is a surprise. Come in out of the cold, lad. You must be frozen to the bone."

"Hello, Mrs Stuart. Hope I've not come at a bad time." He stumbled into the passage and ducked his head nervously, unable to meet her eyes. Nan smiled warmly at him, for she had always had a soft spot for Rita's 'gypsy'.

"'Course you haven't, you daft h'apporth! It's lovely to see you again. Rita will be so pleased. I know she's been really bothered wondering if you were alright. Thought you were probably working on a merchant ship somewhere. Whenever the weather's bad, she always worries that you're safe."

"I should have let her know, but I'm not much of a hand at writing." He reddened and shuffled his feet, so Nan took pity on his embarrassment, and pushed him firmly into the warmth of the kitchen.

"Look who's turned up, Joan. Our Rita's Matt."

"Well, you're a surprise and no mistake!" Joan went to put on the kettle while Nan helped him off with his coat and settled him before the fire. Miranda and Benjy regarded him with solemn interest, although Luke was now fast asleep.

"I only docked in Liverpool last night, so I came straight here. How is Rita? Is she alright? Is this young Benjy? My word, he's filled out and shot up."

"Well, he needed fattening up a bit. Rita's fine, although I'm afraid she's out at the moment. Gone up West to see the royal wedding, with some of her old girlfriends.

"Now, Benjy, come and say 'hello' to your dad, there's a good boy." Nan lifted him out of the playpen and dumped him unceremoniously on Matt's knee.

Matt held his son awkwardly, and the pair of blue eyes curiously gazed into the pair of brown. Then the little boy reached up to grasp Matt's earring that glinted in the firelight. They both grinned at each other delightedly and Nan turned away with a lump in her throat.

However much she might disapprove of the strange ways of Matt's travelling family, and the fact that he and Rita had never actually tied the marital knot, there was no doubt that the young man was a gentle fellow with an obvious feeling for his son.

Joan came back with a mug of tea and said quietly, "Now you've met your elder son again, you'd better take a look at the younger one", and she nodded towards the sleeping infant.

Matt gazed in amazement across the room, and then asked hesitantly, "She had another boy, then? I bin wonderin' if everything went alright. I wished I could have been here sooner. But it's been difficult, travellin' about to get the work, an' that."

"It's alright, lad, we understand. Luke's a fine boy,

another one for you to be proud of. They're both good little lads and we all love having them here with us."

"I am grateful for what you've done for them - and Rita - Mrs Stuart. I knew she'd be alright once she got home to you. It was a bad time when we had the falling out with my folks. But I hope things will get better now."

"I'm sure they will, my dear. Now I expect you'll be hungry, so I'll just knock you up a sandwich to keep you going till supper time." Nan bustled about, as she mentally reviewed the state of the larder and how it would stretch to feed another mouth.

Rita of course was ecstatic to find Matt waiting for her that evening, and predictably they were soon giggling their way upstairs for an 'early night'. Nan hoped wryly that their nocturnal antics would not be noisy enough to wake Benjy, or Luke in his cot, as they both slept in Rita's room.

Watching the young couple's unashamed joy in each other, as they were unable to keep apart at the supper table, Joan felt a twist of bitter envy. Harry was his usual genial self, teasing them both about their reunion, and showing a friendly interest in Matt's travels on the merchant ship. It seemed in his eyes, as an old married couple, he and Joan no longer needed an active sex life. Companionship was quite enough for him.

Joan admitted to herself that Harry's caresses would not have been welcome, but maybe if he had made the effort, at least for a time it would erase the anguish of her guilty mourning for Oliver. Who knows, she might learn to really love Harry for himself. If only he'd show some signs of needing or wanting her again! Joan felt Nan's thoughtful eyes resting on her and knew that her mother, with uncanny understanding, could almost read Joan's every thought.

Within a few days, the extra adult in the house was becoming a definite burden on their space and rations. Matt himself seemed restless in the confines of the terraced family home, and Nan was not surprised when he came to tell her that he was leaving once more. But this time Rita and the children would accompany him.

"We'll be sorry to see you go, my dear, though I'll not deny it's a bit crowded with all of us under the one roof. But have you got any proper plans for the future? With the two little lads, you can't just hope for the best, you know. They need a proper roof over their heads and regular meals in their stomachs, especially during the winter. And Christmas is almost on us as well. Are you sure you won't wait till the new year?"

"Thanks, Mrs Stuart, but no. I've got a bit saved up now and I reckon I'll be alright for a job back with my cousins in the midlands. They have a snug place for the winter where they keep their travelling sideshow, and I think they'll give me work. I stayed with them when Rita first came back here, and we got on fine. In the new year I want to see my own family and make things up with them. I'd like to get work again on the barges, if I can."

"Well as long as you're sure, Matt. If it doesn't work out, you know I'm always here for you all. Oh, and I do think you could stop calling me 'Mrs Stuart'. I know you and Rita haven't seen fit to make your relationship legal, but in every other way I suppose you could say you're family, which makes me your mother-in-law. So I'm quite happy for you to call me 'Ma' like Harry does, if you want to."

"Thanks, Ma." He produced another of his shy, engaging grins, and once again she reflected wryly that she was quite able to understand where his enormous appeal lay for Rita.

It was certainly a wrench for Nan when the little family waved goodbye from the corner as they set off the next morning. Benjy sat on the end of the old pram, where Luke was warmly tucked under the blankets, and their parents were loaded with bags of all the good things that Nan had been able to muster from her already overstretched larder. They intended to travel by train to the midlands and promised to write soon.

"I'll believe that when it happens," Nan had confided to Billy that evening. It was strangely quiet in the kitchen of number thirty. Harry was working at the shop, Miranda was tucked up in bed and Joan had also retired, with her current library book.

"Well, I reckon they'll always be free spirits, those two. But there's not an ounce of malice in either of them, and they are both devoted to their kids in their own way. So I wouldn't worry too much, if I were you, Nan." He patted her hand comfortingly and they smiled contentedly across the fire at each other.

"Well at least young Mandy will be able to move into a room of her own now. I'll give Rita's room a good cleaning this weekend and perhaps Harry might like to give it a quick distemper if he gets the time."

"I can always do that. Poor bloke works his socks off at the shop. I only hope old Mr Cooper appreciates what a diamond he's got in our Harry. If any chap deserves to get on, it's him. Especially with his handicap an' all." Billy nodded emphatically, and Nan agreed with him.

"I just wish he and Joanie seemed a bit more...together. I do worry about them, Billy."

"I know you do, love. But they'll just have to find their own way. It's something you can't sort out for them." And

Nan knew that he was right. If she could have foreseen the events of the coming year, her worries would have weighed even heavier on her shoulders.

Apart from the pleasure of watching Miranda (or Mandy as she was more often called now) enjoying the excitement of opening her pile of gifts, Christmas was a very low-key affair at number thirty.

The boxes that arrived from Mavis and Irene were much appreciated as a means of supplementing the seasonal fare. Nan was delighted to also receive from Mavis a large coloured photograph of her fourth 'grandchild'. Joanne had been born in November and of course was enjoying all the benefits of the luxurious home that Mavis and Irvin inhabited.

Since his father had diversified his business interests after the war, Irvin was in charge of the Californian manufacturing company, which was doing very well indeed supplying components for the automobile market.

Mavis also sent photographs of their lovely home in Beverley Hills, as well as several poses of herself beside the huge swimming pool. Now nearly twenty-six, she was lovelier than ever with her auburn curls elegantly styled, a tanned figure showing no traces of her recent pregnancy and pert features beautifully made up.

"Her dreams certainly came true, didn't they?" Joan asked in bitter tones, as Nan showed her the pictures. "She always wanted everything that money could buy and now she's got it!"

"Yes, I grant you that, love. But I wonder if it will really keep her happy? I hope so, I'm sure. And her little Joanne looks a poppet. Same red hair as her mum, I see."

"Well, I don't suppose we're likely to meet her. Unless

Mavis can't resist playing Lady Bountiful in the slums - if Irvin has to come over on business."

"Oh, Joan, that's not very kind, is it? I know Mavis does keep ramming her posh lifestyle down our throats in all her letters, but you have to admit she is very generous. That's a lovely dress she sent Mandy for Christmas, as well as the toys. And we'll all be glad of the tinned fruit and other food in her parcel."

"I know, Mum. I'm being a right cow. It's just I get so depressed with everything, I have to take it out on someone. At least she can't hear me, all those miles away!"

It was just a few weeks before Mandy's third birthday in April that disaster struck number thirty. When Nan came home from her work at the town hall, she found Joan at the kitchen sink, rinsing out one of Mandy's nightdresses.

"She's not right, Mum. Has hardly eaten anything all day and now she's been sick. She's ever so hot as well."

"Don't worry, Joanie. It's probably just some kiddy's illness. They can be up one minute and right down the next. Never mind if she's not eating, just make sure she has plenty to drink. Has she got a rash at all? It might be something like measles or chicken pox. There's always plenty of them about."

"She's so fretful. I've tried to make her drink, but it's a real battle. I can't see any spots, though."

Nan went up and stayed with the little girl for a while. She certainly was very hot and flushed, and whimpered whenever they touched her. Nan tried to calm Joan with comforting words about childhood ailments that came and went over night, but privately she was experiencing a rising panic.

When Harry came home from the shop they talked it over and he went off to phone the doctor. He returned with the news that several cases of measles had been reported, so the spots would no doubt be apparent soon.

"Just keep her comfortable and give her plenty of fluids, he said. If she seems worse tomorrow, he'll call in to see her. Don't worry, Joan, measles are just a common kid's illness. She'll soon get over it." Harry patted her arm and she pulled away from his unexpected touch.

"I hope you're right, Harry. But I'm having that doctor round first thing if she's no better. I've got a bad feeling about this." Joan took another glass of orange juice upstairs and Nan almost echoed her daughter's words.

After a very restless night, Mandy's face was on fire and she was whimpering that it hurt too much to turn her head. At seven in the morning Harry went off to phone the doctor, requesting an immediate visit.

When he arrived, Nan and Billy (who had not opened his shop that day) waited in silence in the kitchen, straining to hear the movements and voices above. They had not long to wait. Harry clattered down the stairs two at a time, putting his head round the door to gabble, "Doc says he's sending her into the cottage hospital. He's really concerned. I'm off to ring for an ambulance," and left Nan and Billy staring at each other in consternation.

The next hours were a terrible nightmare for all of them. It was heartbreaking to watch the little girl carried out to the ambulance, swathed in blankets, with just a pink ribbon visible on one pigtail. Joan and Harry went with her to the hospital and Nan and Billy waited on events in the awful silence of number thirty.

By mid afternoon Harry was back to say that the little girl was undergoing tests and the doctors were taking her symptoms very seriously.

"Her temperature's really high and the stiff neck is a bad sign." Harry clenched his fists as he strove to control his voice. "They think it could be meningitis, Ma."

"Oh, Harry." She put her arms round him for a moment in a vain attempt at mutual comfort, and then pulled herself together.

"I'll get off to the hospital, love. Joan will need another woman at a time like this. I expect you'll want to get round to the shop and explain to Mr Cooper. Billy, could you call at the town hall and tell them I won't be in for a while?

"Now, I'll make you a cup of tea and a sandwich, Harry. You must keep your strength up - Joan will really need your support now. Then I'll get my hat and coat on."

The next hours crawled past as the two women sat hand in hand on the hard seats outside the isolation ward where Mandy was lying. White-gowned figures tended her, but little was conveyed by the eyes above the surgical masks as they passed the two waiting women.

"If only we could sit with her for a while. But the doctors say she's resting and mustn't be disturbed. How long will it take before they get the results of all these tests? They've already taken several different lots of blood. Poor little mite, I should have been holding her hand when she had to face those needles. They've even taken tests from Harry and me, in case it's something catching." Joan's voice shook, and she twisted her crumpled handkerchief between damp palms.

Nan wordlessly embraced her daughter, her own eyes swimming in tears. She was not a churchgoer, but that afternoon she sent up endless appeals to her Maker. Harry came back in the early evening and took Nan's place beside

Joan. Stretching her aching muscles, Nan went off to find a telephone box.

"I'm going to ring Irene, Joanie. She'll want to know what's happening, I'm sure. It's lucky they've got a phone at the farm. The Tregarons can pass on a message for me. You'll be alright if I leave you for a while, won't you?"

"Don't worry, Ma. I'll be staying now. I'll look after her." Harry gave her a weary smile and put his arm around Joan. For once she appeared to gain some comfort from his touch, resting her head on his shoulder, which brought a glimmer of hope in the darkness of Nan's despair about Mandy.

By late evening the doctor was telling them all to go home and return in the morning.

"There's nothing you can do here. She's asleep at the moment and if she sees you it may unsettle her. Perhaps by tomorrow we'll know a bit more. Try and get some rest yourselves. It won't do her any good if you keel over."

It was too late to catch a bus, so they got a taxi back to Holgate. Joan sat like a zombie in the corner, but allowed Harry to retain her hand in a firm grasp. Nan wished desperately that David was waiting for them back home. As a doctor he could have explained all the likely possibilities and would have made her understand Mandy's chances.

But when they walked into the kitchen, the sight of Billy, with a saucepan of soup keeping hot on the stove and the inevitable pot of tea waiting to be poured, was an enormous balm to her troubled soul.

None of them slept much that night. Nan heard footsteps pacing backwards and forwards in the room above her head in the early hours and guessed that Joan was finding it impossible to remain still in her bed. They were all relieved when it was time to come down for some toast and tea, and then set off to catch the early bus to the hospital.

With churning stomachs Nan and Joan waited outside the isolation ward while Harry went into the sister's office to ask for information.

"Oh, Mum, what shall I do if she dies? Kiddies often do with meningitis. I've been so horrible to Harry lately - so critical of him all the time, and full of self-pity. I've kept thinking how much I miss Oliver, and wishing Harry was him. All the while I've been so lucky having Mandy, and Harry's such a good father to her.

"The long hours he spends at the shop, I've resented him showing no interest in me, but he's only working so hard to give Mandy and me a good life. If she just gets better, I swear I'll turn over a new leaf and be a better wife to Harry. He's been so good to me through all this, such a comfort..." and her body was torn with sobs. Nan murmured soothingly as she gathered her daughter in her arms, all the time watching over the other's shoulder for Harry's reappearance. When he came a shaft of pure terror went through Nan as she saw the tears trickling down his thin face and he put out a hand to steady himself against the door-frame.

It's happened. Dear God, Mandy's dead, thought Nan. Instinctively her hold on Joan tightened, as if to shield her from the terrible blow about to fall.

"Joanie." Harry's voice cracked as he reached out and turned his wife to face him. "Joanie, Sister's just told me..." He swallowed painfully and then an enormous smile transformed his expression.

"She's alright, sweetheart. Mandy's fine. Her

temperature's back to normal and her neck isn't stiff any more. There's no sign of anything serious. They think it was just some children's virus. A twenty-four hour thing. Oh, Joanie!"

Wordlessly they clung together, weeping in silent relief, as Nan swayed and then sank down on a bench, her legs threatening to give way beneath her.

The rest of the morning passed in a happy daze. They were allowed to visit Mandy, who was sitting up in bed playing with a hospital teddy bear. Joan stayed with her while Harry and Nan went home to collect her clothes, since the doctor had said she might come out that afternoon.

Nan remembered to stop at a call-box and pass on the glad tidings to the Tregarons, so that Irene should be put out of her misery. Then she stopped in the local toy shop, unable to resist buying a new doll to celebrate Mandy's recovery. Over the next few days a wonderful air of euphoria pervaded number thirty. Joan sang about her housework in a way that Nan could not remember her doing for months. There was a warmth between her and Harry that was unmistakable, and although Nan and Billy did not discuss it, they were both aware of a new depth in the young couple's relationship.

Harry managed to get home earlier from the shop in time to watch Mandy having her bath and bedtime story, and he and Joan would often share a joke as they talked over the happenings of their day. The weather seemed to improve to match their mood and the air held a promise of springtime.

"Harry's talking about us having a day out at the weekend. Thought we could take Mandy down to Southend on the train. The sea air will bring the colour back to her cheeks, and I reckon it'll do us good to get away for a break." Joan smiled brightly at Nan as they folded the sheets between them for ironing.

"Just what the doctor ordered, love. Nice trip out, the three of you. Matter of fact, Billy and I were talking about going out this Saturday. One of his mates will mind the shop and we thought we might go up to Kew Gardens and have a look at the bulbs. Should be a picture at this time of year."

Nan and Billy set off early on Saturday morning to catch the bus to Wood Green, where they would get the tube up to London. Nan wanted to have a look at Piccadilly Circus, where Eros was now back in place at long last. There was a lot of excitement being generated in the capital by the Olympic Games, which were being held in England that summer, and Nan fancied a stroll about before they went on to Kew Gardens. They had a wonderful day, which was much enjoyed because it was such a rare treat for them both. Billy usually kept very busy at his small greengrocery shop, and Nan worked hard in the welfare department at the town hall. She enjoyed her job, which had been a natural follow-on from her war work. Sorting out problems of homeless families, the elderly or the widowed was exactly the right outlet for energy and compassion.

But to have a whole day sauntering along in the sunshine with Billy - lunching in the café at Kew - and then revelling in the scents and colours of the spring flowers was absolute bliss for Nan.

When they walked through the street door in the early evening she was tired but content, and looking forward to soaking her throbbing feet in front of the kitchen fire. She was surprised to find the gas unlit and thought the others had not yet returned, but then a sound made her realise that Joan was sitting in the fading light, her head in her hands.

"Whatever are you doing here in the dark, Joan? Aren't you well? Has something happened? Mandy's not been taken ill again, has she?" Nan's heart sank as she took in the desperate expression on her daughter's face.

Joan was chalk-white and her eyes were swollen and red from weeping. In the few hours since that morning it appeared to Nan that she had aged ten years.

"It's not Mandy - at least not directly. She's upstairs in bed, asleep. I took her for a long walk at Ally Pally this afternoon. I don't know where Harry is. He walked out."

"Walked out! What d'you mean, he walked out? Whatever's been going on?" Nan stared in consternation at her daughter, whilst Billy lit the gas and then left the room in his usual tactful way.

"Mum, it was dreadful. He looked so awful, so hurt and betrayed. I felt like I'd killed something inside him. Oh, God, I was always afraid this would happen some day!" And Joan hid her face in her hands once more.

Nan pulled a chair close to her daughter's and said quietly, "You'd better tell me all about it, Joanie. Though I think I can guess what you're going to say. Harry knows about Mandy, is that it?"

"Yes, it happened this morning. That new doctor paid us a visit. Just as we were about to go off to Southend. We were all so happy together. Mandy was really excited, Harry was going to build her a sandcastle and promising her a train ride along the pier... Oh, Mum!"

"Come on, love. Pull yourself together and tell me what happened. What did the doctor want, then?"

"He thought he was doing the right thing, I suppose. He called in to check on Mandy, because the hospital had sent the results of all the tests through to him as a matter of procedure. He was saying what a relief it was to know that she was alright. Said what a lovely child she is. How proud we must be of her.

"Then he asked me if she was born in hospital. When I said no, he looked a bit odd and then asked if she was by any chance adopted. Harry laughed and asked him whatever gave him that idea. By this time I was starting to have a terrible fear of what might happen.

"The doctor looked very awkward then. He apologised and said that as he was new to the area he didn't know much about the family history, but that he was puzzled by something he'd noticed in the blood tests we'd all had done. He was worried there might have been a mix-up when Mandy was born - if I'd had her in hospital. You did hear of such things happening, especially during all the chaos of wartime."

She stopped, recalling the awful moments of the conversation they had with the doctor that morning.

"Then he said, if that wasn't the case, there was nothing to worry about. He got up, made as if to leave, but Harry stopped him. Of course he could tell from the doctor's face that something wasn't right.

"He was very insistent the doctor told us what the tests had shown that was so unusual. Eventually he made him say it. The blood groups for Mandy and me and Harry were three different ones. Mine was group A, Harry's was B and Mandy's was O. If her blood was different from mine, then it must be the same as her father's. But she and Harry had different groups, so that meant he couldn't be her father!"

"Oh, merciful heavens! What a terrible thing, Joan. Poor, dear Harry. Whatever did he say?"

"There was silence for a minute. The doctor just stood there all red and embarrassed. He could tell what a shock it was for Harry and I suppose I must have looked as guilty as hell!" Joan's face had flushed scarlet at simply remembering the dreadful shame of that moment.

"Then the doctor said he was sorry to have caused any upset, but he felt it was his duty to check things were alright in case there had been a mix-up of babies. Then he just sort of backed out the door ever so quietly, leaving Harry and me and Mandy together."

"Did Mandy realise anything was going on? There wasn't any row in front of her, was there?" Nan asked anxiously.

"No. Harry just told her quietly to go and play in the garden because we weren't going out after all. Said he had to go to work. You know what a good little thing she is; she just went outside with her dolls' pram.

"I started to speak, tried to say how sorry I was that he'd found out like this, but he wouldn't listen. He stood looking down at me with so much suffering on his face - I don't think I've ever seen such a look of naked betrayal." Joan's voice broke as she remembered the agonising fear and shame she had experienced at that moment.

Harry's voice had been raw with pain as he strove to keep it steady. He had simply asked questions, breaking into her gabbled protestations of sorrow and remorse.

"Is it still going on between you and Miranda's father?"

"No, no, Harry! He's dead - he was killed just after the D-day landings. He was a pilot, shot down over the Normandy beaches."

"One of our brave boys in blue, eh? How long did it go on between the two of you?"

"Only a matter of months, Harry. It was after they told me you were believed killed on Sicily. I was desperately unhappy when I thought I'd lost you. Oliver was at the same airbase in Kent as me. His whole family had been killed in the Blitz, so he could understand what I was going through. He was kind."

"Obviously! So you 'comforted' each other while I was lying out of my head in that god-forsaken cave in the Sicilian hills having my arm hacked off with a kitchen knife! Very pretty, Joan, very nice!"

"I'm so sorry, Harry. I had no idea you were still alive. I'd never looked at another man before when you were away. I honestly thought you'd been killed - I was so lonely and afraid..."

"Don't make excuses, you faithless bitch! Even if there was some excuse for what you did - believing you were a widow - nothing could excuse the deceit after I came back, when you knew you were pregnant with another man's child. Letting me believe she's mine. Letting me love her! When all the time she's the result of your cheap little affair. Just because you couldn't face a lonely bed."

"I'm so desperately sorry, Harry. I thought it was all for the best. When you came home you were in such a bad way - so exhausted and shocked by losing your arm. I didn't think you'd be able to face what had happened. Oliver was dead and I thought that becoming a father would help you rebuild your life. Help us to start again, as a family."

"So it was all for my own good, was it? You hypocritical cow! It had nothing to do with you wanting a father for the bastard you were carrying? It wasn't because you needed a way out of the shame you saw ahead of you? You must think I came down in the last shower expecting me to believe that!" Joan had sunk lower in the chair, her body racked with sobs as he flung out of the room and ran upstairs. She heard the sound of drawers and cupboards being wrenched open and then he was clattering down the passage to the front door. Shocked into action she rushed out of the room, calling his name in panic.

"Harry! Harry! Where are you going? What are you going to do? Don't leave us. Please don't go!"

"There's nothing on earth would make me stay another second under the same roof as you, Joan. I can't bear to look at your cheating face. Tell Mandy what you like. I can't bring myself to look at her either. I've got to get out of this place before I do something I'll regret."

He had crashed out of the basement door and she heard his boots stumbling up the area steps and then the house was enveloped in a terrible silence.

"So you don't know where he's gone, then?" Nan listened to her daughter's pathetic narrative and was struggling to hold back her own tears.

"No, I told Mandy he had to work late when she asked why he wasn't there to say good night. But I don't know what I can tell her when she realises he isn't coming back. Oh, Mum, it's such a dreadful mess! Whatever shall I do?"

"For now you'd better try and get some sleep. Things always seem better in the light of day, and you look exhausted. You've got to make everything seem normal for Mandy tomorrow and you'll need your wits about you to do that.

"Harry may calm down once he's got over the first shock and then perhaps you can make him understand how it really was - so terrible finding yourself pregnant just after he got back. Perhaps he'll let me talk to him. After all, I'm the one who persuaded you to keep it all a secret from him." Nan shook her head and her shoulders were bowed as she felt an awful mantle of guilt descending upon her, recalling her own involvement in Joan's deception.

"You said what you thought was right at the time, Mum. And it was me that made the final decision. I knew what I was doing." Joan brushed the hair back from her damp cheeks and Nan's heart went out to her troubled daughter.

Although Joan slept the deep sleep of emotional exhaustion, Nan tossed and turned and eventually came down at first light to make herself some tea. She was stirring the embers of the fire into a tiny blaze when Billy quietly entered in his old grey dressing gown.

"Couldn't sleep, ducks? Anything you want to tell me about?" He fetched himself a mug from the scullery and filled it from the pot that Nan had just brewed.

"It's not really my business to discuss, Billy. But you'll have guessed that Harry's left. He and Joan had a terrible falling out yesterday and that's the long and the short of it. I can't tell you any more than that. But I'm half out of my mind with worry, that I do know."

"Walked out has he? Well that's not good. Young Mandy will be getting upset when she realises he's missing. D'you reckon he'll be back, Nan? Surely it's just a storm in a teacup? They seemed so much happier recently - Mandy's illness really drew them together. And Harry's not one to shirk his responsibilities."

"No, he's not, Billy. But it's not that simple, I'm afraid."

They sat in silence for a while and Nan could hear the rising crescendo of the dawn chorus in the back yard. Always a nature lover, she delighted in leaving scraps for the birds and they usually had a few feathered visitors outside the scullery door.

Listening to their song gave her a sudden inspiration and she sat up straighter in her chair.

"I've got an idea, Billy. At least it may help sort things out in the short term. I'll ring Irene and ask if Joan and

Mandy can go down and stay for a little holiday. She knows about the scare over Mandy's illness and I can tell her that Joan is in need of a rest and a break. If she wants to tell Irene all about the business with Harry, that's up to her. At least being away from home, Mandy won't keep fretting for her dad."

As usual, when she could take some practical measures in an emergency, Nan felt better at once. As soon as she was washed and dressed she went down to the phone box on the corner and rang the Tregaron farm. She explained matters to Betty Tregaron and asked if she would pass on the message to Irene.

It was arranged that Irene would be at the farmhouse to take another phone call later that afternoon, when either Nan or Joan would make more definite plans with her.

Billy cycled up to the station to find out details of times of trains and what changes would have to be made on the journey, so that by the time Joan came downstairs later in the morning, Nan had all the plans ready to lay before her. "Well I can't think straight, Mum, and that's a fact. If you believe it will help, us getting away for a few days, then I suppose we might as well. At least Mandy will enjoy living on the farm and the country air will be good for her. I'd better speak to Irene myself this afternoon and tell her the whole story. She's going to have to know eventually, like everyone else I suppose. I just hope we won't be too much of a bother for her."

"Of course you won't be a bother. She'll be thrilled to see you both. Every time she writes she keeps saying she wishes we could see their little cottage and all the work they've done on it. Springtime in Cornwall should be lovely and the peace of the countryside is just what you need, my girl."

Nan and Billy took Mandy out for the afternoon to Hampstead Heath on the bus, so Joan could spend time getting their luggage packed and some of Mandy's clothes washed and ironed in readiness for the trip. She was half hoping the door would open and Harry come in, ready to talk at least, but the house remained silent.

Nan walked up to the station the next morning to see them off. Joan was laden with a suitcase, which balanced across Mandy's folding push-chair, as well as carrying a bag with food for the long journey and some of Mandy's toys to keep her happy on the train.

"Now you'll be fine when you get to King's Cross, Joan. You can get a porter to help with the luggage and find you a taxi across to Paddington to catch the express. Robert will meet you at the other end, so you'll be well taken care of, love.

"You be a good girl, Mandy. Send your Nan some drawings of all the nice cows and horses on Auntie Irene's farm, and have a lovely holiday by the sea." Nan gave her daughter and granddaughter a final hug, and waved till the train had rounded the bend in the track. Then she had to hurry off to the town hall and apologise for her unusual lateness.

The next days were silent ones at number thirty. Nan waited eagerly for the postman to bring news from Cornwall. She was weighed down with worry about Joan, and strove to find a solution to her's and Mandy's future. Billy had told her that he had caught sight of Harry working in the wireless shop as usual - so at least he was managing to go through the motions of normal living.

"I expect he's staying with old Mr Cooper in the flat

over the premises. But he'll have to come round some time and talk over the future." Nan looked across at Billy, who sat by the table working on some tiny furniture for Mandy's new dolls' house that he was building for next Christmas.

"You don't have to tell me anything private, Nan, or break any confidences. But perhaps I should say that I've already guessed what their trouble is all about. I've wondered over the years if Mandy might be Oliver's child, not Harry's. There's a look of Oliver about her eyes, and she's got his gentle smile.

"I suppose somehow or other Harry's found out and that's why he left. It's a sorry business and no mistake. He's always been a good father to Mandy - the apple of his eye she's been - and it will be a sad day if he decides he can't accept her as his own.

"But he's a sensible chap and when he thinks it all over, he'll realise that Joan wasn't being unfaithful to him in the real sense - believing as she did that he'd been killed. She was just taking a bit of comfort at a time when we all thought we might not live to see another morning!"

"That's what I keep hoping, Billy. But every day that goes by without any word seems to make it more unlikely that he'll come round. I don't know whether I should pay him a visit or keep out of it. God knows, I don't want to interfere, but I do feel responsible." She looked at him with tears threatening to overflow her swimming eyes.

"Since you've guessed this much, it won't hurt to tell you that it was me that persuaded Joanie to keep the truth from Harry. I just felt he couldn't cope with it - such a wreck he was when he first came home. I honestly believed it would help their marriage to succeed, if he believed he was a father."

"And so it did, Nan. You've no reason to reproach

yourself, my dear."

When Nan received a short note from Joan, it did little to set her mind at rest. The long journey to Cornwall had gone smoothly. As usual, Mandy had behaved well, and Robert had met them at Penzance station. Joan said nothing of her current state of mind, but the brevity of the letter conveyed more to Nan of her daughter's anguish than pages of emotional outpourings. If Nan could have seen Joan, she would have been even more concerned.

From the moment of their arrival at Tregaron cottage, she had simply given up all pretence at coping with this crisis in her life. Irene had been waiting in the doorway as they walked up the pathway from the car, and wordlessly gathered her elder sister into her arms. Robert was carrying the sleeping Mandy, who had succumbed in the car on the drive through the darkening lanes.

"Oh, it is lovely to see you, Joanie. It seems such ages since we were all together last year. Now come inside and sit down by the fire, while I make you a cuppa. You must be exhausted after that long train journey. How was Mandy? Did she get very bored sitting still?"

Without waiting for a reply she bustled Joan into the comfortable kitchen-cum-living room and settled her beside the enormous old fireplace. A glowing log fire excluded the chill of the April evening, and there was a fragrant smell of baking bread and a savoury stew, which was simmering on the range in the scullery through the open doorway.

Robert settled Mandy in the depths of a large sofa, and, murmuring something about shutting up the hens for the night, tactfully left the sisters alone. Joan listlessly removed her coat and hat and sat with them on her lap, as if unable to summon the energy to deposit them anywhere else. Irene, after a searching look at her sister's white, haggard face, quietly poured a cup of tea, sugared it as liberally as if rationing had never been heard of, and pressed it between Joan's cold fingers.

"There you are, love, drink it while it's hot. That'll put some heart into you. Then you can come upstairs and have a nice, long bath. There's plenty of water. I'll bring your supper up on a tray, so you can have it in bed, if you like."

"Oh, Irene, you can't think how awful I feel! And now you're being so good - it's such a relief just to give in, after pretending all day for Mandy's sake. What am I going to tell her? How can I explain what's happened to her daddy - except he's not her daddy, is he?"

Joan allowed her sister to take back the cup and then enfold her in a silent embrace, which lasted for several minutes while she finally gave way to rending sobs. She had kept her emotions on a tight rein ever since she had left Holgate, but now that she had let herself relax, her whole body was shaking violently. Irene wisely said nothing, but simply stroked her tangled hair and gently patted her back.

When the storm of grief eventually seemed to be abating, she passed over a clean handkerchief and rising, said, "That's probably just what you needed, Joanie. Now come on, up the apples and pears, as Mum would say. Don't worry about Mandy. She's dead to the world for the moment. I'll put her in the little box-room, next to the spare bedroom where you'll be sleeping. There's a towel on the side of the bath, and you can use my dressing gown when you've finished your soak. I'll be unpacking your bags while you're doing that. The sooner you're tucked up in bed the better".

By the time Robert came back, Irene had finished unpacking for their two guests, and was ladling out the hot stew into bowls on the kitchen table. Mandy still slumbered on obliviously.

"Joan gone up, has she? She certainly looked pretty shattered. Just about ready to pass out when she stepped off the train."

"Oh, Rob, she's in a terrible state! I think all the strain of keeping this secret from Harry has taken a dreadful toll on her nerves. Now that he knows the truth, coming on top of the awful meningitis scare over Mandy, well she really looks on the verge of a complete breakdown to me. We're going to have to treat her very carefully, I think."

"Well if anyone can sort her out, it's you, sweetheart." Robert smiled at her lovingly as he pulled off his boots and sat down opposite her at the table. She was such a wonderful woman, his Irene.

Even her husband would not describe her as beautiful, but a quality of strength and calmness of spirit emanated from her sturdy figure. Her fair hair had been bleached to gleaming gold by the sun, but was habitually arranged in two sensible plaits that encircled her head. It was a nightly pleasure for Robert to watch as she swiftly removed the pins and brushed it down to her shoulders. No wonder his parents loved her like a daughter; he thanked his lucky stars for that faceless bureaucrat in the Land Army who had assigned Irene to Tregaron Farm.

Mandy continued to sleep peacefully while they ate their supper, and afterwards Robert quietly carried her up the winding staircase, built inside the kitchen cupboard, and laid her on the camp bed Irene had made up in the box-room.

Hearing their footsteps, Joan dragged herself wearily out onto the landing. She had been sitting, with an untouched supper tray on her knee, gazing unseeingly through her bedroom window. Having spent all her adult years in London, the only other time she had witnessed such complete darkness was in the wartime blackout. It seemed a fitting reflection of her gloomy mental state. No light at all at the end of a claustrophobic tunnel, she thought despairingly.

She watched apathetically as Irene gently removed Mandy's shoes and outer garments and then tucked her under the bed clothes, making sure that her favourite teddy was settled in the crook of her arm. "I'll leave the door ajar and the landing light on, Joan. Then if she wakes in the night she won't be frightened in a strange bed on her own," Irene said as she and Robert came out to Joan.

"Thanks, Irene. And you, Robert. It's ever so good of you to take us in like this. I'm sorry to land on you with all my problems. I didn't know what to do and when Mum suggested coming here, well it seemed like a safe haven." Her lip trembled and she twisted her already-shredded handkerchief between shaking fingers - once again the sobs began as she leaned against the wall, legs threatening to give way beneath her.

Irene looked across at Robert and wordlessly shook her head, with a 'what did I tell you?' expression on her face. He gave a sympathetic grimace and with a quick pat on Joan's shoulder and a muttered "Try and get some sleep, Joanie, things will seem better tomorrow", he thankfully left his wife to deal with the situation.

"He's right, Joanie. You'll feel more able to cope after you've had a proper rest. Have a good lie-in. Don't worry about Mandy, I'll listen for her. She'll be alright with her auntie Irene. We got on fine last year, didn't we, when she was my bridesmaid?" Keeping up a flow of comforting banalities, Irene helped her sister climb between the crisp, lavender-scented sheets, and pulled the patchwork quilt around her shoulders. Joan closed her eyes at once, thankful to shut out reality for a while.

Tiptoeing down the stairs, Irene gave a rueful smile. She did not underestimate how demanding the next few days were likely to be. She was well aware that much as she loved Joan, they were two very different characters. Irene was essentially a calm, well-organised, uncomplicated woman who was absorbed in her fulfilled life with Robert, on the farm that she loved.

She would deal with problems as they arose, in a logical fashion, and had never agonised over a decision in her life. She knew that the feelings she cherished for her husband were nothing like the grand passion that Joan had entertained for Oliver, but Irene was also totally sure that she would never experience the remotest attraction towards any other man than Robert.

She would do her best to support Joan on a practical level in this marital crisis, but she knew that her ability to share her sister's emotional turmoil would be somewhat lacking. *I suppose Mum's the only person who really knows how Joanie feels,* she thought, *but since she's not here, I'll just have to do the best I can.*

Over the ensuing days, that resolution was to be sorely tested at times. But although Irene occasionally experienced a decided urge to shake her miserable sister until her teeth rattled, she made an heroic effort to conceal her feelings beneath her usual placid exterior. The saving grace of course was young Mandy. Irene made the little girl's welfare her prime consideration, ensuring that she saw as little of her mother as possible. This was achieved by devising a daily timetable where Mandy spent all of her waking hours involved in the working life of the farm. As usual, they were up early the next morning to set about the farming chores. A quick glance had revealed that Joan was dead to the world, worn out after hours of tossing and turning and intermittent weeping. Mandy, however, was quietly playing with her teddy, and two big eyes were fixed on the door as Irene pushed it wide.

"Hello, lovie, remember your auntie Irene, do you?" She bent to give her niece an affectionate hug that was returned with warmth. "Now let's put on your dressing gown and take you downstairs for breakfast. How would you like some porridge, with milk that uncle Robert's just brought in from our cow, Daisy? I expect you'd like to see her later on, wouldn't you? And there's all the other animals for you to meet. Pigs and sheep and lots and lots of hens. If you like, you can help me feed them after breakfast, and maybe collect the eggs."

Chatting away, she shepherded her niece downstairs and installed her at the table in the sunny kitchen, where Mandy was soon spooning up her porridge and drinking a glass of foaming milk.

Robert had already eaten and departed for his day's work up at the farmhouse with his father, so Irene and Mandy had time to become re-acquainted on their own. Of course the little girl vividly remembered the wedding the year before, and being habitually an outgoing, trusting child was quite at home in the new surroundings.

Irene was very much Nan's daughter, so the little cottage exuded the same air of homely comfort as number thirty back at Holgate. Robert and his father had done an excellent job of renovating the property, and Irene was proud to keep it spotless and comfortable. Downstairs was the one large room that doubled as kitchen and living room, whose main feature was a wide stone fireplace, flanked by twin sofas piled high with patchwork cushions. Beneath the window at the front of the cottage was a scrubbed pine table, surrounded by matching chairs, and in its centre a large china bowl that at present held some vivid pink hyacinths whose perfume mingled with the smell of Robert's breakfast bacon.

The stained wooden floor was covered by several home-made rugs, passed on by Robert's mother, and the walls were decorated with gleaming ornaments such as warming pans or horse brasses. In one corner a grandfather clock ticked an accompaniment to the crackling logs on the fire which was usually burning, except on the very hottest days. One wall was practically covered by an enormous wooden dresser that had also been handed on by Robert's family and now held most of the young couple's china and glass collection.

The door to the scullery at the back of the cottage was permanently open and Irene was able to keep up a cheerful conversation with Mandy while doing the washing up. The scullery held the old-fashioned range where all of the cooking was still carried out. Robert had installed electricity as part of the renovations and offered to buy Irene a modern electric stove, but she had already mastered the range up at the farmhouse, and was happy to do her cooking in the traditional way.

There was a large butler's sink and draining board set beneath the window overlooking the back garden, with an array of earthenware pots on the sill, containing Irene's herbs. In one corner was the walk-in larder, lined with shelves of home-made jams and preserves, and from the ceiling, apart from a clothes airer high on a pulley above the range, bunches of onions and dried flowers festooned the old rafters.

The view from the window was spectacular and when Mandy came through to have her fingers wiped after her meal, Irene lifted her up to see out. The garden itself was a vivid mass of spring flowers growing between some ancient gnarled fruit trees. To the right a separate fenced enclosure held the kitchen garden, which was Irene's special pride and joy. She had always enjoyed helping Nan grow the vegetables for number thirty on Nan's allotment, but here there was far more space and Irene even had a netted fruit cage that Robert had built for her currants and berries, to protect them from the birds.

Beyond the garden fence, a stream gurgled, and then there were several fields sloping gently away. Wild flowers sprouted between their dry stone walls, and finally the open grassland of the cliff tops was rimmed by the silvery blue Atlantic on the near horizon.

"There you are, Mandy, that's the sea, with the sun shining on it. Shall we have a walk over there later on so you can have a proper look? We can go down on the beach and you can throw some pebbles into the waves. If it's low tide, you'll be able to have a look at all the rock pools. There's crabs and shrimps and all sorts of tiny fish in them. Would you like to do that?"

The brown head nodded vigorously. "My daddy was going to go to the sea with my mummy and me. But we couldn't go. Daddy had to work. Is he still working? Will he come to the sea today?" The brown eyes looked seriously into the blue ones - Irene swallowed uncomfortably, but managed to produce a cheerful smile.

"Not today, sweetheart. He's had to stay at the shop near your Nan's house. I expect Mr Cooper is very busy and needs your daddy to help him sell all those wirelesses. But I know he's thinking about you a lot and hoping you're having a lovely holiday down here on the farm, with your mummy."

"Is Mummy still asleep? Will she come down the stairs in the cupboard soon? Will she come to the sea as well?" There was a faint quiver of anxiety underlying the questions and Irene knew that somehow Mandy had already sensed her mother's turmoil and was aware that all was not well in her hitherto secure little world.

"Oh, I expect she's having a nice long lie-in. That's what mummies do when they're on holiday. She knows I was looking forward to having you all to myself this morning. I haven't got a little girl of my own, so I'm going to borrow you for a while. That's what aunties like doing."

"Alright." She wriggled down to the floor and solemnly hopped across the lines dividing the scrubbed flagstones. "Will you have a little girl of your own someday? I could play with her then, couldn't I."

"You certainly could. And yes, I really hope I will have my own little girl - or boy - very soon." Irene smiled as she thought of the secret possibility that she had been hugging to herself for the last couple of weeks. Fortunately Robert was not particularly observant in some areas, and she was anxious to wait a little longer and be utterly certain before she imparted the wonderful news to him and their two families. What a perfect Christmas present it would be if she had got her dates right!

By the time Mandy had been taken upstairs to the bathroom, converted from the third bedroom, and washed and dressed in her Fair Isle jumper and dark green kilt, Joan was emerging from her room. With her eyes deeply shadowed and puffy with weeping, skin pale and drawn, straight dark hair tangled about her shoulders, she was not a cheerful sight.

Mandy greeted her with an exuberant hug as she chattered happily about Irene's plans for their day. The eyes of the two sisters met above her head and Joan attempted a grateful smile.

"Well, it sounds as though you're having a lovely time, darling. You make sure you're a good girl for Auntie and do everything she tells you, alright?"

"I'll make you some tea and toast, Joan. Did you manage to get some sleep?"

"Just tea, thanks. I don't feel like anything to eat. Yes, I finally got off in the early hours, but then I had some awful dreams."

"Well, there's plenty of hot water, if you want a bath. I'll make the tea - I usually take Robert and his dad a flask in the middle of the morning - and then Mandy and I will get off. I've got the hens to see to, and I thought we could have a look at all the animals. I know Robert's mum is dying to see Mandy again. She really took to her at the wedding. You too, of course. She wants us to have a meal with them one evening this week."

"Oh, Irene, I don't think I can face anybody now. I really just want some peace and quiet to try and sort things out..." Her voice was rising to a note of near-panic and noticing that Mandy was regarding her mother with a puzzled, slightly alarmed expression, Irene swiftly interrupted her sister.

"It's alright, Joanie. I've told Robert's parents that you've come down for a good rest after all the recent stresses and strains, and they know you're not feeling too bright at the moment. They'll quite understand if you don't want to be sociable for a while. We'll wait till you're stronger. Now come on, young lady, let's get your coat and pixie hood. It's a lovely sunny morning, but that wind's still a bit nippy off the sea, so you'll need to wrap up warm."

Joan gave her daughter a swift hug and then turned back to her bedroom before the threatening tears could overflow and worry the little girl. One of the worst parts of the nightmare was wondering how long she could put off telling Mandy something about the true situation with Harry. If he really was adamant about not coming back, she couldn't begin to imagine the effect on her daughter, who absolutely adored him.

The days passed and the inmates of Tregaron Cottage adopted a new pattern to their lives. Robert and Irene did their usual morning chores and had breakfast together, which became a cherished time of privacy for them. Mandy usually came down just as Robert was leaving for his day's work and would chatter happily to Irene while having her breakfast and then completing her toilet. Although she would go into Joan's room to give her a morning kiss, she never minded leaving her mother still in bed, and cheerfully joined Irene as she carried out her jobs around the cottage and farm.

Isaac and Betty Tregaron became very fond of the child, and always welcomed her up at the 'big house'. Mandy took after her grandmother in her love of animals and from the farm tabby cat right up to the huge shire horses was in her element with so many creatures to pet. By the time she went back with Irene and Robert for a lunch-time sandwich or a bowl of soup, Joan would be up and about. She willingly helped out with the washing and ironing and even some cooking, but her mind was obviously dwelling on other matters. She drifted through her days, a figure of acute depression who was a source of considerable worry - not to mention irritation at times - to her younger sister.

Apart from her brief note to Nan, advising her of their safe arrival, she had attempted no contact with Holgate. Nan had written back, mentioning that she had seen Harry at his usual duties in the shop and had bumped into Mr Cooper in the Post Office. He had shaken his head sadly over 'the young people's falling out' and told Nan that Harry was installed in the spare bedroom above the shop - news which she had passed on to Joan.

While she and Billy had been out at work, he had also returned to number thirty and removed some more of his belongings, which she decided not to mention.

Mandy spoke of her father from time to time, but the new and exciting surroundings kept her occupied and cheerful. When Joan or Irene replied to her queries, they would tell her he was extra busy helping Mr Cooper, and she appeared content with the explanation. Nan sent the little girl a short note each week, which Joan would read to her, and sometimes Mandy would send back a drawing in reply. Irene kept her mother up to date in her own weekly letter, but as she said to Robert, there was little cheerful to report.

"I don't know how long Joan plans on staying, but she can't let things drift like this forever. She'll have to see Harry and have a proper discussion about the future. They owe that to Mandy, if nothing else." Irene shook her head as she counted the stitches on the needle of the cardigan she was knitting for her niece, and wondered if someone else shouldn't contact Harry and suggest a meeting with Joan. When Irene had tried to persuade her to write to him, she had practically had hysterics at the thought of confronting his anger and betrayal once again.

April had given way to May and the profusion of wild flowers had made the Cornish countryside even more beautiful. Mandy had been promised an afternoon walk to the beach across the fields and Irene suggested Joan come with them.

"Do you mind if I don't come, Irene? I just feel so tired, I think I might have a lie-down." Joan sighed heavily, and positively drooped as she stood by the sink with a tea towel in her hands. Irene bit back the reply which rose to her lips, to the effect that her sister had only been up for about two hours, but then seeing the unhealthy pallor and haggard expression on the other's face, allowed her natural good nature to reassert itself.

"No, that's alright, love. You do look a bit peaky. And you've hardly eaten a bite the last few days. You must keep your strength up. It won't solve anything if you make yourself ill, will it?"

"I know. I do feel a bit under the weather. I suppose it's because I'm not sleeping very well. Everything keeps going round and round in my head. I just don't know what I'm going to do about it all, Irene". Joan bit her lip and stared pleadingly at her sister, as if she might produce some magical solution from her fount of practical wisdom.

"Never mind, Joanie. It'll all sort itself out somehow, you'll see. Maybe you'll hear from Harry tomorrow. Mum said she'd told Mr Cooper you were staying here, and asked him to pass the news on, so p'raps he'll write soon and tell you he wants to talk things over. If you want to go back to Holgate and see him on your own, we'd be quite happy to keep Mandy here with us, so she doesn't get any wind of what's going on. I'm sure she wouldn't mind."

"I know she wouldn't. She loves it here. But I just can't seem to make any decisions, Irene. I know how daft that must sound - you're always so sensible and positive about everything. I used to think I was the same - but now I feel like I'm in some sort of limbo, where nothing's real any more."

Irene tried hard to think of some bracing sensible words that didn't sound unsympathetic, but suddenly the pattern of sunlight on the scullery flagstones was moving in a strangely unreal fashion and whirling faster and faster before her startled gaze. Muttering, "Sorry, I feel a bit odd myself," she staggered forward and, clutching the doorway for support, slipped quietly down to the floor in a dead faint.

She was only unconscious for a few moments, but it achieved what all her previous attempts had failed to do. Joan was shaken out of her self-absorption in the shock of seeing her invincible sister actually vulnerable for once. Administering a cold flannel and glass of water, she helped Irene to sit up gradually and then supported her through to the sofa in the kitchen.

Having removed Irene's shoes and propped her feet up, supported her with cushions and produced a cup of hot sweet tea, Joan herself looked enormously improved at suddenly having to take charge of someone else's welfare.

"I'm alright, Joanie, there's no need to fuss," Irene protested when her sister was eager to run up to the farm and fetch Robert. "As a matter of fact, I know what's the matter and I've been planning to tell him - and everybody else of course - but I wanted to be absolutely positive."

"You don't mean you're...? Oh, Irene, that's wonderful! I am pleased for you! You must be so excited!" Her own depression finally pushed to one side, Joan clasped her sister tightly and beamed at the good news.

"Yes, I am thrilled. I'm hoping it'll be the best

Christmas present Robert's ever had!"

"Well, you must ease up a bit. No more waiting on me hand and foot. I feel awful when I think how I've let you do so much, and I've been lazing about like some wilting lily, wrapped up in all my own worries. You know the first three months you have to be extra careful, even if you are as fit as a flea!" Joan poked the fire into a cosy blaze and fetched a quilt from upstairs to tuck round her sister.

Mandy, who had been outside in the garden playing, now came in and watched the unexpected role reversal between her mother and Irene. "Isn't Auntie Irene very well? Can't we go to the sea this afternoon?" She gazed anxiously at Joan, who smiled reassuringly.

"Don't worry, love. Auntie's just a bit worn out so we're going to leave her to have a nap, and I'll come with you instead. But you'll have to show me the right path, where Auntie usually takes you. Alright?"

It was a beautiful day, and the sun held the promise of real warmth at last. After lunch, wandering across the fields and watching Mandy prance along in some imaginary world of her own, Joan finally found within her spirit some sense of purpose. She accepted that she must now go back to Holgate and confront Harry. They would have a calm discussion and she would make him understand that she had never been unfaithful to him. Her relationship with Oliver had been something totally separate. It had only happened because she had honestly believed that Harry was dead.

She would remind him of the happy times they had spent together with Mandy and point out that he would always be the little girl's father in every way that mattered. He must believe how much he meant to the child, and how devastated she would be if he were no longer a part of her life. Joan knew that, on her side, she must put the memories and mourning for Oliver out of her mind once and for all.

If Harry could be persuaded to make a new beginning and forget the past, her part of the bargain must be to strive with all her willpower to form a committed and loving relationship as a wife to Harry. Who knows, she thought, maybe we'll have a baby of our own soon. That would really cement our new beginning.

Thinking of Irene's pregnancy, Joan suddenly stopped in her tracks. It suddenly occurred to her that her own body had recently deviated from its normal timetable. Her mind had been in such a turmoil, she hadn't realised... She did a few mental calculations - thought back to the nights of renewed closeness with Harry after the terrible scare over Mandy's suspected meningitis - and the certainty hit her. The recent days of lethargy and general queasiness, the other bodily signs, all attributed to her emotional trauma, could simply be the symptoms of early pregnancy!

How wonderful if it were true! But would Harry be pleased, or not? Supposing he was so disillusioned with her that even the prospect of fatherhood would not be enough to effect a reconciliation between them? Joan mentally shook herself. No, she would not return to the endless mental treadmill of 'suppose?' and 'what if?'. From now on she would make some positive decisions and act on them. If the worst happened, she would deal with it. It must be living with Irene, she thought ruefully. That's just how she would be thinking!

Firmly pushing all thoughts of the future to the back of her mind, Joan set out to enjoy some time with her daughter - a pleasure that she had foregone over the last weeks. Mandy skipped along until they reached the stile and the path across the cliff top. Here she took Joan's hand, unasked, obviously having been indoctrinated by Irene over the dangers inherent in this part of the walk.

Steps were cut down the side of the cliff face, leading to the small rock-strewn beach. Once here, Mandy happily trotted off on her own pursuits, and Joan strolled along behind. She was realising that her daughter was becoming more self-sufficient and even appeared to have grown taller since their arrival in Cornwall. She kept calling her mother to examine the various rock pools and their exciting inhabitants.

Irene had schooled her well and she was enthusiastically pointing out the waving tentacles of the delicate sea anemones and the transparent antics of the tiny shrimps. They gradually reached the tide line and investigated various objects that had been washed up by the ocean, in between attempts at skimming pebbles across the curling wavelets. Unusually for this northern coast, there was very little wind, which normally brought the high seas crashing over the rocks at the boundaries of the small cove.

Looking at her watch, Joan realised the afternoon was more advanced than she had thought, and she told Mandy they must turn back.

"I want to get home in time to make supper for Auntie Irene this evening. She really needs a good rest after taking care of us, so it's our turn to spoil her for a change. After supper I'll give you your bath and read your bedtime story. I haven't done that since we first came to the farm, have I? Then Auntie and Uncle can have a nice chat by themselves." She smiled as she pictured the scene when Irene broke her very special news to Robert. Joan determined to have yet another early night herself. But this time it would be a tactful decision, rather than hiding away with her miseries. It was only when they reached the top of the cliff that she realised they had come up a different path, further to the western end of the beach. There was another stile which lead to an area of wild headland covered with gorse and wild plants, encompassing the edge of the Tregaron property. But in the distance she could see the rooftop of the farmhouse itself, so decided they might as well take this route back. It would be quicker than retracing their steps to the beach and the other cliff path, and although Mandy was an energetic little girl, Joan knew that she would be flagging by the time they got home to the cottage.

Sure enough, when they were half way across the headland, Mandy was muttering that her legs were 'wobbly' and she needed a rest.

"Come on, sweetheart, it's not far now. And it looks like it's going to rain." Joan eyed the clouds sweeping over from the sea, and thought they might be in for a storm.

"Tell you what, I'll give you a piggy-back for a while, shall I?" She bent down and hoisted up the sturdy figure, tucking the legs round her waist and little arms about her neck. Mandy was not terribly heavy, and with her weight settled comfortably, Joan set off at a steady pace. There was a small dip in the ground ahead and she knew that once she crested the rise on the other side, she would be almost at the fence that surrounded the Tregaron fields.

It was as she plodded across the middle of the depression that disaster struck.

A section of the tussocky grass seemed to slip sideways beneath her foot, then the whole area was caving in below her, with a terrifying rumbling noise. Joan was flung forward onto her knees and then found herself sliding backwards into the large hole that had now appeared in the ground. Desperately her fingers clawed for support, but the clumps of grass and wild plants slid through her grasp and she hurtled downwards with gathering momentum into the yawning darkness.

It all happened with considerable speed, but at the time to Joan it seemed to be in slow motion. Simultaneously she was aware of Mandy's screams of panic and the pain of the tiny fingers pinching the tender skin of her neck, as the child clung more and more tightly in the extremity of her terror. Then with an awful jarring sensation, that almost drove the breath from her body, Joan's descent was abruptly halted as she slammed into the broken rungs of a ladder that was precariously hanging on the side of the hole into which she had plummeted.

Clods of mud and grass mixed with stones continued to shower down on the two figures for several moments, and Mandy instinctively buried her face against her mother's back, whilst Joan bowed her own head beneath the stinging onslaught from above. When it ceased there was a long silence, as even Mandy stayed quiet in the shock of what had occurred. Joan gradually recovered some presence of mind and was able to take stock of their situation.

They were about ten feet below the ground and by the light from above, Joan could see they were in some sort of disused shaft. She had heard about the Cornish tin mines, and guessed at once that this must be its original purpose. Steeling herself she tightened her grip on the ladder's rung and peered below. But was none the wiser. The ladder that had broken their fall, where it was hanging away from the shaft wall, simply descended into the depths of total blackness.

Looking up at the hole above them, Joan knew there was no way that she would be able to ascend the shaft whose sides were lacking in any handholds. Trying to shift her position so that Miranda's weight was more comfortable, she discovered to her immediate panic that the ladder rocked precariously at her slightest movement. An awful vision of it suddenly ripping away from the rest of its ancient fixings and sending them hurtling into the stygian darkness flashed across her mind.

Fighting to retain some calmness, she froze against the shaft wall and endeavoured to reassure her daughter.

"Well, this is a pretty pickle we've got ourselves into, isn't it, Mandy? Just like the pussy-cat falling down the well in your nursery rhyme. Do you remember the picture in your book?"

"I'm frightened, Mummy. I don't like the dark and I've got bits of grass in my face and stones fell on my head. It hurts, Mummy." The voice quavered, but at least she was no longer wailing.

"I know, darling, it's not nice at all. But you be a brave girl and hold tight to Mummy, and we'll soon be out of this..." Joan bit her lip, her own voice threatening to break as she mentally reviewed her choices. She couldn't go up, so she must either remain still, or else risk descending into the unknown.

If she stayed on the ladder, it might suddenly give way and who knew how far down they might fall? She was sure that Irene would start looking for them relatively soon, but could she retain her precarious position for any length of time? And more to the point, could Mandy? On the other hand, if they managed to climb down the ladder further, it might lead to an even worse situation. The bottom of the shaft might be flooded. There might be more rungs broken or missing, which could lead to another fall.

The longer she reviewed the unpleasant options, the worse their plight seemed. As she lifted her head to the distant light above, she received stinging raindrops on her upturned face and faintly the sound of thunder rumbled in her ears. Mandy was not very happy in a storm at the best of times, and in their present situation, Joan realised she might panic so much that she would lose her grip. Joan knew she had no choice.

"Right, Mandy, we can't stay here on this old ladder, can we, sweetheart? We'll go down to the bottom and make ourselves comfortable till auntie Irene and uncle Robert come and fetch us. At least then we can sit and have a cuddle and keep ourselves warm. I think I've got some toffees in my pocket, so we'll pretend we're having a picnic, shall we?"

"Is it far? My arms are aching holding on, Mummy."

"I know, pet. Just hold tight a bit longer and we'll soon be there." Praying that this would prove to be the truth, Joan risked removing one hand briefly from the rung to pat her daughter's leg, before summoning all her courage to move her foot to the first rung below.

Each step seemed an eternity in the awful downward journey that followed. Every movement caused the ladder to swing violently, no matter how gingerly Joan shifted her hands and feet. Thankfully Mandy had a child's unquestioning trust in her mother's abilities and simply held on in a stranglehold around her neck, with eyes tight shut against the horrors about her.

After the first step, Joan realised that she had sustained some very painful injury when her body had slammed into the ladder. Her thighs and abdomen had received the worst of the impact, and she was afraid that something inside was badly hurt. Waves of pain washed over her at every motion, but she gritted her teeth and suppressed the groans that rose to her lips. As she placed each foot, she was terrified that the rusty rung might give way beneath it. Or that she would find a section of rungs missing altogether.

The lower they descended, the darker it became, and this was intensified as the storm approached above. The rain was pouring steadily down on them now, and introduced the extra hazard of the ladder becoming slippery beneath Joan's wet grasp.

How many minutes that nightmare journey took, Joan could not gauge, even if there had been enough light to see, her watch had been broken in the initial fall. Several times her courage failed her when the ladder's swings had been especially violent, and she stopped and took deep breaths in order to find the strength to continue. She could sense that her daughter's panic was also mounting and threatening to overwhelm her, as she became aware of the rumbling thunder above.

Finally Joan's groping foot was unable to find a purchase. Dear God, was this what she had dreaded? Had the ladder broken away again and they were marooned halfway down the shaft? She peered below, although she knew it was fruitless trying to see her way through the blackness. Then, fortuitously, a vivid flash of lightning gave a brief and blessedly reassuring glimpse beneath.

The ladder had reached the rock-strewn floor of the tunnel at the bottom of the shaft. With a whimper of gratitude, Joan carefully stepped down. Crouching against the wall, she eased Mandy off her back and into her arms, with crooned murmurs of comfort.

For a while they clung together in a tight embrace, both crying with relief that the awful journey was over. Successive flashes of lightning, although still frightening Mandy with their accompanying thunder, were a boon to Joan as she was able to briefly take stock of their surroundings.

The shaft was at the confluence of three identical tunnels. Their walls were slimy and the floors damp and uneven, with scattered rocks that had fallen from the roof. In the shaft bottom there were some large puddles, but Joan wasn't sure if these were caused by the presently falling rain or by continuous leaking from the concealed entrance above. Beside her, she found the old metal grill that had protected the top of the shaft, and over the years had gradually become hidden by the grass on the headland. Her unwitting footsteps just happened to be the ones that finally caused its rusted support to give way and fall into the old mine workings, with Joan and Mandy in its wake.

Joan settled herself with her back to the wall and Mandy on her lap. She wiped both their faces with her handkerchief and found three toffees left in her pocket from that week's sweet ration. Talking all the while, she popped one into her daughter's mouth and was relieved to find the little girl's terrified shaking was gradually abating as she cuddled into the warmth of her mother's arms, wrapped inside her opened coat.

The passing of the storm overhead also helped her recovery, but unfortunately meant Joan's only means of light had gone. The pinpoint of the ever-darkening sky high above did nothing to illuminate their surroundings, and in the wake of the storm, night was falling earlier than usual.

If only I knew the time, I could guess if Irene has raised the alarm yet. Joan tried to reason it through. When we're not back by tea-time, she's bound to start worrying. She knew we were going to the beach, so she'll get Robert to look for us there. It's not that far across the top of the headland, so surely it won't be too long before he sees the hole in the ground.

I wonder if I should try calling out. But she was wary

of frightening Mandy by shouting for help - it would emphasise the perilous situation they were in. I'll wait until I hear sounds overhead, then I'll call up to them, Joan decided. So for now, it would have to be a case of patience and keeping Mandy occupied.

The steadily falling rain made their position even more unpleasant, but Joan was reluctant to move away from the bottom of the shaft. While there was even the faintest glimmer of daylight overhead, she needed to see it. Also her own physical problems made any sort of movement an increasing agony. Thankfully Mandy had not suffered any real injury Joan guessed, except a few scratches from the falling debris. So while Joan kept her occupied with a succession of stories and nursery rhymes, she was not too miserable.

Time dragged by and the light from above was almost nonexistent. Joan was in pain all the time, and even when she was quite still it seemed to be fiercer by the minute. Mandy would ask at the end of each story or rhyme, "Are they going to fetch us soon, Mummy" and Joan would strive to sound optimistic as she invariably replied, "Not long now, sweetheart."

Eventually as Joan's voice was becoming hoarse, she realised that Mandy had finally nodded off on her shoulder. At last the rain had stopped, but there was a monotonous dripping from the foliage surrounding the hole above. It seemed incredible that no one had yet come to find them. It was now completely dark, and Joan knew that it must be well into the evening. What was taking them so long?

The pains in her back were getting worse as well as those in her abdomen, and she was horribly aware that there was a spreading wetness below her that was not simply the dampness of the tunnel floor. Her body was feeling icily cold now and even her teeth had started to chatter. She tried to control her shivering for fear of disturbing Mandy, but an increasing giddiness and a draining weakness was sucking her into unconsciousness.

"I must keep awake. Mandy needs me. Surely they must find us soon." Muttering aloud in her delirium, Joan slipped down further against the tunnel wall, and by the time the longed-for voices finally resounded down the echoing shaft, Mandy was the only one who heard them.

The first news that Nan heard of the drama unfolding in Cornwall was a banging on the door late that evening. She and Billy were sitting over their bedtime cocoa and, with a mother's premonition of disaster, Nan hurried along the passage. Harry stood in the area. By the light of the street lamp his face was thinner and more haggard than she last remembered it.

"Hello, Harry, it's good to see you. I've been hoping you'd come round..."

"Ma, it's bad news! I've just had a phone call at the shop from Robert." He was gasping for breath and had obviously been running. Wordlessly Nan drew him inside and closed the door. Her stomach twisting in fear, she forced herself to wait in silence, although she experienced a desperate urge to shake the words from his trembling lips.

"It's Joan and Mandy, Ma. They've had a bad fall - down some old mine shaft - Mandy's not badly hurt, but Joan's in hospital. Robert says it's serious, Ma!" The wide terrified eyes stared into hers beseechingly, and Nan found herself gripping his shaking shoulders. "Take your time, lad, tell me exactly what Robert said."

"They fell quite a long way, and then Joan climbed down to the bottom with Mandy on her back. But she took the worst of the fall and it's damaged her inside. Apparently they were there for hours before they were found and she lost a lot of blood... God, Ma, if anything happens to Joanie, I don't know what I'll do!

"I've been such a fool these last weeks. Brooding over the past when she believed I was dead - and now this. I may never have the chance to make it up with her."

Nan held him tightly while his thin frame was shaken with sobs. She struggled to control the waves of terror that were sweeping through her own body as she pictured her beloved Joanie and her little granddaughter huddled in the blackness of some dreadful hole in the ground. But Harry needed her strength and as always Nan responded to the call of her family.

"Alright, son. We must go down to Cornwall straight away. Joan'll be in good hands - Irene and Robert will see to that - but our little Mandy needs all the loving family she's got with her mummy so ill. Especially after what's happened to her today. The person she'll be wanting the most will be her daddy."

She looked Harry straight in the eye and there was an infinitesimal pause as she willed him to make the right response. Then he nodded and said softly, "That's right, Ma. She'll be needing me as much as I've been wanting her the last few weeks."

As ever in a crisis at number thirty, Billy proved what a Trojan he was as he quietly took charge of the situation. He made them all a cup of strong tea, then got out his bicycle and went off to the station to enquire about the earliest trains and connections for Cornwall. Nan sat at the kitchen table making a list of things to organise. "I'll get Billy to contact the town hall and tell them I won't be in for a few days - they'll understand, it's a family emergency.

Now what must I pack? Washing things, night clothes, skirts and jumpers. Better take a 'good' dress in case Isaac and Betty ask us round. I wonder if I should take a few of Mandy's toys? Joan couldn't manage to carry much when they went down, so I expect she'll be glad to see a few of her favourite books and cuddlies."

The sound of her own voice dealing with all the simple practicalities somehow kept the full horror of the worry over Joan's condition at the back of her mind, although she knew it would pounce as soon as she allowed herself to rest for a moment. Harry too drew comfort from the sight and sound of Nan's calm efficiency. While she was there, the situation somehow under control in her capable hands, he could let himself believe that everything must come right and life would eventually get back to blessed normality.

When Billy returned they arranged to meet Harry at Holgate station in time to get the milk train up to London and then the first express down to Penzance. Harry would ring the Tregarons so that they could pass on a message to Irene and Robert.

"Tell them not to worry about meeting us at the station if they're too busy looking after Mandy or waiting with Joanie. We can get a taxi and go straight to the hospital," Nan instructed Harry, who really looked as though shock had robbed him of any ability to make decisions for himself.

Throughout the next days, she would continue to be the bulwark against which Harry thankfully leaned. The train journey seemed unending and although they tried to doze, neither having slept the previous night, it was a futile exercise.

When they pulled into the Penzance platform, Isaac

Tregaron was waiting by the barrier. He gave Nan a warm hug and shook hands with Harry before taking charge of their luggage and shepherding them out to his car. "I expect you'll want to go straight to see Joan. Irene's there - has been all night - and Robert's at home with young Mandy. My Missus is at the cottage as well, so the littl'un's in good hands. But the doctor gave her something to help her sleep - probably be late afternoon before she wakes, he said."

"Thanks ever so much for meeting us, Isaac. We were going to get a taxi. I expect you're busy on the farm." Nan tried to smile, but the burly Cornishman's kindness was threatening to undo her rigid self-control.

"Have you got any more news since we spoke last night?" Harry's voice cracked with tension and his jaw clenched as he steeled himself for the reply.

"No, lad. They say there's no change at all. But once you get there, you'll be able to see for yourself. It's not a long drive."

Nan was scarcely aware of the passing views of the choppy grey sea, or the thronged pavements of the busy holiday town. When they reached the hospital, Isaac led them through an echoing corridor and at the end, the lone figure of Irene rose hurriedly from the bench where she had spent the long hours since Joan's admission the night before.

"Oh, Mum, it is good to see you!" They fell into each other's arms for a brief embrace, before Irene held out her hand to Harry. "It's so good you came, Harry. If anything will help pull her through, I'm sure it's knowing that you're beside her."

"Tell us, love, just how bad is it?" Nan and Harry gazed at Irene's exhausted face and she bit her lip as she tried to phrase the bad news she had to impart.

"She fractured the top of her leg and she's broken her pelvis. She's got some bad cuts on her head from falling rocks, which may have caused concussion. They think the shock of the fall and the hours in the wet tunnel has brought on pneumonia. But the worst part of the injuries - I'm so sorry, Harry - but it seems she was pregnant. The fall brought on a miscarriage and she was haemorrhaging really badly for quite a while. So the loss of the blood coupled with everything else... Well, she hasn't regained consciousness at all."

"Pregnant! And she's lost it! Oh my God, I had no idea!" Harry passed a shaking hand across his face and practically collapsed on the bench. Isaac murmured that he'd get back to the farm, and they must ring if they needed anything, anything at all. Irene and Nan gripped hands and sat beside Harry.

Quietly Irene described the events of the previous evening. How she had gone out to help Robert with a difficult calving and they had been late back, finding the cottage in darkness. They had set off at once to search the immediate area. Armed with torches they had followed the path down to the beach and then decided to take the other path across the headland.

Irene recalled the horror of finding the hole and dreading what might be in its depths. She and Robert had knelt in the wet grass and called urgently below, shining their torches as far down as they could reach. She described the awful silence that ensued. It took Mandy a few moments to wake up and then of course she had been terrified at finding herself in the dark with a silent mother. But eventually she had responded to the familiar voices above.

"Mum, it was awful. She kept saying her mummy wouldn't wake up! I had to keep her talking while Robert ran all the way back to the farm to call the ambulance and police and get some rope. He and Isaac came as fast as they could, but it seemed like hours..." Irene's voice faltered and Nan squeezed her hand tightly.

The rescue services had been wonderful. Robert had gone down on a rope and comforted Mandy and then she had been gently pulled up to safety with him, held securely in his arms. A doctor had descended and given Joan immediate first aid and then she had been carefully taken up to the waiting ambulance.

"It was such a relief to find she was still alive, although the doctor said straight away that her condition was very serious. But we've just got to keep hoping, haven't we, Mum?"

"'Course we have, love. She's a fighter, our Joanie. Besides she's a mother and she knows Mandy will need her more than ever after the experience she's just been through." Nan smiled stoutly at her daughter and son-in-law, and wished she could feel inside the confidence that she had managed to instil in her voice.

It was a confidence that was sadly strained over the next hours as she took her turn sitting beside Joan's still form. The ghastly pallor of her face was relieved only by the purples and yellows of the scratches and bruises that covered it - a legacy of the falling debris that had battered her. Her breathing was horribly laboured and a cradle lifted the bedclothes above the shattered leg and pelvis. Nan held her hand, which was pathetically limp and cold, and prayed that this daughter who had endured so much tragedy in her short life might be spared for a happier future. It was clear from the tortured expression on Harry's face as he maintained the vigil by his wife's bed that there would be no question of any further jealousy over her past. She was his adored Joanie, and no matter who Mandy's natural father might be, she would always be Harry's daughter as she had been since her birth. It had taken this awful tragedy to put his feelings in their true perspective. How ironic it was, Nan thought, that Joan had actually been pregnant with his child, and now that poor infant was lost. Life was sometimes a tragedy waiting to happen, she sighed.

While the doctor was doing his examination in the early evening, Nan, Irene and Harry waited outside. All three were exhausted mentally and physically, but equally reluctant to leave the hospital until there was some sort of change.

But when the doctor reappeared he was adamant that they should go. "The blood transfusion is finished and the haemorrhaging is under control. We've dealt with the fractures of the thigh and pelvis so now it's the effects of shock and pneumonia that we are fighting. It's a question of time, to see how she responds to the drugs we're giving her. If she can hold her own for the next few hours, she should be out of the woods.

"Now I'm going to insist the three of you go and get some rest. Come back first thing in the morning. And have some proper food as well. Whatever happens, you'll none of you help her by collapsing round her bed!"

Accepting his logic, they trailed out to the reception hall and Irene rang her in-laws to ask Robert to collect them. Within the hour they were being welcomed into the warmth of the kitchen of the lovely old farmhouse.

"We've put Mandy upstairs in Robert's old room so that we can look after her while you're all at the hospital. She woke up for a while this afternoon and had some food, but soon went back to sleep. She's worn out, poor little thing. We told her that her mummy was in hospital, but she seemed fine when we said her daddy had come down to be with her. I think it will help her a lot when she sees you tomorrow, lad."

Betty Tregaron smiled warmly at Harry as she passed him a plate piled with shepherd's pie and home-grown vegetables. She knew of course that the young couple had been having problems though not the actual reason for their break-up, so was pleased that it looked as though at least some good had come out of the accident.

Everyone forced themselves to eat something, but no-one had any real appetite. Nan had been given the guest bedroom and Harry had Robert's old room. When he tiptoed in, Mandy was fast asleep on a little camp bed. Her face was very pale and there was a sticking plaster on one temple. Harry's heart turned over with love as he bent down and softly stroked the silky hair back on the pillow. He was unaware of Nan standing in the doorway behind him uttering a small prayer of thanksgiving that at least one worry was behind her. She knew that the issue of Mandy's parentage, which had always been a dark secret from the past, was once and for all laid to rest.

Irene and Robert went back to sleep at the cottage, and he made a private resolution that he would definitely organise a telephone of their own in the very near future. All the to'ing and fro'ing with messages from the farmhouse in this sort of emergency was really unacceptable. Had he but known it, Nan had been thinking exactly the same during the train journey from London. If you lived a long way from your loved ones, at least a phone could bring them nearer in times of crisis.

Nan was up at cock crow and had just accepted a cup of tea from Isaac, who was off to milk the cows, when

Harry appeared downstairs with Mandy in his arms. The little girl beamed delightedly at the sight of her grandmother, who gave her a cuddle while swallowing a huge lump in her throat as she remembered the awful ordeal this little girl had just endured.

"Daddy's come for a holiday now, Nan, and I'm going to show him all the animals and the sea and everything!" The dark eyes were sparkling and she certainly appeared to have put the recent drama behind her for the moment.

"That's lovely, sweetheart. Perhaps we can all have a walk later on. I'm looking forward to getting some good sea air into me."

"Is Mummy coming home today? Is she better now?"

"We'll have to see what the doctor says, Mandy." Harry looked at Isaac. "D'you mind if I ring the hospital now, Isaac?"

"'Course not, lad. You don't have to ask, you know that."

The news was still 'no change', so they all had breakfast and then Robert arrived to drive Harry to the hospital. Irene came to amuse Mandy, so Nan was free to accompany the men.

The next hours crawled. Sometimes Nan and Harry would sit on each side of Joan's bed, then one of them would go outside for a break or to fetch a cup of tea from the canteen. Occasionally they had to wait in the corridor while a doctor or nurse administered to the patient, but no one could give them any new information about her.

Nan had finally dozed a little beside the bed in the warmth of the small room, as all the stress eventually caught up with her body. But suddenly an urgent whisper from Harry jerked her into wakefulness.

"Ma, Ma! I think she's coming round, look!"

Joan was muttering a little as she moved restlessly beneath the confines of the cradle over her lower body and sensed the bandage round her skull. Some of the falling rocks had caused a nasty gash that had required several stitches. As consciousness returned, her first sensation was one of pain in what seemed like all of her being. Then she managed to open her eyes and stared muzzily into Harry's.

"Joan, darling, it's me. Are you alright? Can you hear me? How are you feeling?"

"Harry, is it really you? I think I must have had a nightmare... I was in the dark - Mandy was with me - and then it was raining and I was in terrible pain... Harry where are we? Oh, Harry it wasn't a nightmare, was it? Mandy! Where is she, Harry? What's happened to Mandy?"

"It's alright, love. Mandy's quite safe back at the farm with Irene. You're in hospital, and you've given us all a fine scare. Been dead to the world for nearly two days, you have!" Nan took her daughter's hand and squeezed it gently. "Brought Harry and me rushing down here in a right panic."

"Oh, Mum, it is good you're here. It was so terrible in that dreadful hole. I thought they'd never find us again. And Harry, you came..." Her eyes gazed into his face which was looking down at her with so much love in his expression. "It's wonderful to see you - you can't guess how much I've missed you. I'm so sorry for all the pain I've caused, about Mandy, and Oliver." Her voice faded as the sedatives carried her back to sleep, but she did register Harry's words before reality finally receded.

"I'm the one who's sorry, Joanie. I've been such a fool to let the past take you and Mandy away from me. But never again, I swear! Just get well, sweetheart, and the three of us will make a new beginning."

Looking at his bowed head, listening to his voice breaking with sincerity, and knowing that Joan had finally started on the road back, Nan could allow the tears of relief to flow at last.

After that, it seemed life could get back to normal for the whole family, with a settled future before them. Harry and Nan remained at the farm until Joan was well enough to leave hospital and stay on in Cornwall for her convalescence.

What a welcome she received from the Tregarons when she struggled out of Robert's car, leaning heavily on Harry's arm. Everyone was in the mood to celebrate as Irene had now broken the news of her pregnancy to the whole family. Isaac and Betty were ecstatic at the thought of being grandparents and Nan of course was thrilled at the prospect of her third daughter producing another grandchild for her.

The one sad note was the thought of Joan's miscarriage, but in view of her reunion with Harry and the knowledge of her own near brush with death, she was able to accept this loss and, as Nan would put it, 'count her blessings'. Besides, she was very anxious to spend all her energy (which was still depleted) on the wellbeing of her daughter. Mandy had made a remarkably swift recovery from her ordeal, but still had the occasional bad dream, which was only to be expected.

Once Joan was out of hospital, Nan had decided to return to Holgate, leaving Harry in Cornwall. She felt guilty at being away from her job for too long, not to mention from Billy. She knew he would have held the fort back home, and they had spoken on the phone several times, but she guessed he would be feeling lonely.

She had fallen in love with the Cornish countryside, as

Irene had always predicted, but felt Joan and Harry needed time to have a holiday together which would cement their new-found understanding. So she was quite happy to settle into her corner seat on the London express and wave to the little group on the platform as the train pulled out.

Well, that's another drama over and done with, she reflected. It's back to the old routine and we can all get on with our lives. Then closing her eyes, she enjoyed the rare luxury of complete relaxation on her journey back to Holgate.

PART II : 1948 - 1952

For the next two years, it seemed that Nan's prophecy was coming true. Life at number thirty settled into a staid routine like that in thousands of other post-war homes. Housewives everywhere continued to battle with stringent rationing conditions. Clothes were no longer rationed after 1949, but meat was reduced to only 8d worth per person per week. Milk and egg rationing finished in 1950 but it would be 1954 before meat rationing finally ended. As Britain concentrated on her export drive to try and recover from the vast debts incurred during the war, life seemed to be one long round of shortages in the shops. Aside from food, houses, furniture, cars and luxury goods all seemed out of reach to the average citizen.

For Joan and Harry, the housing question was solved on their return from Cornwall. Nan knew they wanted to make a completely fresh start in a home of their own and was absolutely delighted when Harry received the news that Mr Cooper had decided to leave him running the shop entirely, while he took up residence with his married daughter in Surrey.

"She was widowed in the war - her husband was lost on the Burma Railway, poor devil - and she hasn't got any children, so Mr Cooper has decided to up sticks and go to Guildford. But he doesn't want to sell the business, especially as he thinks it will be a real money-spinner if we can expand into television sets, so he's asked me to manage it for him. I'm getting a good rise and I'll have a percentage of the yearly profits."

"Harry, that's really wonderful! What a chance for the future! But it's only what you deserve, lad. You've worked so hard there, he knows he can rely on you."

"Well, Ma, I won't pretend I'm not tickled pink!" He gave her his old cheeky grin. "The best part is, Joanie and me can move into the flat above the shop. It's got two bedrooms, so Mandy can have a nice one of her own. There's a big living room and a kitchen, and a fair sized bathroom. It all needs doing up of course, and I'll probably have to scratch round to get paint and paper, but in the end it should be really smashing!"

"It's come at just the right time. I can't say I won't miss having you here, because I will. But you're only up the High Street, and I daresay Joanie'll still be glad to have me baby-sit sometimes!"

"'Course she will, Ma. There's a yard at the back of the shop. It's full of rubbish and stuff at the moment, but once I've given it a good clear out, I expect she'll be asking you to help her grow some flowers there. A few pots of plants, and maybe a swing for Mandy, and you won't recognise it."

He was bubbling over with so much enthusiasm, it did Nan's heart good to see him. Joan sat quietly sewing a new nightie for Mandy, a gentle smile on her face as she listened to her husband's excitement. Nan could see the depth of her tenderness for him. Although it was not the sort of passion to set the rooftops on fire, it would do very well for a start. Maybe as the years passed and the tragedy of her love for Oliver receded, Joan's feelings for Harry would gradually strengthen. Nan certainly believed they had a good chance of happiness together, as she listened to their laughter and excitement explaining their ideas for the new home to Mandy.

By the end of 1948 they had been settled into the flat above the shop for several months and Harry had taken on an assistant to help him with the business. Mr Cooper would pay a visit every month or so, but was quite satisfied to leave all the decisions and running of affairs to Harry. Occasionally Joan would help out with some of the paperwork, and Nan was delighted that the young couple seemed to have more shared interests.

In mid December, news arrived from Cornwall that Irene had been safely delivered of identical twin boys, whom they called Christopher and Callum. Nan was longing to see her new grandsons, but she knew that Betty Tregaron would be a good support for Irene immediately after the birth, and with Christmas so near she decided to postpone a visit to Cornwall until the new year.

There had been no news of Rita and Matt for months, and Nan was amazed and delighted to receive a Christmas card from them with the news that Rita had a baby daughter called Kate, who had arrived a few weeks previously.

"Well, that's three youngsters they've got now - one a year - she must have her hands full and no mistake! I do wish she'd give me a proper address so I could go and see them. But they're still on that blessed canal boat and travelling all over the midlands. I don't know what sort of life those children will have as they get older. There's schooling for a start!" Nan shook her head over the strange lifestyle that Rita was now living, and as on many previous occasions, reflected what varied homes her girls all had, and how differently they were bringing up their offspring.

It was a strange Christmas for her and Billy, the quietest she could remember. Joan and Harry naturally wanted to spend the day in their new home, so apart from a brief visit in the morning for Mandy to open her presents, Nan saw nothing of them. It was the smallest Christmas dinner she could ever remember cooking, although with rationing still so bad that was just as well. Billy smiled at her across the hearth as they sat by the old range, listening to the King's speech on the radio and sipping their glass of seasonal port - a present from one of his grateful customers at the greengrocery.

"I bet you're thinking of all those grandchildren spread out across the country and wishing you could have had them all round this table, aren't you, old dear? That would be the sort of Christmas you'd really like, wouldn't it?"

Nan smiled and nodded. "You know me so well, don't you, Billy? Yes, I do miss having a houseful, but between you and me, I quite enjoy the peace and quiet, just being the two of us."

"I'm so glad, Nan. Because you're all the family I could ever want, you know." He reached across and took her work-roughened hand and lifted it gently to his lips. They exchanged a long and loving smile and Nan, as on so many occasions in the past, blessed the fates for bringing this dear friend into her life. While he was sharing her home, she could never be really lonely. Surely no physical marriage could offer a deeper or more committed companionship than that shared by them for so many years?

1949 was an uneventful year for the whole family - no new grandchildren and life proceeding smoothly. Nan was busy in her job at the town hall, and branched out into an evening class to learn typing. "My handwriting's getting worse, and you never know I might decide to write me memoirs one of these days," she jokingly said to Billy.

"Well I reckon you lived enough in your early life to fill a book, Nan".

"Let's be truthful, Billy, anyone who lived through the two wars could probably do that!" They sighed and fell silent, briefly recalling some of the terrible scenes they had both witnessed during life in the London Blitz; and years before that, the family and comrades sacrificed in the 'war to end all wars'.

But in July 1950 their quiet life came abruptly to an end one Saturday morning when Nan was summoned by a knocking at the basement door. Speechless as she gazed at the beautifully dressed young woman who stood outside, she wished she could have experienced genuine pleasure at the sight of this member of the family who had been absent for nearly five years.

"Mavis! What a surprise! You're looking very well, I must say. Come in, then." Nan held out her hand and brought the elegant stranger into the passage. Mavis bent and lightly brushed Nan's cheek with her own. Her very high heels made her taller than the older woman, and she brought with her a cloud of expensive perfume. She wore a smart blue two-piece, which matched an off-the-face hat. The stylish ensemble was completed by black suede shoes, gloves and bag.

"Hello, Mother. You look exactly how I remember you." There was a very faint transatlantic drawl that seemed to lend an undertone of irony to all that Mavis said. Her beautifully made-up face was quite flawless, and when she removed her hat, Nan saw the familiar red-gold hair was cut in a fashionable urchin style. Mavis had obviously achieved all the wealth and polish that she had so desperately craved as a young girl, and was now happily flaunting it back in her working-class origins.

She sat at the kitchen table, nylon-clad legs elegantly crossed and sipped the cup of tea that Billy placed before her.

"When did you arrive in London, Mavis? Are you stopping for long?" Billy was his usual friendly self, but with an underlying wariness, for he knew Mavis bore no love for Nan. She believed that Nan was her natural mother but did not hide the gulf between them, although she still resented Nan's affectionate bond with the other three girls.

"I arrived in this country two days ago. I'm staying at the Dorchester and I've been recovering from the journey. I flew over and it's quite tiring, although so much quicker of course than coming by sea."

"So is Irvin here with you? And what about little Joanne? I'm so looking forward to seeing her." Nan tried to sound as warm and caring as she would with any of her other girls and their children.

"Heavens, no! She has a perfectly good English nanny who looks after her. She's far too young to drag all this way. Besides Irvin's father lives nearby and he absolutely adores her, so she'll probably be spoiled rotten by the time I get home."

"What about Irvin, then? Is this a business trip or a holiday for you both?" Nan was jarred by Mavis's off-hand tone about her only child and decided on a quick change of subject.

"No, I'm on my own. As a matter of fact Irvin's gone off to Korea."

"Korea? You mean to the war?" Billy gaped at her astounded. He had only been reading in the paper that morning about the awful conditions the soldiers were fighting under, and as a survivor of the trenches in the First World War, had felt immediate sympathy for them.

"Yes, I'm afraid Irvin and his father haven't been seeing eye to eye lately - they have very different attitudes to the business. Actually Irvin's quite useless in the office - hasn't a clue how to negotiate a good deal. He certainly isn't like his father at all. Aaron is a very sharp cookie indeed!" Mavis smiled reflectively as though recalling some of her father-in-law's particularly clever financial strokes, and, from the expression on her face, Nan intuitively guessed that Mr Goldwyn senior was not averse to sailing a little close to the wind, legally speaking.

"But surely having a row with his father is hardly reason for going back in the army, is it?" Nan looked sharply at the spoilt face across the table, and as always could read Mavis like a book.

"If you must know, Irvin and I haven't been getting along ourselves. He idolises Joanne, but of course is desperate to have a son to carry on the family name. I think he feels that if he manages that, his father will forgive his ineptitude in other directions." She shrugged. "However, I've made it very plain that I've absolutely no intention of going through all that wretched experience again. It was nine months of sheer hell, not to mention actually giving birth! It's beyond me how any woman ever wants more than one child. I had to really work at getting my figure back! So there will definitely be no more little Goldwyns."

"You and Irvin had a really big row, then?" Nan looked at Mavis sadly. With Charlie and Nan's own irresponsible sister, Ruby, as parents, it was hardly surprising she had turned out such a selfish, shallow creature. But Nan still felt a terrible sense of failure. After all, she had had the responsibility of bringing Mavis up from birth - surely her own efforts at instilling some decent standards should have had some effect on the woman before her?

"Yes, his father and I showed him how useless we thought him, both at work and at home. So in a fit of temper he rushed off and rejoined his old unit. Left a note saying that at least he had felt of some use in the army - I ask you! A grown man with every comfort money could buy, and he rushes off like a spoilt child!"

"But aren't you worried about him? They say the conditions out there are terrible where the fighting is." Nan knew it was pointless asking such a question, even as the words left her lips.

"If he gets into trouble, it's entirely his own fault. But of course Aaron thought I would be upset and suggested a little trip to visit my family might cheer me up. He's quite a poppet really, and I can twist him round my little finger." A self-congratulatory smile curved the crimson lips, and for a moment it was exactly as if Ruby had been sitting in front of Nan.

"So tell me, what news of the twins and dear Joan? How many more grandchildren are they all producing for you, Mother?" The plucked eyebrows lifted superciliously while she raked Nan with her eyes, as if noting every detail of the cheap cotton housedress and flat sandals.

Nan was never very conscious of her own looks, but suddenly she felt every inch a dowdy, middle-aged grandmother, well aware of the lines on her face devoid of make-up and the few streaks of grey in the neat bun at the back of her head.

Determined not to let Mavis realise she had riled her, Nan smiled brightly.

"Oh, I don't suppose you heard before you left California, but Irene had a baby girl at the end of last month, so they're calling her June. It'll be lovely for the twin boys to have a little sister, though I expect it will be really hard work with them all so small at the same time. Still, Robert's mother is very good and the farm is a wonderful place to bring up children.

"Billy and me have been for a couple of holidays and of course Joan and her family are always welcome down there. I expect you remember from my letter that Joan is expecting again. They're so pleased because they've been trying for quite a while, I think."

"Well, I suppose dear old Harry will be thrilled to have a child of his own at last. It can't have been easy supporting some other man's child, can it?" Mavis stubbed out her cigarette in her saucer, and fitted another one in the long silver holder, which matched her cigarette case and lighter.

When the truth about Mandy's parentage had all come out back in 1948, Joan had explained the situation in one of her letters to Mavis. She had felt that as the rest of the family now knew the facts, it was only right that Mavis should also be aware of them.

Nan bit back the sharp retort that immediately rose to her lips. If anyone knew the anguish of bringing up someone else's offspring, she had suffered it with Mavis over the years, and was still doing so. But she swallowed her anger as usual and said quietly, "Harry has always loved little Mandy like his own daughter. I know that's how he thinks of her. She has grown up believing it to be true, and there's no reason why anyone should tell her otherwise. But that's up to Joan and Harry when she gets older. I do know they're all looking forward to the new baby. But I'm sure it will make no difference to the love that Harry has for Mandy."

"How very sweet and cosy. So are they still living in the flat over the shop? A new baby will make that a little cramped, surely?"

"As a matter of fact, Harry has got his eye on a small house that's up for rent. It's in Muswell Hill and would be quite convenient for him travelling to the shop, just a couple of stops on the bus."

"My, we are going up in the world - Muswell Hill! And what about dear Rita? Still roaming around with her gypsy brood is she? How many infants has she got at the last count?"

"Two boys and a girl - Benjy, Luke and Kate, but she's expecting another one in February. She sent me a card recently to let me know. I'd love to see them all, but they're always on the move with that canal boat. Still, delivering the cargoes is Matt's job and at least it's a roof over their heads and keeps them all fed and clothed."

"How the other half live!" Mavis looked at the slim gold watch on her wrist and rose to her feet. "Well, I must be off as I've one or two old friends I want to look up. But perhaps you'd like to meet me in London one day next week, Mother. I could give you lunch in a decent restaurant and we could do some shopping.

"Obviously I'll get all my nieces and nephews some presents while I'm in England. Perhaps you could arrange for Joan and Harry to come over here one evening for a little get-together? I know how you always loved to see us around the table enjoying one of your cosy family dinners!"

Nan was aware that she was being sarcastic, but chose to take her literally. "That would be lovely, Mavis. I'll give Irene a ring as well. It might be that they could manage to come and stop overnight. I'm sure she would love to see you while you're here. Robert's got a nice car now, and they can do the journey quite quickly."

"So you have the telephone, do you? And I see the old gas lamps have all gone now. Electricity at last!"

"Yes, Harry and Billy did most of the work between them, and one of Harry's pals did the rest. The family all clubbed together to get it for me for my Christmas present last year. It's a real boon, I can tell you. And of course it's lovely having the phone so I can speak to Irene - makes her seem that much nearer somehow."

"Well, the family were always the be-all and end-all for you, weren't they, Mother?" Mavis gave a hard little laugh. "I'm afraid I'll never be the domesticated little woman, myself. I obviously don't take after you, do I?"

Watching Mavis climb into the hired car that was still waiting and waving her off, Nan didn't know whether to laugh or cry. Billy gave her a hug and said with a chuckle, "Leopards don't change their spots, eh girl?"

And smiling back, Nan said, "No, Billy, but I'd say she was more of a peacock than a leopard these days!" and they both thankfully closed the door and went into the kitchen, which was their safe haven against all the vicissitudes of the hard world outside.

Joan and Irene were both intrigued at the thought of seeing Mavis again, and Nan was delighted when they were able to settle on the following Saturday evening for their family meal. Irene and Robert would bring baby June with them, which really pleased Nan who was longing to see the newest grandchild, and the twin boys would be left with the Tregarons. Joan and Harry arranged for a local friend to sit in with Mandy, and so it was all arranged quite easily.

Nan made a big effort to produce a special, celebratory meal, which was something she enjoyed doing. Irene had promised to bring a chicken up for a roast, and Billy could be relied upon for plenty of good quality veg. A first course of grapefruit and a dessert of fruit salad completed the meal.

Nan surveyed the table, laid with her best china and a

pretty centre-piece of carnations from the garden, and decided it might not be as posh as the Soho restaurant that Mavis had taken her to earlier in the week, but it was certainly fine for a rare family gathering.

"It's such a shame Rita and Matt can't be here - then we'd all be together. That hasn't happened since the end of the war, Billy." Nan took off the apron that was protecting her best dress of flowered silk, with a peplum at the back. She was wearing white court shoes with higher heels than usual. Her dark hair had been freed from its customary bun and was caught up at each temple with a small pink comb that matched the lipstick she was wearing. Billy thought she looked quite lovely, and told her so.

"Well, I know it's silly, but that madam makes me feel like some terrible old hag, so I thought I'd make an effort tonight. Daft at my age, I know."

"What age? Fifty-six? You're as young as you feel, Nan. Isn't that what you're always saying? And I reckon you look more like the girls' sister tonight, not their mum." He gave her a peck on the cheek and Nan squeezed his hand gratefully.

The evening started well. Irene and Robert had arrived in the late afternoon and Nan was able to coo over baby June in her Moses basket. She was a throwback to her grandparents and, instead of being fair like her parents, had a mass of dark curls. She was a placid baby who quite happily settled in a spare bedroom when she had taken her evening bottle.

Joan and Harry were the next to come, bearing some bottles of beer, and port for the women. They were all enjoying a glass when Mavis arrived. In spite of the fact that it was a July evening, she wore a mink coat draped over her shoulders. Underneath was a cream taffeta cocktail dress, with ornate draping picked out in black around the hips to a bustle effect behind. Black patent leather shoes and bag completed the outfit and diamond drop earrings matched a choker and bracelet.

"Talk about overdone!" Joan and Irene signalled each other with their eyebrows, and stifled giggles as they both watched their respective husbands reacting to the expensive fashion plate before them. Mavis as usual was unable to resist playing to any male audience. She was a little more subtle than she had been as a provocative schoolgirl, but the intention was the same. No matter how hard they tried, Harry and Robert both found her body language disturbing and embarrassing, particularly as each was well aware of the amusement it was causing the other women present.

Mavis had come loaded with gifts for all the family, purchased from the West End. She also brought several bottles of champagne to accompany the meal, as well as brandy and whisky for afterwards. Although her ostentation was resented, the family soon found the alcohol had the effect of relaxing the situation and making conversation flow easily.

They quickly started reminiscing about the old days when the girls were growing up, and even Mavis appeared to enjoy the anecdotes from their happy family life. Looking round at the laughing faces as they recalled the various shifts Nan had been put to when she was refurbishing their clothes during the wartime shortages, their mother felt a warm glow that wasn't just the champagne.

This was the reward for those endless years of skimping and scraping; the gruelling hours labouring in the fish and chip shop and scrubbing floors in Muswell Hill. She had done what she had vowed all those years ago in Canada, when Charlie had first abandoned them. She had brought up her girls single-handedly and they all had happy memories of their childhood. The lack of a father had not scarred them in any way. Nan allowed herself a moment to revel in her success.

As though she was reading Nan's self-congratulatory thoughts, Mavis's voice cut sharply across the table.

"Don't any of you ever wonder what it would have been like if our father had still been around while we were growing up? Maybe we'd have turned out quite differently if we'd had two parents like normal families."

There was a brief silence as all eyes turned automatically towards Nan. Then Joan said firmly, "I'm sure we were much better off without him, from what Mum's always told us. Any man who would leave his wife and four children to starve in the middle of nowhere wouldn't have been a very good influence, would he?"

The others nodded and murmured agreement, except for Mavis who, smiling sweetly, said, "Of course we only know Mother's side of the story, don't we? I mean we're all married ourselves and let's be honest it takes two to make or break a relationship doesn't it? I'm sure there must have been faults on both sides, weren't there, Mother? After so many years, I expect you can see things more in perspective, can't you?"

"I'm afraid a hundred years wouldn't change my feelings about Charlie Stuart, Mavis. I never said much about him to any of you because it didn't seem right to condemn a father to his own children. Believe me, if I wanted to justify my loathing for him, there are plenty of details I could give you. But after all this time, there's little point in raking up the past that is still very painful for me. Now, who's for another helping of fruit salad. Harry?"

"No!" Mavis spoke sharply and Nan almost dropped

the glass bowl she had picked up. "I think we all have a right to know about our father. You owe it to us."

"Mavis, that's enough." Joan and Irene both glared at her and glanced at Nan who had visibly paled.

"It's alright, girls. If Mavis is so keen to delve into the past, I suppose, as she says, it's her right. Yours too, for that matter. But why you should need to know anything more about a scoundrel who would abandon his wife and three children, I can't imagine, Mavis. Still, ask me any questions and I can assure you, they'll get a truthful answer. I've nothing to hide, that I do know."

"Very well, Mother. Then why is it you've always maintained that he abandoned three children, and you brought four of us back from Canada?"

"Don't be stupid, Mavis. You know you were only a baby when we all got back to England. Obviously Mum was pregnant when he went off. That's what made it even worse - leaving a pregnant woman on her own to cope with three toddlers." Irene looked contemptuously at Mavis and deliberately finished her glass of wine.

"Yes, that seems the logical explanation, doesn't it? But I'm afraid it wasn't quite like that." Mavis took a deep breath and Nan had a sinking feeling that her long-protected secret was about to be divulged to the whole family. "If you remember, when I first went to America to marry Irvin after the war, his family had only just moved their business down to California. Previously they all lived in North America, very near the Canadian border. They still retained interests there and occasionally Irvin and his father went on business trips up north. After Joanne was born, I suddenly had the urge to go along with them and visit my birthplace."

She looked at Nan. "Surprised, Mother? I expect you never thought of me as sentimental, did you? Well, maybe it was just that I've always suspected you've kept something hidden all these years and I was determined to find the truth." She smiled triumphantly.

"In the end it wasn't that difficult. Naturally I had my birth certificate - you had given me that when I went to America - so I was able to find the address of the farm where I was born. Of course, after all these years the ownership had changed but one of the old labourers did remember an English woman and her children who lived in a shack on the farm property. Said they'd all been snowed up and a new baby had almost died.

"When I showed an interest, and offered some money to buy him a drink, he suggested I pay a visit to old Jessie Campbell in Welland. Apparently she was a friend who knew the English family well."

"Jessie Campbell! I haven't thought of her for years." Nan looked at Mavis eagerly, her premonition of disaster forgotten for a moment. "Did you find her? Is she well? She was quite a bit older than me. Treated me like a daughter back in those days. I don't know how I'd have managed without her at times."

"I did find her, yes. But she's hardly 'well'. She's in an old folks' home and her memory has practically gone now. Widowed years ago and her children scattered. But when I told her I was Nan Stuart's child she was quite rejuvenated. Rambled on about the trip out from England when you first met and then all about your children being born.

"Quite boring of course most of it. But then she opened up her old photograph album and showed me something very interesting indeed." She paused to light a cigarette, and her audience waited in silence, rivetted as she knew they would be.

"She showed me a picture of you standing outside that

hovel where you lived, in the back of beyond. There was a pram with the twins sitting in it. Joan was holding its handle and you were caught unawares, hanging up some washing. So your figure is shown very clearly. You looked incredibly thin, Mother, Obviously the privations you had endured were really telling on you." She sighed and shook her head in mock sympathy, then fixed Nan with glittering eyes.

"The amazing thing about it was the date, Mother. It was printed on the back of the photo - February 1922. Apparently Mr Campbell had taken the picture to show his wife you were alright. She couldn't make the journey herself because she had young children of her own.

"Now this is the interesting part. As I was born in March 1922, how come you were stick-thin a matter of weeks previously?" She opened her bag and pushed the photograph across the table.

"Does that look like a heavily pregnant woman to you, MOTHER?"

Nan gazed down at the faded images and was transported back to the bitter cold of that Canadian winter. She remembered how quickly her fingers had become numbed as she fumbled with the pegs, hanging out her washing in the attempt to catch some warmth from the pale sunshine. It had been such a terrible struggle to dry the children's clothes inside the shack, draping them on lines above the smoky fireplace. She had worried that the steam would be bad for the girls' health.

She even recalled that incident when Mr Campbell had caught her unawares on his camera. He said that Jessie had been fretting about Nan and how she was managing. Although he had done his best to reassure her, he said she wouldn't be satisfied until she could see for herself.

Nan's eyes filled as she remembered the huge debt she

owed that whole family. So sad to think of Jessie living out her last days alone, her mind practically gone, and no relatives to comfort her.

Mavis took back the photograph and passed it round the table. The others looked at it in silence and then all eyes turned to Nan. "Mum, what does this mean? Is there some mistake with the date?" Joan and Irene looked bewildered and anxious. The men appeared somewhat embarrassed, Billy red with anger that Nan was being so upset. He was the only other person who knew the truth, which Nan had confided years ago, and realised how much she must be hating to have these old wounds reopened.

"Well, Mavis, you've obviously done your snooping out in Welland very thoroughly, and it seems I shall have to tell you all - a secret that I've kept since those days, because I made a promise. But if it's the truth you want, Mavis, then you shall have it."

She looked across the table directly into the other woman's eyes. Mavis was very pale now, and Nan could see her hands were trembling as she grasped the old photograph. Whatever her motives had been, it was clear that she was undoubtedly genuine in her eagerness to know about her own origins.

"You're quite right, you're not my daughter. Although God knows I've always struggled to treat you like one. That was the promise I made to your mother, you see. I delivered you myself with no other help, out in that 'hovel' as you called it. And it was there that your mother died when you were scarcely an hour old.

"It was hardly surprising, after what she'd endured. Abandoned, penniless, by your father in America, left to struggle across the country, back to Canada, while heavily pregnant. She must have suffered the most terrible hardships, and at the end of the journey she walked through that winter storm to find me. She knew, you see, that I'd always taken care of her and I'd look after her, come what may."

Nan's voice broke and she was unable to continue for a moment, remembering Ruby as a little girl, falling over in the garden of number thirty and running to Nan with a bloody knee to have it 'kissed better'.

"Don't upset yourself, Nan. There's no need for all this." Billy glared at Mavis, but she ignored him and said implacably, "So who was this pathetic creature that you did so much for? And who was the scoundrel who left her pregnant? Or didn't she tell you that on her deathbed?" The bitterness in Mavis's voice was so sharp that Joan and Irene both felt a moment of real sympathy for her, in spite of their anger on Nan's behalf, who was so obviously distressed.

And Nan too felt only pity at that moment for the woman who was putting her through this ordeal, as she said very sadly, "That 'pathetic creature' Mavis was my sister, Ruby, who was just 20 years old when she died in giving birth to you. As for 'the scoundrel' who fathered you - I had good reason to know his name, without her telling me. It was Charlie Stuart, my husband."

The silence was broken only by the gasps of shock from Joan and Irene, but Mavis said nothing for long moments, her eyes still locked with Nan's. Then she whispered venomously, "No wonder you always hated me. I was a living reminder wasn't I of how he betrayed you, with your own sister? And you had to be saddled with their little bastard because she made you promise!

"God, what a perfect opportunity for martyrdom! How you must have hugged your secret sacrifice all these years.

Telling yourself how wonderful you'd been, bringing up an ungrateful little wretch like me. But don't kid yourself you really kept that promise, MOTHER. You never made me feel that you cared for me as you did the other girls. Even that stupid bitch Rita meant more to you than I ever did. I knew that you see, and that's why I went to Canada to find out the truth. So all your lies have finally been shown up and that hollow martyrdom meant nothing after all."

She rose to her feet, gathering up her bag and mink coat. "Don't worry, MOTHER, I shan't be telling anyone else about my dubious origins. After all, Irvin's family would hardly be impressed, would they? And I certainly don't intend saddling Joanne with this sort of pedigree. We'll all go on with the sham as before. Except of course that your own family can now see you for the lying, devious woman you really are.

"The mother who so virtuously instilled those standards of honesty in her offspring was all the time living the ultimate lie. Oh, but of course, you did show your true colours back in the war didn't you? When you encouraged Joan to try the same course and foist another man's baby on to Harry?

"Quite sure about the father of this other arrival you're expecting, are you Harry? Once a fool always a fool, they say, don't they? After all, who could blame dear Joanie for looking elsewhere, now that her husband's only half the man he was!"

"That's enough you wicked harpy!" Robert walked swiftly round the table and gripped her arm. "You're not dripping any more of your poison into this family. You're leaving, now."

There was silence as their footsteps receded down the passage and then a crash as Mavis slammed the door behind her.

Joan was very pale and struggling with tears. Irene was red with anger but smiled proudly at Robert as he came back into the room and sat with his arm round her. Billy was gazing at Nan, who had buried her head in her hands and was sobbing quietly. But Harry was the first to move towards her. He pushed a clean handkerchief between her fingers and spoke tenderly as he bent over her.

"Come on, Ma. No need to break your heart. Don't give that cow the satisfaction. She's found out what she wanted and now at least you can be glad it's all out in the open. You've no call to reproach yourself with anything."

"Oh, Harry, that's just it. I do! You must all think I've lied to you, and you'll never be able to trust me again. You especially; it's the second lie I've lived with you."

"Ma, there's lies and lies. I know and the rest of the family knows you're as honest as the day is long. Both those lies were good lies, told for the very best of reasons. Told with love, Ma. I forgave you long ago, just as I forgave my Joanie, so that's a closed book. And as for the past, it seems to me you deserve a medal. Not just for taking on your husband's bastard by your own sister - but managing to go on pretending to that little madam that she was your daughter all these years. I reckon that makes you a saint in my book!"

"Oh, Harry. Oh, son, where would we be without you?" Nan howled in good earnest now, and Harry gave up his place beside her to Joan and Irene, who both put their arms around her and whispered words of comfort and love.

Harry looked at Robert and Billy and said with a rueful grin, "How about a game of darts down at the local for an hour? I reckon we might do well to make ourselves scarce for a bit, don't you?"

In their absence, Nan and the girls were able to talk calmly together and she finally poured out to them all the pent-up details of her awful betrayal by Charlie and how deeply she had been scarred by his affair with Ruby.

She described in vivid detail how she had discovered them together in the old shack in the woods and how he had then run off, a fugitive from the police. He had been wanted for making moonshine whisky and then smuggling it across the border at Niagara Falls and into America, where it was banned by the Prohibition.

"I believe he was probably on the run from others as well. I heard that he was heavily into gambling, and no doubt owed a lot of money to the other low-life in Welland. I do know he even took the last pennies of my housekeeping money from the old tea caddy." Nan sighed as she recalled the terrible predicament she had been in and how supportive Jessie Campbell and her family had proved.

"Not exactly the sort of father to be proud of, was he?"

Joan stood up and massaged her aching back. The baby was kicking and the emotions of the evening had exhausted her.

"Not then, Joanie, no, he wasn't. But I suppose you have to try and see the other side of the coin. He'd had a terrible upbringing - abandoned outside an orphanage as a baby, then the cruel life he led there. Ran away as soon as he was old enough and lived off his wits. After that it was the merchant navy, before enlisting and being sent off to war in the trenches.

"When we met I loved him for his sense of humour and his carefree attitude, but of course he should never have married and had a family. He wasn't cut out for responsibility or settling down to domestic life. I'm not making excuses for him - I'll never, never forgive him for what he put us all through, Ruby as well, but I suppose I can understand a little of what made him the person he became."

"I wonder what happened to him in the end." Irene looked at Nan. "You never heard any more did you?"

"No love, not from that night he slammed out the door of the cottage. When David and I talked of marriage, he said that he would get his solicitors to try and trace Charlie. If he was found I would have divorced him. If they couldn't find him, I believe in law he could be pronounced dead after seven years, and I'd have been free to marry David.

"The last Ruby saw of him was somewhere in the mid-west in America, but she never told me much because she was in no state to talk - delirious most of the time, as well as in terrible labour with Mavis."

"Well, Mum, I think we must all put it behind us now. Mavis will probably leave you in peace since she's got what she wanted. We certainly don't blame you for anything at all, so you can consign it all to the painful past, where it belongs." Irene gave her mother a loving smile, and Nan told herself yet again how blessed she was in this most practical of her daughters.

Two months later Joan gave birth to Donald - Donnie as he was always known. It had been a difficult labour and he was rather underweight and sickly. She struggled to make him take his bottle, being unable to breastfeed, and his health was a constant worry. But otherwise he was a great joy to them all. Harry adored his little son, being always careful to share that love equally with Mandy. But there was never any hint of jealousy as she idolised her brother from the first moment that Joan brought him home from the hospital.

They had now moved from the flat above the shop and were settled in the little 'semi' in Muswell Hill. Nan was almost as thrilled with it as Joan, and they happily cleaned from top to bottom and organised the little garden, front and back. Harry installed a sand-pit and a new swing for the children and Mandy was given a patch of earth where she was encouraged to make her own little garden. This was a great success and she had obviously inherited her grandmother's love of growing things.

Plans were laid for the family Christmas to be held at the new house and Nan and Billy had promised to stop overnight on Christmas Eve so that she might help out with the cooking as Joan had her hands full with the baby. Then their lives were all changed once again by another new arrival.

This one was heralded by a letter in unknown handwriting, which Nan opened curiously one breakfast time. Billy looked up from his porridge as she suddenly exclaimed, "Well, I never!" and her hand rattled her teacup as she replaced it in the saucer.

"What's up, Nan? Not bad news, is it?"

"No, nothing like that. It's just so unexpected." She looked up, her lips trembling a little, as she was obviously trying hard to keep her emotions in check. "It's from David's nephew, Adam. He's in London and he wants to visit me."

"I didn't know he had a nephew, Nan. I never heard him talk about family. I assumed he didn't have any close relatives."

"He told me about an older brother - James he was called - but they didn't get on very well. Not much alike in temperament. You know David was always wrapped up in his work after his wife died. His brother apparently was a businessman, had a big timber firm I think. He moved away from Welland in the late twenties. They kept in touch, but not very often. I do recall David mentioned there was a nephew, said he was in the Canadian Air Force during the war, but I don't think they'd seen each other for ages."

"So why's this chap writing to you, Nan?"

"Apparently his father died recently and he's been sorting out the estate. He came across some letters David had written during the war - he'd told his brother about us, said we were going to be married - but that was the last letter he wrote before he left England on the ship." Nan's voice faltered as she still found it hard to talk about the terrible tragedy, when the ship carrying all the refugee children along with their doctors, including David, had been sunk by a German U-boat.

"Adam kept my address and as he's now in England he wanted to pay me a visit. For David's sake. It sounds as though he was very fond of his uncle, had more in common with him than his own father, and wants to meet me."

"Well, that's really nice, Nan. You'll see him, will you?"

"Oh, yes. I want to meet him. Though it's strange to think of this contact with David's family - unexpected. Well, I must write back and give him our phone number. If he rings we can make arrangements to have him round one evening. His address is a hotel in Bayswater, so I wonder how long he's staying. I suppose he's having a holiday." She sounded slightly vague, and Billy could see that this echo from the past had had a profound effect upon her. He just hoped the proposed meeting would not upset her too much.

Adam phoned very promptly, the same day that he received Nan's letter. His pleasant Canadian voice brought back so many memories, but Nan was able to chat to him quite calmly on the phone and he was eager to pay a visit the next night. Nan decided not to invite him for a meal, until she saw how they got on together. Time enough to offer further hospitality if things went well.

When she opened the street door, it was quite hard for her to greet him unemotionally and take his proffered hand. He was taller than David had been and a slighter build. His hair was brown, a lighter shade than she remembered David's - but the latter's had been heavily streaked with grey. However, when Adam smiled and moved as he spoke, the mannerisms were like looking at David. A certain shy hesitancy in his speech; a sense that this was not a very gregarious animal, one who enjoyed his own company and was not at ease with social chit-chat.

It was odd to think that although he seemed young to her, he must be older than David had been when they first met. He was thirty when he had delivered Joan, although he had appeared older to Nan at the time. Probably because of the air of authority that he had exuded when acting in his professional capacity. Which was how she had always regarded him back in Canada. It was only when he had come to England in the war, years later, and Nan fell in love with him that she saw the vulnerable personality beneath the professional facade.

Nan led Adam into the front room, where she had purposely lit a fire. It was a room they rarely used, but she had felt entertaining this stranger was a special occasion that warranted the effort. A bronze jug on the side table had been filled with yellow chrysanthemums and their scent pervaded the air.

She settled him in an armchair and asked if he would prefer a hot drink or a glass of beer.

"A cup of tea would be great. Your English winters

aren't as bad as our Canadian ones, but it's still pretty chilly out there tonight." He held his hands towards the cheerful blaze and Nan bustled out to the kitchen to fetch a tray. In truth, she was glad of the opportunity to catch her breath, emotionally speaking. Billy had tactfully made himself scarce, visiting Muswell Hill to assist Harry with some shelves he was putting up in the kitchen, so Nan quickly laid a tray for two, with a hand-embroidered cloth, her best china and a plate of home-made scones with jam.

When she returned to the other room, Adam was examining various photographs that were arranged on the mantelpiece. In one silver frame was a snap of Nan and David, which had been taken on the Embankment by a street photographer. Her arm was tucked through his and both were smiling warmly. It was the only one she had of the two of them together.

"You and uncle David look really happy there." He accepted his cup of tea and sat down by the fire. "He was a great chap, what I remember of him, although we didn't meet that often."

"Yes, he was a very special person. I still miss him." Nan handed him a plate with a scone and sipped her tea, striving to retain her composure.

"He and my dad didn't have much in common. Dad was every inch the businessman and he was eight years older than uncle David. So there was seventeen years difference between us two. I admired the work he did in his field, both as a G.P. and then his specialised area of psychiatry. I imagine he helped a lot of those poor kids back in the war. Especially the Jewish refugees."

"Yes, he was dedicated to his job. You could hear it in his voice and see it in his eyes - the enthusiasm, the commitment." Nan was silent, remembering it was the same dedication which had sent him on the refugee ship to Canada, looking after his young patients, that had stolen him from her.

"So, what about you, Adam? What work do you do? Did you follow in his footsteps?"

"Gosh, no! I became a teacher when I left school. Much to my dad's disgust. He wanted me to carry on in the family timber business, but I'm afraid that wasn't for me. I went to college, got a degree and then taught in a school in Toronto. I enjoyed it, but when the war came I enlisted with the Canadian Air Force. I think that was the only time Dad really approved of me!"

"Did you see a lot of action in Europe?" Nan refilled their cups, just enjoying the sound of the familiar Canadian accent.

"Here and there, and then I was shot down and spent the last couple of years in a P.O.W. camp in Germany. Not much fun, but it could have been worse, I guess. After I was repatriated I found it hard to settle down - like thousands of others I suppose - so I took off on my travels. Went all over the place, working on farms or doing other labouring jobs to earn enough to buy my next ticket and pay for my next lodging house. It was a nomadic sort of life, but it was what I needed for a while. Certainly broadened my outlook.

"Then when my father died earlier this year, I came back to Canada to sort things out. My mother had died just before the war, so there was no one else to keep me there. I sold the firm and packed up all the personal belongings and rented out the house. I couldn't quite bring myself to sell it yet.

"When I was briefly based in England during the war I thought I would like to see more of it, and now seemed like a good time. There was a teaching post advertised in north

London so I decided to take the plunge. And here I am." He smiled David's slow smile and Nan's heart missed a beat to see it.

"Say, these scones are great. Did you make them yourself?"

"Yes, I did. It's funny; your uncle always loved my scones. I'd make them as a special treat, when I could scrounge the ingredients during the war."

After that they chatted easily, and the more he relaxed, the more Nan enjoyed his company. She told him about the family and showed him pictures of all the grandchildren. He seemed fascinated, and it was obviously all foreign to him, being an only child. Nan had the impression he was quite a lonely person, who had found it impossible to put down roots after the war.

"No plans to settle down with a wife and family yourself, Adam? Or doesn't that appeal?"

"There's nothing I'd like better, Nan - it's O.K. if I call you Nan, is it? - but I've already met the woman I wanted to marry, only sadly it wasn't to be."

"I'm sorry, lad. I didn't mean to pry."

"It's alright. I guess it's not a very unusual story, and ancient history now. My fiancée was attached to the Canadian Air Force. She came from Quebec and was bilingual. When she heard about the resistance workers in France, and how the S.O.E. were sending men and women out there to live under cover and help prepare for the invasion, she volunteered to join them.

"Lucille was always a dare-devil sort of girl - just the opposite from me - but don't they say 'opposites attract'? She loved rock-climbing and canoeing and it was just like her to join something as dangerous as the Maquis. Anyway, it all went wrong and she was captured by the Gestapo in the last months of the war."

He was silent for a moment and stared into the depths of the fire, his jaw clenched and a bleak look of pain transforming his placid features. Nan waited until he said, quietly, "They interrogated and eventually executed her. I had a letter from another member of her resistance group afterwards. He said how incredibly brave she had been - how much they all adored her..."

Nan reached out and took his hand. They sat in silence for a long moment and then he squeezed her fingers with a gentle smile and said quietly, "Bloody war, eh, Nan?"

And she replied, "Bloody war, Adam."

Adam's arrival brought a new happiness to Nan and he was also soon a great favourite with the rest of the family. As Christmas was almost upon them and he had made no plans, it was suggested that he join them at Muswell Hill for the festivities. It was obvious from his easy ways with Mandy that he would be a good teacher and was equally relaxed cradling Donnie in his arms when the baby was particularly fractious.

Joan enjoyed his conversation about books, as she was an avid reader like her mother, and the three of them would eagerly discuss their latest library offering. Harry and Billy found him a useful pair of hands with their latest D.I.Y. project as well as a relaxed companion at the local pub for a pint or a game of darts. Sometimes the three of them would reminisce about their own particular war experiences and then the women would leave them to get on with it.

Joan and Nan knew that this sort of talk was a necessary catharsis for all three. Their male chat over shared bad memories was a healing balm to all three. For Adam and Harry the wounds were still quite raw whereas

Billy's days in the trenches were far behind him, but the scars were lasting, both physical and mental.

In the course of conversation, Adam revealed that he was searching for a permanent base, as he was tired of living out of a suitcase at the hotel. Harry then casually mentioned that the flat above the shop was still vacant, since he and Joan had moved to Muswell Hill. One quick visit showed Adam it would be ideal for his purposes, only a short train ride to the school where he would be working.

So in the first weeks of 1951 he installed himself, after a trip round the local shops to purchase the bare essentials for furnishings. It was clear that money was not a problem; the sale of his father's business meant that he had a comfortable nest egg wisely invested, apart from his somewhat meagre earnings as a teacher.

The year was only a couple of months old when Nan received a brief letter from Mavis. After the traumatic evening at number thirty, they had heard nothing further from her during her London visit. But a Christmas card had arrived as usual - an elegantly engraved offering, with no personal signature - and all the family had sent their own individual cards to her. As Nan had reminded them, it was important for little Joanne's sake that her English family keep in touch. Irvin being an only child meant that her American relatives were few, and every youngster needed to feel part of a family, was how Nan saw it.

When she read the contents of Mavis's letter, she was even more determined to keep in touch with this granddaughter/niece. Irvin had been killed in the ferocious winter fighting in Korea. What a sad waste of a young life, thought Nan.

Mavis made no attempt to sound devastated at his loss,

any more than she had ever pretended he was the great love of her life, even before their wedding. She had simply regarded him as a passport to the lifestyle of ease and luxury that she had always craved. Now she could continue to enjoy that existence without even the necessity of pretending to consider the wishes of her doting husband.

The rest of that year passed uneventfully. Mandy was doing well at Holgate mixed infants school; Harry's shop was thriving and so was Billy's; Nan still enjoyed her work at the town hall. Donnie was a continuing worry to Joan, managing to catch every cough and cold that was around. But Nan was thankful that he had proved the final ingredient needed to cement the strong marriage his parents now enjoyed.

Adam would have a meal with Nan and Billy every week and occasionally invited them to eat at his flat, as cooking was a favourite pastime of his. Sometimes he would join the whole family at Muswell Hill for a Sunday roast. In the summer they took several outings to the Festival of Britain in London and marvelled at the vast exhibition with its Skylon tower and huge Festival Hall. Irene and Robert came up from Cornwall to stay for a long weekend and Nan was in her element looking after the twin boys and little June, who was now toddling everywhere, while their parents also spent a long day on the South Bank.

Nan sometimes felt that she and Billy rattled around in number thirty with two spare bedrooms unused for much of the time, but on occasions like this it was wonderful to have the space to accommodate the rest of the family.

In the year that followed, Nan was to look back on that summer as one of the last happy times, before the comfortable, secure routine of her life was rocked by an event that left her devastated.

Indeed the omens for tragedy were in the air early in 1952 as a stunned nation heard on the wireless on February 6th that King George had died in his sleep. The death of the monarch who had so endeared himself to his people by standing shoulder to shoulder with them throughout the horrors of the Blitz seemed like a personal loss. Nan and Billy made the journey to London and joined the queue of mourners filing past the catafalque in Westminster and she wept unashamedly with thousands of others. It wasn't just the loss of a king, it was the end of an era for her generation.

The winter dragged on and Londoners battled with the dreadful smogs that seemed a seasonal feature now. Indeed that year some four thousand died from their effects. Smog masks were a common sight on pedestrians and Joan was terrified to take Donnie outside the house for fear of his delicate chest. Billy too was looking his age now, although he still kept active with his little greengrocery shop. Nan wondered if she would be able to persuade him to retire in a year or two and take a well-earned rest.

Life was still not particularly easy at that time; prices seemed to be forever climbing and their income did not keep pace. Nan had become an expert in frugal living when the girls were young and managed a lot better than most. She still grew quite a lot of their food on the allotment and would often receive a welcome parcel of preserved goods from Irene. Joan and Harry were reasonably comfortable now, and although there were not many spare pennies, they managed to have a week's holiday with the children down on the Tregaron farm in the summer.

They had just returned when the country was horrified by the flash floods that led to the devastation and loss of life in Lynmouth on the Devonshire coast. Among the casualties, sadly, Issac and Betty Tregaron were numbered. They had been staying in a small cottage owned by old friends, having left Robert to manage the farm while they took a week's break. Like so many others, they were swept away in the violent torrent that undermined the foundations of the cottage, situated on the river bank down in the gorge. It was in the middle of the night and they did not have a chance of escape from the terrible onslaught of the waters.

Robert had the dreadful task of identifying their bodies among so many dead, and then, of course, the full responsibility of the farm descended on his and Irene's shoulders.

"We'd only been talking last summer when they stayed here about them doing an extension to the cottage, now the children are getting bigger. That box-room really isn't big enough for little June, and they've no spare room for family going to stay. Now they'll be moving up to the farmhouse to live, and will have all the room they need.

"Poor Isaac and Betty, they were such a lovely couple. I know Irene thought of him as the dad she never knew. And they doted on the little ones." Nan blew her nose and wondered if she should try and take some time off and go down to Cornwall and see them through this crisis. But Irene as usual was coping magnificently and told Nan not to worry.

"We'll not be moving for a while, Mum, no sense in rushing into it. We've managed in the cottage so far, and a bit longer won't hurt us. I think it will be easier for Robert if we change a few things round, have a good clear out of furniture and redecorate the rooms before we start living in the farmhouse. Otherwise it will seem like we're staying in his parents' place rather than in our own home."

"Alright, love, just as you say. But let me know if you do need me when the time comes, and I'll sort it out at the town hall, so I can come down for a week or two."

"Thanks, Mum, you're a treasure. Got to ring off now, I can hear Robert and the twins are back from the milking, so I'd better get their tea."

What a boon it was having the phone, thought Nan. And now she and Billy had been talking about buying a television set from Harry's shop in time for the coronation next year. The main debate was where to put it. Such an important item really should go in the front room with all their good furniture. But since they lived most of their lives in the kitchen, they would probably put it behind the table, in one corner. She rarely used the old sewing machine which stood there at present so maybe that could go up in one of the spare bedrooms to make some space.

The children had offered to all chip in towards a set as a Christmas present for her and Billy, and Harry of course would do them a special price. You are going up in the world and no mistake, Nan Stuart, she thought with a little smile as she sat down to write her monthly letter to little Joanne in America. Wait till Mavis knows about this!

News from Rita was spasmodic as usual, but she did write to tell Nan about the birth of a second daughter, Sally, in late September. "Two of each, I wonder if they'll stop at that, love? What d'you think?" Billy smiled as he read the misspelt postcard she had shown him.

"You tell me, pet! I'm not sure they've discovered where the babies are coming from, knowing what a daft pair our Rita and Matt are! Still, that's them, and I'm just thankful as long as they're happy together. I'm not sure it's the way I'd choose for my grandchildren to grow up - always on the move in that narrow boat, with no real roots.

Still, who's to say they're not a lot happier than Mavis's young Joanne with her nanny and her pony and her wardrobes of posh frocks?"

"That's true, ducks. I reckon your Rita has more genuine maternal instincts in her little finger than that fashion-plate, Mavis!"

In October the papers were full of the Mau Mau terrorist atrocities in Kenya, and Nan felt the familiar twinge of sympathy for relatives of the servicemen being sent out to fight a different kind of war from the two she had experienced. With constant scare stories of the 'Cold War' between Russia and America and its attendant threatened repercussions, it seemed there was global gloom and despondency.

"And we thought all our worries would be over when Hitler finally went for a Burton!" Nan shook her head over man's stupidity as she waved Billy off on a rare visit to an old army friend in the suburbs.

She first heard of the disaster that was to have such a crushing effect on her life when she switched on the wireless that evening to hear the news. A huge railway collision in Harrow had led to a terrible death toll. It was feared that over a hundred had perished with a vast number injured.

Even as her legs turned to jelly and her whole body started shaking in fear, there was a banging on the front door, and the sound of Harry's voice as he let himself in.

"Ma! You in, Ma? Have you heard the news about the train smash? Hey there, easy Ma!" She was sheet-white and swaying on her feet. He guided her to a chair, and swiftly fetched a glass of water from the scullery. "Now have a sip of that, and take some deep breaths. That's the ticket."

"Harry, I just heard on the wireless. I'm so scared that Billy might have been involved. I expected him home by now and it was on his way from his mate's house. Oh, Harry, do you think he could have been hurt or...?" The usually strong Nan found herself unable to voice the awful dread that was threatening to send her off in a faint at any moment.

"Now, Ma, don't start thinking the worst. I expect lots of the train services have been delayed because of the crash, so he's bound to be late. But why don't you come back with me to Muswell Hill and stop with Joanie while I pop up the police station and ask them? They'll know where to make enquiries about the casualty list, I expect. I know the sergeant there quite well - he'll be able to find out something for me, I'm sure."

"Thanks, son. I can't seem to think straight for worrying. But I'll stop here in case Billy comes back. As you say, it's probably just delays on the trains making him late." She made a valiant attempt at a smile, but the quivering lips ruined the effect.

Harry knew better than to try and persuade her so he set off for the police station, briefly stopping on the way at Adam's flat. Once he knew of Nan's distress the older man immediately grabbed his jacket. "Don't worry, Harry, I'll go straight round to number thirty. You're quite right, she shouldn't be left alone to wait for news."

"Thanks, mate. I just hope to God that this is all a storm in a teacup. If anything happens to old Billy I don't know what she'll do. They're like Darby and Joan those two, even if they never actually tied the knot."

But Harry's prayer was not to be answered. Enquiries at the police station soon discovered that Billy's body was one of the first to be listed - dead when he was removed from the wreckage. Harry afterwards told Joan that it was the hardest moment of his life when he walked back into the kitchen of number thirty and had to face Nan.

She was still in her usual armchair by the fireplace, Adam opposite her. In the background the wireless made a low noise - they had left it on in case any further news was broadcast about the crash. Harry hesitated in the doorway and she rose to her feet, eyes meeting his in a mute question that received its answer from the expression of infinite sorrow on his face.

"He's gone, Harry, hasn't he?" She waited to hear the sentence pronounced in so many words - "I'm so sorry, Ma. They found his name on the first list that's been released. Oh, Ma, I don't know what to say..." His voice broke at the desolation in her eyes and in a quick stride he was by her side, his one arm holding her tightly to his chest.

Those were dark days that followed for Nan. Harry and Joan insisted she stay with them, while she dealt with the inevitable formalities that always ensue with sudden death. Harry and Adam saved her the macabre duty of identifying Billy's remains, for which she was eternally grateful. Like most Londoners, she had witnessed some gruesome sights in the Blitz, especially as an Air Raid Warden, but there was no way she could have faced up to the sight of Billy's poor broken body on some mortuary slab.

She insisted on organising the funeral herself, with the mourners invited back to number thirty afterwards. Billy had made a will, which he had told Nan about years before. His small savings, and the remaining lease on the shop, he had left entirely to her. He had also asked that he should be buried in Holgate cemetery, as he had never liked the idea of cremation.

Years later Nan was to be glad of that request. Although not a religious woman, and with a practical streak that made her declare cremation was more sensible than burial - "Look at all that land wasted in graveyards all over the place, that could be used for houses or growing food!" - Billy's grave proved to be a place of comfort for Nan.

When life was particularly difficult, or she felt more lonely than usual, she would be glad to pay a visit to this quiet corner, kneel down with her scrubbing brush and give his headstone 'a good going over'. The inscription was simple: *William (Billy) Wright - A true friend to Nan Stuart and all her family.*

She always ensured there were fresh flowers growing above him, even pansies during the winter-time and a holly wreath at Christmas. As she weeded and dug, she would hold a conversation with him, usually in her head, but increasingly as she got older, it would be whispered out loud - it brought her enormous comfort in times of tribulation.

But that was in the future. In the immediate aftermath of the funeral, Nan was functioning like a zombie, and her life was going through such a time of blackness that she was hardly aware of any conscious thought at all. Throughout her waking hours there was just a sense of aching loss, and incredulity that it could have happened in this shocking, unexpected manner.

All the family rallied round her. Irene and Robert came up for the funeral, although it was only a matter of weeks since his parents' double one. Rita of course did not know as they had no way of contacting her. But Mavis sent a condolence card and had an ornate wreath delivered. It was a hollow gesture, Nan felt, but she supposed it must mean something.

Watching his coffin covered in the flowers that he loved, she allowed her mind to drift back to the day they had met. Funny, it had been a tragic accident that had first brought them together. Her brother Fred, a shell-shocked victim from the trenches of the first war, had gone onto the ice at Alexandra Palace lake trying to retrieve a doll of young Joan's which a stray dog had snatched.

Poor Fred. The ice had cracked and he had been drowned before the eyes of Nan and the girls. Billy had been a chestnut vendor in those days. He had been a tower of strength, taking charge in the crisis as he had done so many times in the years that followed, when he had become a dear friend and lodger at number thirty.

When the other mourners had gone and only the family members remained, Joan and Irene tried to persuade Nan to go away for a while. "You know you're welcome to come back to Muswell Hill with us again," Joan said kindly.

"Or come down to the farm for a few weeks. You love Cornwall and the change of scene will do you good. You always say a breath of sea air works wonders". Irene put her arm round Nan, secretly shocked to see her mother looking so beaten and fragile. This was not the strong Nan they were all used to, dealing with any emergency and a support for everyone else.

"No, I don't think so. Thanks, both of you. I know you mean well, but I really can't face the upheaval now. I just want to stay here at home with my own things around me. I think I need to be alone for a while, if you don't mind. I'm not ungrateful, but I don't want anyone else at the moment. I'm sorry."

She picked up a tray of cups and drifted out to the scullery and they could see her dispiritedly filling the washing-up bowl. Joan and Irene, Harry and Robert all exchanged glances, unsure whether to try harder to persuade her.

Adam said, quietly, "I think you'd do best to listen to her. She knows how she feels. I'm sure there'll come a time when she will need you, and when that happens, she knows you'll all be there for her."

The others nodded, reluctantly, and eventually they all left with final embraces and whispered words of love and condolence. Nan seemed to hear and feel them all through a grey veil of pain and disbelief. When they had finally gone, she looked round the kitchen trying to focus on routine actions. Mechanically she banked down the fire and locked up. The October night was already bringing a wintry chill with it. Strange to be doing the jobs that had always been Billy's domain. Switching out the light, she slowly ascended the stairs to her lonely bedroom.

Of course they had never shared a room, but there had been a comforting familiarity about the sound of his footsteps behind her; exchanging a peck on the cheek outside their respective bedroom doors; and if she woke in the night, hearing the creak of his mattress or the faint sound of the occasional snore. Now all was silent and, for the first time since David's death, she felt utterly alone. She was filled with terror at the prospect of living out the rest of her days without that familiar shoulder on which to lean in times of joy and sadness. Billy was gone. How would she ever cope without him?

In the ensuing months, the rest of the family became increasingly concerned about Nan's mental and physical well-being. They were so used to their mother's huge strength and resilience in adversity that deep down they all expected her to recover from Billy's death quite soon. Of course she would grieve for him, but she would simply get on with things as she had always done. But this time, everything had changed.

Nan had gone back to her job a few days after the funeral and she carried out her duties as efficiently as ever, but she was simply going through the motions. She would dread coming home at the end of the day. Entering the dark house, drawing the curtains and then preparing her solitary evening meal - it was like some sort of nightmare.

Cooking became an enormous effort, and usually she would simply heat a tin of soup or boil an egg. There seemed no point in laying the table for one, and she would sit by the fire in her old armchair with a tray on her knees. She was loath to lift her eyes for the sight of the empty armchair opposite was such a painful reminder. Not that she needed any reminding. All her thoughts were filled with Billy these days.

She flayed herself with recollections of all the times she had been grateful for his unstinting care without speaking of her gratitude. Now she was convinced he had been unaware of how much his love was reciprocated.

They had both known that no man could ever replace David in her affections, but slowly over the years since David's death, Billy had come to mean as much to Nan, but in a different way. She had just not realised it until he had been taken from her life so suddenly and tragically.

When Joan and Harry came to visit, which they did several times a week, they noticed that even the daily chores of keeping number thirty clean and tidy were becoming too much of an effort for Nan. A thin film of dust lay along the mantelpiece and over Nan's cherished family photographs; the lino needed sweeping; the plants on the scullery window-sill were drooping for lack of water; and the copper jug on the table was empty of flowers, which Nan would never normally allow - even in the depths of winter she would find some greenery to brighten the room. Now it was all too much effort.

"I'm so worried about her, Irene." Joan spoke on the phone to her sister. "She's getting terribly thin and her face is so haggard, with great shadows under her eyes. I'm sure she's not sleeping. Or cooking proper food. I've asked her to come to us for Sunday roast each week, but she says she doesn't feel like going anywhere. Honestly, I'm at my wits' end at the moment, I can tell you!"

"Well, I suppose we've just got to give her time. Billy and she were like an old married couple - they'd shared number thirty for so many years. That's another problem - what's she going to do with the house? I mean she can't intend staying there on her own, can she? It's far too big for her now. I should think all those empty bedrooms must be a bit scary at night, the state she's in at the moment."

"Well, I did ask her if she might be better off getting a flat nearby. I suggested she have a word with her landlord. He might have something suitable on his books and I'm sure he'd be glad to have a whole house vacant to rent out to a big family. He could probably get more for it."

"So what did she think?"

"She really got on her high horse. Said she'd been born and brought up there and had no intention of moving into some poky little flat. When I pointed out that she'd find it hard to pay the rent without Billy's contribution, she almost told me to mind my own business! Oh, I didn't take offence, I know it's just the way she is at the moment, but she'll have to make a decision soon." Joan sighed and Irene echoed her down the telephone line. They only wanted the best for Nan, but at the moment it was hard to determine exactly what that was.

Even the prospect of Christmas, which Nan usually adored organising, was not successful in shaking her out of her apathy. When Joan suggested that Nan might like to have them all to number thirty that year, she was told that her mother 'didn't feel up to all the effort'.

"You have it at Muswell Hill, Joanie. It'll be easier for you to keep the kiddies in their own home with all their presents. I expect Adam will come, and I'll be round for my Christmas dinner. I don't suppose Adam will mind giving me a lift in his car."

So they all made enormous efforts to produce the appropriate air of festive jollity, especially in front of the children. But it was an obvious sham, and when Nan quietly asked Adam to kindly drive her home shortly after tea, they were almost thankful to put an end to the farce.

Adam was secretly as shocked and worried as the family about Nan's deterioration, and that Christmas Day impelled him into action. He told Harry that he would not return to Muswell Hill after dropping Nan home. "It'll be nice for you and Joan and the kids to have some time to yourselves this evening, so I'll go back with Nan and keep her company for an hour or so. Maybe we'll have a game of cards or listen to the wireless, eh Nan?"

"If you like, Adam. I don't mind being on my own. I expect I'll have an early night."

"Nonsense! Can't go to bed early Christmas night, it's not allowed!" Adam refused to be dissuaded and when they arrived in Holgate he poked the fire into a cheerful blaze, refilled the coal scuttle for her and then went into the kitchen to produce what he called his 'Christmas Special'.

He had been given a bottle of brandy by Joan and Harry and he liberally laced a large pot of coffee with this, and poured them both a cup. They settled by the fire and

Adam gradually made Nan relax as he chatted about Christmas in Canada when he was a child, and drew from her reminiscences about her life there with the girls. Making sure her cup was refilled, he could see her visibly relaxing and at last her tongue was loosened by the warmth and alcohol.

From talk of the old days in Welland, she progressed to the early years bringing up the children in Holgate - the shifts she had been put to, scrimping and scraping to make ends meet - and of course Billy's name then entered the conversation increasingly. Adam felt this was a good sign, because over the past weeks she had been loath to mention him at all, but now she talked of his humour and strength and the way the girls had all regarded him as a surrogate father.

"Life is strange, Nan. Out of tragedy so much good can often come. If it hadn't been for your brother drowning, you'd never have got to know Billy and think what a loss that would have been to the whole family."

"Yes, you're right, lad. Life's full of surprises, the way things work out. But you can't know it at the time. You just have to keep going the best way you can. Find some meaning to it all. But God knows, it's not easy. Not when you lose someone like Billy so suddenly. Then you keep asking yourself, what's the point in carrying on at all."

"Surely the point, Nan, is other people? The ones that need you?"

"Oh, Adam, there's no-one who really needs me now! Joan and Irene are settled and happy with nice homes, good husbands and lovely children. Even Rita lives her life - strange as it seems to me - without my help. I haven't seen her in years and I wouldn't recognise my own grandchildren now."

"I think you're wrong, Nan. As an outsider, I can see

how very pivotal you are to all the family. You're the rock they can always cling to in times of trouble. When their lives are running smoothly, sure they don't need you, but when things go wrong, that's a different story.

"It seems to me that right now, you have to find a purpose for getting up each morning. Your job is not that demanding for you and I reckon you need a new challenge. It seems to me your kids have always been the most important part of your life, so if you feel they don't need you so much, then look round for some other people who do?"

"You mean do some charity work in a children's home, that sort of thing?"

"No, I was thinking more on the lines of taking some youngsters into your home. You don't want to leave number thirty, I know, but realistically it's too big for you, and too expensive to rent on your own. Why not take in a couple of youngsters as lodgers? Kids who don't have proper family homes of their own. I'll bet your welfare department at the town hall would know of cases where youngsters need a decent lodging, at a reasonable rent.

"But you'd give them more than that, Nan. Because that's your talent. Caring for people. I know when I arrived in England I immediately felt I was being welcomed into a loving, warm home. Believe me, you'd be filling a very important gap in someone's life. Since the war, there are an awful lot of people who've lost great chunks of family and security, and I reckon you could make a lot of difference to some of those. You could pick and choose who you took into your home - decide the most needy cases if you like. And you'd be getting some financial help with the rent."

Nan lay back in her chair, pleasantly relaxed and, she knew, slightly tipsy. She listened to his words and she heard David's accent and Billy's caring common sense. At some level, she had known with a feeling of shame these last weeks that she had become a dreadful worry to the family, but she had been unable to shake herself out of her torpor. But Adam had put his finger on the problem. Nan was first and last a mother and she needed to be needed. While Billy was alive, the fact that the girls were grown up and independent had not mattered too much, but in this new lonely existence, it was suddenly mattering very much indeed. "Yes, lad, I know you're right. I should pull myself together and stop wallowing in self-pity. I owe the girls that much, even if I can't do anything else for them." She looked round the familiar surroundings and shook her head, sadly.

"I'm ashamed of this place. I haven't given it a proper going over since Billy went. I've let everything slide. I know there's things I should be sorting out. The solicitors have written several times - there's legal matters to arrange. Billy left me everything and I should decide what to do about the shop. There was a lump sum from his life insurance as well."

A thoughtful expression passed over her features and she sat up straighter in the chair. "I don't know how much it all comes to, but if I sold the lease on the shop, I think it would be a tidy sum. What you're saying about taking in lodgers to help pay the rent - I'm wondering if I should think about buying number thirty myself? That way, I wouldn't have to worry too much about what I charged the lodgers - if they needed somewhere to stay, I could keep the rent down till they could afford to pay more. I wouldn't run a charity home of course, that wouldn't be the idea at all. But if I own the house, it would put a different complexion on matters."

Adam was so delighted he could have laughed aloud. At last echoes of the old Nan were coming through the defeated, lonely woman who had taken over her personality these last weeks. They talked far into the night about the sort of young people she might be able to help and where she should go for advice about the project. She decided to look for boys or girls who were old enough to be working or even college students, but were far from home, or alone in the world - they would be the sort she would welcome.

In the early months of 1953, these plans came to fruition. Adam was an enormous help sorting out the legal and financial details with her. She sold the lease on Billy's shop, finalised the legalities of his estate and then bought number thirty with the proceeds. There was not much left over, but with help from Adam and Harry she redecorated the two bedrooms at the top of the house, keeping one spare one next to her own on the floor below.

"I want the girls to always know I've got the space for them to stay here if ever they feel like it." She was determined that her own family should not be excluded by the lodgers. The 'front room' was also redecorated so this would be used by the lodgers as their own sitting room. Nan had been used all her life to living in the kitchen and would be quite happy to carry on that way. She envisaged that her paying guests would probably join her there a lot of the time if they really came to look on number thirty as their home, but she still wanted to feel some sense of privacy for herself and family visitors.

So the pattern for Nan's life was set that year. The lodgers that she was to welcome into her home over the decades ahead would be many and varied. Some stayed a few months, others years. Some were locals, others came from all over the country and even from abroad. All came to look on her as a surrogate mother or grandmother. All called her 'Nan' and all of them learned to rely on her cheerful common sense and intuitive sympathy in times of trouble.

As the years passed, her Christmas post would become larger and larger. News of her extended family, which gradually spread out far and wide, was to be a constant source of pleasure and pride in her later years. When she talked about it, she always credited Adam with having the foresight to pull her out of her depression after Billy's death, and produce the idea that was to enrich her life from then on.

Indeed Adam himself was the source of much of Nan's happiness over the next eight years, but he was also to unwittingly take the central role in a heartbreaking episode of Nan's life, which was a secret she vowed to carry to her grave.

PART III : 1961 – 1963

By 1961, Nan had retired from her job at the town hall but her life was very active and full. She still enjoyed producing a lot of her vegetables and fruit on the old allotment, and was physically very fit. Indeed, her looks and manner belied her sixty-seven years. She was slim, upright and full of energy. The dark hair was only touched with grey and although her face was certainly lined, the fine bone structure remained a source of mature beauty and strength. Her smile had lost none of its warmth and her sense of humour had kept pace with modern life, so that her grandchildren all adored her and thought her very liberal in her outlook. More so in fact than their own parents at times.

The grandchildren were an ongoing delight for Nan - as they grew up she was able to see them more often. In 1953 Irene and Robert's family had been completed by a third son, Malcolm, so June was very much out-numbered by her three brothers. In the same year Rita and Matt had produced a third daughter, Beth, so Nan's grandchildren now totalled eleven, or twelve if she included Mavis's daughter, Joanne. Although their parents all knew the truth about Mavis's parentage, the grandchildren still believed that she was Nan's own daughter, not her niece, so they all counted Joanne as another grandchild of Nan's.

Life was good to all the family over those eight years. Irene and Robert's farm was thriving, their children all making good progress at school. Harry had persuaded old Mr Cooper to extend his premises when the shop next door came up for sale, and now they covered a wide range of luxury electrical goods as well as radios and televisions. Joan often helped out in the shop and did most of the paperwork for Harry, as she had more time on her hands with the children both at school.

Mandy was a source of great pride, having passed her eleven-plus exam and been accepted at Holgate Grammar. She was a serious, shy girl who worked hard at her studies with a quiet determination to succeed, rather than possessing a native brilliance. No beauty, but very bony and awkward as she reached adolescence, her best feature was her huge dark eyes. But at twelve she was forced to wear spectacles when she had been found unable to read the blackboard in class. Some unkind contemporaries took great delight in telling her that 'boys never made passes at girls who wore glasses' so her self-confidence was eroded still further.

Her skin was beautiful and blessedly free of teenage spots, but in the summer it was dusted generously with freckles, which she hated. Most of her contemporaries had more curves than she did, and whatever clothes Joan bought for her they always seemed to swamp her thin form. Her hair was very fine and silky, but without any sign of a curl. She wore it long and in a pony-tail, which was the fashion while she was growing up but did nothing to improve her overall appearance.

Nan sympathised totally, as she had been so like Mandy herself as a young girl.

"I was flat as a board, love, and I was always wishing my hair would curl like my sister Ruby's. But you'll fill out a bit as you get older, see if you don't. And I daresay your mum would let you have your hair permed if you were to ask her nicely. I'll treat you for your birthday if you like."

"Would you, Nan? I was wondering if I might get myself a bra as well. Then I might look a bit more...well..."

"Curvy? Don't want to turn into a beauty queen do you, Mandy? With your brains, you can do something more with your life than that." Nan smiled lovingly at her. She invariably stated that her grandchildren were all loved equally, but deep down she had a very special place in her heart for this particular granddaughter.

Donnie's health was still a source of constant anxiety to Joan. Sometimes Nan thought she was almost too excessive in her vigilance over him. He was a happy soul, with a lovely smile and always cheerful, in spite of the fact that he often missed out on boyish activities because of his delicate constitution. He was very much Harry's son, with his friendly disposition and kind heart.

Like his father, his strengths lay in practical directions rather than with his school studies. He would soon be sitting his eleven-plus exam, but if he passed it would be a miracle, thought Nan. Joan made excuses for any failures, and sometimes it seemed that she favoured him over her daughter. Whether this was because he was such a worry with his poor health, or whether it was a sub-conscious attempt to reassure herself, and Harry, that his child was loved as much as Oliver's, Nan was never quite sure. Fortunately the two children had always adored each other so there was never any jealousy on Mandy's side. Indeed, she was fiercely protective of her little brother, while he looked up to his older sister.

Adam had become an even closer member of the family over the years and a very special companion to Nan. Their growing closeness had gradually filled the void left by Billy. Although he was twelve years younger than her, the age gap never posed a problem. Physically and in his outlook, he was so like David that there seemed a natural affinity between them.

Since her retirement, Nan had been able to devote more time to reading, a pastime she had always loved, and had enrolled for various evening classes in subjects that interested her. Adam was always encouraging her in these ventures and they would spend hours discussing books and plays. He escorted her on excursions to the theatre and concerts in London, and introduced her to his own love of art. They visited all the big galleries and then progressed to the museums.

Nan counted herself fortunate that her more mature years were filled so happily by the many activities they shared. He seemed quite content in her company, having few friends of his own age. He was very much a 'loner' and Nan suspected that his wartime experiences and the harrowing loss of his fiancée had only emphasised his natural shyness. He seemed to blossom in the company of young people, was a great friend and playmate to all the grandchildren, and was no doubt a brilliant teacher.

He had bought one of the popular Mini cars and at weekends and during the long school holidays he would often propose outings to various stately homes or places of historical interest. Nan would pack a basket for a picnic, or sometimes they would stop at a picturesque country pub. After all the years of rationing, it was wonderful to find the shops full of food and Nan was able to indulge her love of cooking to the full. She would sometimes wake early and, listening to the dawn chorus, would reflect on how much her life had been enriched by her relationship with Adam.

His birthday was in May and it coincided with an early summer heatwave that year. "How do you fancy a drive to the sea, Nan? If we set off early, we could get down to Brighton, have a walk round The Lanes and browse through the little antique shops. We can go to the Royal Pavilion and then find a nice restaurant for a slap-up lunch."

"That sounds just the job, love. And I'll do us a picnic for tea, eh? If you're good, I'll do you some of my scones!"

It was a beautiful morning and Nan felt like a young girl again as she sang cheerfully about the kitchen, packing the basket with her various delicacies. Apart from the famous scones and two sorts of home-made jam, she included sandwiches, sausage rolls and a couple of chicken wings.

Carefully packed in a cardboard box was a sponge cake she had decorated the evening before. She had spent a long time achieving the smooth white surface on which to pipe 'Happy Birthday Adam' in blue icing. "That looks really quite nice, though I says it as shouldn't" she murmured to herself as she put on the lid.

"Good morning, Nan. You are about very early. You are going somewhere special today? With your friend, Mr Adam?" Nan turned and smiled at the petite figure of her favourite lodger.

Eva had been with her since 1956 when she had arrived in Britain amidst hundreds of other refugees from the Hungarian uprising. Then she had been skeleton-thin, with terrified dark eyes in a chalk-white face. She possessed nothing but the contents of the old carpet-bag she carried and the clothes she was wearing. Her English was quite good because she had been a student at the university. When the Russian army invaded she had been among the brave band that had attempted the heroic defence of their country.

It was only after she had been staying for some months

at number thirty that she had finally begun to relax and let down the barriers she had erected around her terrible memories. Then she told Nan of the horrors of watching her friends and classmates, as they lobbed their Molotov cocktails at the Russian tanks rolling inexorably through the streets: how she had witnessed the puny figures crushed beneath the tracks or remorselessly gunned down as they fled through the city.

There were nights when Nan would hear her weeping in her room above, and on some occasions she would be the victim of violent nightmares. When that happened, Nan would quickly climb the stairs and hold the trembling figure until the spectres receded. Then they would go down to the kitchen; Nan would make them both mugs of cocoa and sit with her arms round the young girl, letting her talk through her terrible experiences.

Gradually Eva had become settled in England and came to regard number thirty as her home. She had finished her studies at London University and was now an analytical chemist. She worked in a large pharmaceutical company and although she could have afforded to move to a flat of her own now, she was in no hurry to leave the refuge of number thirty.

Pouring them both a cup of tea she smiled teasingly at Nan as she said, "We are looking very chic today, Madame Nan. It must be a special occasion, no?"

"As a matter of fact, it's Adam's birthday and we're going to Brighton for the day. He's taking me to a posh restaurant for lunch and I've made a picnic tea. So I thought I'd better put on me best bib and tucker".

Standing in the bright sunshine, her dark hair gleaming in an elegant French pleat, instead of her usual old-fashioned bun, Nan did indeed look smart. She wore a pale lemon dress that reached just to her knees - a concession to the incredibly short skirts that were becoming more and more fashionable. The style was straight and simple, which showed off her still-slim figure, and was topped with a matching short-sleeved box jacket. Her legs were still good and were flattered by the navy court shoes that matched the small clutch bag lying on the chair. Her face was lightly made-up with a pretty pink lipstick and powder, and her skin was glowing with a healthy tan from the hours spent on the allotment.

Adam gave an appreciative whistle when he appeared in the doorway. "Well, I'm going to be the envy of every man we meet today, Nan. A real head-turner you look in that outfit. What is it Mandy says, 'Really fab!'?"

"Don't you start, young man! Happy birthday, my dear." She reached up to kiss his cheek and his arm tightened round her shoulder for a moment. She caught the faint tang of his crisp after-shave and suddenly was a young girl, excited to be off on a date. Ridiculously she felt herself blushing as she stepped back, and to cover her awkwardness, picked up the brightly wrapped package on the table. "Here you are. I know you've got shelves of books already, but these are two new ones that have come out. The man in Smiths reckoned they'd both be good reads."

"'Catch 22' by Joseph Heller and 'The Old Men at the Zoo' by Angus Wilson. Why thanks, Nan, these look great. You spoil me." He smiled what she privately called his 'David smile' and she beamed back at him.

Eva thought what a lovely pair they made and was pleased that Nan was having a day out. She worked so hard looking after number thirty and the lodgers; it was good to see her being taken care of for a change.

The day was perfect. A golden time that Nan always

remembered as very special. Everything conspired to make it so. The weather was warm as they strolled through the crowds along The Lanes and Adam insisted on buying Nan a brooch shaped like a seahorse that she admired in the window of a bric-a-brac shop. It was not really valuable but very pretty, and the marcasite glittered in the sun when she pinned it on her jacket.

The restaurant was excellent. There was a tiny courtyard at the back and they sat outside to eat their meal. A fountain splashed among tubs of tulips and wallflowers, which pervaded the air with their velvety scent. The food was wonderful. Nan felt very sophisticated as she ate her prawn cocktail, followed by a fluffy Spanish omelette and finished with a crème brûlée. Adam chose a delicate rosé wine to accompany the food and, greatly daring, Nan was persuaded to have a Cointreau with her coffee.

"Well, I don't know about you, love, but I feel as though I've put on about a stone in weight. I don't think I needed to bother with a picnic tea - I'm certain I won't feel like another thing till tomorrow!" Nan smoothed down her skirt and had to admit she felt ever so slightly woozy when they stood up to leave.

They strolled slowly back to the car and then drove inland away from the town, which had become more crowded with day-trippers. Adam kept off the main roads and they meandered through tiny villages with thatched cottages and gardens bright with spring flowers. Eventually they came to some open countryside and parked the car at the start of a footpath leading on to the downs. Adam took a rug from the boot and they strolled slowly along, chatting and enjoying the view spread out below them.

Nan was becoming breathless as they neared the top of the path and Adam laughingly took her hand to pull her the last few yards. Then he spread out the rug and they sprawled side by side, talking at first, but then both dozing off as the heavy lunch and the warm sun had their way with them.

It was about an hour later when Nan awoke and, on opening her eyes, found Adam sitting upright beside her, a gentle smile on his face. "Enjoyed your forty winks, sleepyhead?"

"I certainly did. I just couldn't keep me eyes open. Don't tell me you didn't have a nap as well?"

"I have to admit I may have rested my eyes for a few minutes!" He grinned at her with the sort of cheekiness that might have been young Donnie's and she pushed him jokingly in the chest, saying, "Go on with you! I bet you were as spark out as me".

He caught hold of her hand and said quietly, "Thanks for today, Nan. And all the other days like it. Your company means an awful lot to me, you know." His eyes gazed into hers very seriously and she felt there was a deeper meaning underlying his words that he was trying to convey.

Ridiculously, her heartbeat had quickened and she was very aware of the warmth of his fingers on hers. Her voice sounded oddly breathless in her own ears as she answered him.

"You don't have to thank me, Adam. I'm the one who should be thanking you. All the time and trouble you spend on an old woman like me. There's not many young men who'd be so kind. I feel very selfish at times - when I think that while you're out and about with me, you could be meeting some nice young girl and settling down with a wife and family."

"Oh, Nan! I'm not exactly a 'young man' myself any more! Remember I'm fifty-five today! And I don't think I'd have a lot in common with some youngster in a mini skirt who wants to listen to the Beatles and Rolling Stones all the time!

"And as for you being an 'old woman', that's crazy. You're just a girl at heart, Nan, and you look at least ten years younger than you are, so in my book I reckon that makes us contemporaries!" He squeezed her hand and then jumped to his feet energetically.

"Now how about racing me down the hill to the car, just to prove what a couple of spring chickens we both are? I don't know about you but I reckon my appetite's coming back and I could really do justice to your picnic."

The intimate mood was broken, but Nan was strangely shaken by it. Beneath their relaxed chat and laughter as they ate the picnic beside the car and then enjoyed the evening drive back to London, she felt that, as far as she was concerned, their relationship had subtly altered. Whether Adam had deliberately intended this, she was not sure, but the new dimension to their companionship had opened her mind to ideas that until now she had studiously refused to recognise.

As Adam concentrated on his driving when they entered the busier suburbs, she allowed herself to think in a dreamlike way about the future. He had emphatically pointed out that the difference in their ages was totally unimportant to him. They had many of the same interests in common that she had enjoyed with David. Was she really too old to think about a new partner at her age? As Adam had said, just because she was sixty-seven it didn't mean she had to be old in spirit. She was active and enjoyed life and today, with him, she was aware of stirrings in her body that she had assumed were long forgotten. Suddenly the future was full of glowing possibilities and Nan wanted to sing for the joy of living.

This radiance lasted just as long as it took them to reach Holgate High Street. Adam was about to drive past his flat over Harry's shop in order to drop Nan home when he realised there was some sort of incident occurring. There was a police car and a knot of interested onlookers.

"What's going on, I wonder? Do you think we should stop and find out, Nan? If there's a problem - perhaps a burglary - Harry may want some moral support."

"Yes, love. I must find out, or I'll only be worrying all night. It's probably the alarm gone off by accident, but we'd better make sure."

Adam drove the car round the back to the small parking area and then used his own key to enter through the rear door. A police constable appeared from the room that was used as a storage space for electrical items being repaired. When Harry had expanded into the second shop he had taken on another assistant who was a qualified electrician and that side of the business had been very successful.

"What's going on, Constable? I live in the flat upstairs. Is there some problem?"

"Yes, I'm afraid there is, Sir." His voice was very serious and the sombre expression on his face hit Nan like a physical blow to her stomach. A premonition of some terrible occurrence made her sway where she stood.

"My son-in-law manages this shop. What's happened? Is it serious?"

Before he could answer, a distraught figure pushed past him from the store-room. "Mum, Mum! Thank God you've come! Mum, it's Harry. He's dead!" With an awful howl, Joan flung her arms round Nan and practically knocked her to the floor with the force of her anguish.

In the hours that followed, Nan found the necessary strength to support her daughter and her grandchildren, although it felt as though a small part of her own spirit had died with the lovely man that she genuinely regarded as her son.

Bit by bit the details of the tragic accident emerged. Harry had come down to the shop in the afternoon to do some odd jobs that had piled up. He had wanted to reorganise the store-room over the weekend while the shop was closed. He had always been so determined to overcome the difficulties of his disability, but with only one arm most tasks were more time-consuming for him than other people and he was often painfully aware of his own clumsiness.

On the workbench there had been some small electrical appliances that his assistant, Jim, had been in the throes of repairing. Reaching across these, his hand had unwittingly brushed against the flex of an electric iron. He had been unaware that the problem Jim had yet to fix was that the flex itself was badly frayed and so the live current was unprotected.

"It would have been instant, Joan. The police keep saying that and you must believe them, lovie. He wouldn't have known a thing."

"But it's all so senseless, Mum. Such a stupid way to die. He was ever so careful and methodical with his work. He always said that when you were around electricity you must never take chances. I just can't believe it! I shall never forget the way he looked when I found him." Joan shook her head and gazed desperately at her mother.

"I know, lovie, it's just not fair. But accidents can happen to the most careful of us. The constable said the vacuum cleaner was plugged into the socket next to the one with the iron. They think that Harry must have switched on the wrong socket and as his arm moved back from it, he just brushed against the iron's flex.

"The vacuum was in the middle of the room, so he was probably just about to clean up the dirt on the floor. He'd been moving boxes around and there was a lot of dust. It was just a split second of inattention that led to tragedy. It can happen, sweetheart, and it's nobody's fault. That's what makes it so hard to accept."

During the weeks that followed the whole family struggled to come to terms with Harry's death. He had been a well-liked member of the community, which was obvious from the large number of local friends and shopkeepers who attended his funeral. Joan was enormously touched by all the messages of condolence and the many floral tributes. Even the local paper did a small piece about the one-armed hero from the war who was such a cheerful friend and devoted family man.

Mandy and Donnie looked like two little ghosts as they sat on each side of their mother at the church service, and Nan wished the school term would soon be over so they could get away to stay with Irene in Cornwall for a few weeks.

"A change of scene is just what they need at the moment, Joan. You as well for that matter."

"Oh, I don't know, Mum. There's so much I've got to sort out here. Poor old Mr Cooper is bedridden now and his daughter has got to make all the decisions about the shop. I think he always felt that Harry might buy her out when he died - none of us dreamed that poor Harry would go first."

"So do you think she'll sell, or put in another manager?" Nan was glad to distract Joan with practicalities even if only for a short time. At least it kept her from dwelling on her grief.

"I think she'll sell. So that may mean Adam will have to leave the flat if the new owner doesn't want to rent it out. I don't know what I'll do myself. I'm not sure I can manage to keep the house on now. I'll have to look round for a job, I suppose. I used to take a wage for the paperwork I did at the shop, but I'll need to earn a lot more than that to support the three of us. Goodness knows the widow's pension isn't much, and with Mandy at grammar school, I've always got my hand in my pocket for her.

"And Donnie's shooting up like a broomstick now. None of his clothes last for long. Even though he didn't pass to start at the grammar school, he'll still need some new clothes for the secondary modern. Honestly, Mum, it's a nightmare thinking about it all." Joan buried her face in her hands. Putting her arms round her, Nan noticed, with a lump in her throat, that her daughter's dark hair already had as many grey streaks in it at forty-two as her own did, in spite of the twenty-five years between them.

How history was repeating itself, she thought. Whereas she had struggled to bring up four small children, Joan only had to cope with two and both of hers were a lot older, but the strains of being a lone parent were just the same.

Young Mandy was very aware of her mother's financial problems and talked freely about them when she called in on Nan one Saturday morning. She had been attending a rehearsal for the school play, and stopped for her lunch before cycling home to Muswell Hill.

"How did the rehearsal go, love. Remembered all your lines did you?"

"Yes thanks, Nan. I'm really enjoying it. I love acting - English was always my best subject, and it's brilliant playing Viola in 'Twelfth Night'." She smiled a little sadly.

"I can't help thinking Miss Ferris has given me the part because I have to play a girl dressing up as a boy and with my shape that should be easy!"

"Rubbish! She gave you the part because you're a lovely little actress. You've always had praise for the parts you played before, ever since you were a little tot at the mixed infants playing a fairy! I'm really looking forward to coming to see you when the play's on at the end of the term. Adam says he wants a ticket as well."

"I think he ought to get in free. He's been really good helping me with my lines; ever so patient hearing me going over and over them. That was something Dad used to do. He was so sweet because he never understood half of what Shakespeare was talking about but he used to give me my cues and laugh when he got the words all wrong. Oh, Nan, I do miss him so much! And it seems awful to go on enjoying things like the play and he's not here any more."

"I know, pet, I know. It's terrible to lose someone you love very much and there's no easy way to get through it. You just have to keep on doing all the everyday things; stick to your routines even if it does seem pointless at times.

"It's a terrible cliché, but life does have to go on. Your dad would want you to get on with yours and make a success of it. He was so proud of you, you know. He'd hate you to miss out on the fun of things like the school play. And he wouldn't want your school-work to suffer either. He was really keen to see you get some good qualifications and make a proper career for yourself."

"I know. I hope I've done alright with the exams. I think I've just about got through them. But I'm not sure about next year. We always planned I'd go into the sixth form and do my 'A' levels. I think Mum and Dad would have liked me to go to university, but to be honest I never really fancied that. I'm no great brain and I don't know if I could have coped with all that study. What I'd like to do is a secretarial course in the sixth form. That way I'd have some practical qualifications on top of my GCE's (assuming I've passed them), but now I don't know if I should be staying on at school at all next year."

"Why not, love?" Nan was pretty sure she knew what this was all about.

"Well, I know Mum is going to be really hard up now. She's wondering if we can afford to stay on at the house and we may have to get a flat somewhere cheaper. Donnie's only eleven so he's got several more years at school and I think I ought to get a job at the end of term to help out. That way we could probably keep on the house and Mum wouldn't have all the worry of moving on top of being so unhappy without Dad."

"That's very thoughtful of you, pet. But I think you'll find it would be just as upsetting for your mum if you left school earlier than was planned. She'll blame herself for letting you down, you see. I won't pretend it's not going to be a struggle; it is. But knowing your mum, she'll cope somehow. And your old Nan will help where she can."

"I see what you mean, Nan, and I know you're a tower of strength to Mum. She always says so. But I will feel guilty being an extra drain on her finances."

"Let's just wait and see what happens. Things have a way of panning out if you give them time. Never meet trouble half-way, that's what I always say. Now have a slice of my cherry tart and cream. Be thankful you don't have to worry about your weight like most of your girlfriends!"

By the end of the summer term, life had begun to sort

itself out for Joan and her children, largely thanks to Adam's efforts. Firstly he discovered that the post of assistant secretary was vacant at the school where he was now a department head, and he arranged for Joan to be interviewed for the post. Although her shorthand was somewhat rusty, her typing was excellent owing to the work she had done in the shop and she was offered the job on the spot.

"Adam has been wonderful, Mum. He says we can travel together in his Mini, so I won't even have to pay out for fares. I'm so grateful to him. I know I'll be terrified going back to work after so many years, but he's really supportive. It will make all the difference having him around at the school."

"'Course it will, love. Salt of the earth is Adam. I don't know where any of us would be without him." Nan smiled cheerfully at Joan, but thought a little sadly that she had personally done without Adam quite a lot recently.

She was extremely grateful to him for the way he had helped Joan through so many of the practicalities that ensue from any bereavement but it had meant that most of his spare time had been spent at Muswell Hill rather than in his usual visits to number thirty. However, the very next evening he gave Nan a ring, asking if he might pop over for an hour. "Of course you can, silly. You know you're always welcome, my dear. Eva's just rung to say she's having a meal in town with a girl from her work, so you can come and have her share of dinner. I've done a steak and kidney pie and I've got fresh beans and carrots from the allotment."

"There's an offer I definitely can't refuse. You really know how to tempt a fellow, Nan! I'll be round in thirty minutes."

Nan's heart lifted at the prospect of an evening in

Adam's company. Eva was her only lodger at present - the last occupant of the second top bedroom had recently departed. He had been a student at London University and had just completed his three years. So she and Adam would have number thirty to themselves and Nan looked forward to catching up with all the minutiae that made up their two lives, but which became so much more when shared between them. She constantly found herself thinking, 'I must tell Adam' and was quite sure he would often do the same as he always seemed eager to regale her with interesting anecdotes about pupils and the staff-room politics at his school.

They chatted away as easily as usual over the meal and then settled outside the back door in a couple of garden chairs, for the summer night was quite humid and the scent of Nan's tub of night-scented stock was almost overpowering.

"Young Mandy seems to be getting on splendidly with the role of Viola. I think she's going to be the star of the show. You and Joan will be bursting with pride, I'll bet!" Adam brushed away a moth that had settled on Nan's arm.

"Yes, I'm so thankful she's had that to take her mind off everything else. What with worry about her GCE results and of course brooding about Harry, I think she'd be in a really bad state if it weren't for the school play. I know she's also concerned about whether Joan can afford for her to stay on in the sixth form. Poor kiddie, she's always been one for taking life seriously and this has pulled her right down. I hope once term finishes she and Donnie will stay with Irene for a few weeks."

"Yes, I've been talking to Joan about Mandy's future. I know Joan's been worrying about making ends meet, although having her own new job should make a big difference. Whatever happens, she'll never forgive herself if Mandy has to cut short her education." He refilled Nan's glass from the bottle of wine that had been his contribution to dinner, and then said thoughtfully, "As a matter of fact, I think I may have come up with a solution."

"What are you thinking of, Adam? If you're considering offering Joan a loan, I'm afraid she wouldn't entertain the idea. She'd appreciate the kind thought, but she's an independent madam is my daughter. She'll be determined to stand on her own feet, that I do know."

"Wonder where she gets that from!" Adam laughed and then, patting her hand, said "I think I can be a bit more subtle than that, Nan.

"It's rather fortuitous that the new owners of the shop have just written telling me they will be wanting to take possession of my flat, so the manager can live over the premises. Which means I'll be looking for somewhere else to live."

"Really?" Nan's first thought was the empty bedroom on her top floor. How wonderful if Adam decided to move into number thirty. She would be quite happy to let him fill her sitting room with shelves of his books and if he wanted to potter about in the kitchen enjoying his cooking hobby, that would be fine too... Her excited musing was interrupted as Adam continued to explain his idea.

"I don't really need a two-bedroomed flat, to be honest. I know I've got loads of books but, other than that, I don't have a lot of possessions. I've always travelled light. I think it was a habit I picked up during and after the war. So I'm going to suggest to Joan than I become her lodger. She's got a spare bedroom and they rarely have visitors overnight so I think it would be ideal for me. We'll be travelling to work together any way, and I get on well with the kids, so I imagine I'd fit into their routine alright. What's your opinion, Nan? How would Joan take the suggestion, d'you think?"

Nan swallowed hard, as her happy fantasy of Adam's continuous presence at number thirty vanished. Then her natural motherly concern for Joan's best interests took over and she smiled gratefully at him.

"I'm sure she'd welcome the idea, Adam. It's a very kind thought and I should imagine it would be an excellent arrangement. You've all known each other for a long time and that would be much easier for them than having a complete stranger as a lodger. The additional income should be just the financial safety net that Joan needs. And it will be good for Donnie to have a male influence around the house. With Harry gone, I was worrying that he'd be rather suffocated by Joan and Mandy fussing over him whenever he coughs or sneezes, so a bit of masculine company will be a very good thing.

"But are you sure you really want to give up your privacy? Moving into a home with two youngsters, even ones you know, may be more than you bargain for, you know. You'll be hearing more rock 'n roll than classical music and their choice of TV programmes is unlikely to be yours!"

"Oh, I guess I can cope with the change, Nan. To tell the truth, I often feel a bit lonely in the flat - as the years go by, I long more and more for some permanent companionship. Which is probably why you get landed with me so often on your doorstep!"

"No-one could be more welcome, my dear, I'm sure you know that". She smiled tenderly at him and then patted his arm as she went inside to make some coffee. She was afraid to say anything else in case she betrayed the feelings that increasingly threatened to overwhelm her when she was alone with him. Tonight especially, after such a long break since they last spent time together, she had been shaken at how physically she was reacting to his presence in the same room.

Her face was flushed, her hands were unsteady and even her breathing seemed uneven. She had stumbled over her words several times and she was afraid that her laughter had sounded false and nervous. If Adam had noticed anything unusual he showed no reaction, as he helped her with the domestic trivia of clearing the table and wiping up the dishes.

When he rose to leave, Nan accompanied him to the street door and he bent as usual to give her a light embrace and kiss her cheek. But tonight, in spite of herself, her arms tightened about him and she whispered, "It's been a lovely evening, my dear. I have missed you these last few weeks."

"I've missed you too, Nan. You're a very special person to me and I value our time together very much."

As she closed the door behind him Nan felt like dancing along the passage to the kitchen. Telling herself how ridiculously she was behaving for a woman of her years really had no effect whatsoever. Even in spite of her grief about Harry, she was happy, happy, happy and surely that wasn't a crime, was it?

Adam moved into the house in Muswell Hill in a matter of weeks, and Joan told Nan that she was unutterably thankful at the new arrangement. "Adam's so kind and thoughtful, Mum, he's no trouble to have around the place at all. He's ever so good helping Donnie with his homework and Mandy adores him - always bending his ear about some play or other. Listening to them talking about

Shakespeare or modern poetry makes me realise I'm a right dimwit at times, but I certainly feel a lot safer knowing there's a man in the house."

"Yes, every time you open the paper you seem to read about some violence or other. If it's not teenagers fighting outside a pub, it's a race riot. I don't know what the world's coming to, I'm sure. When I was young, you got family fights and the odd drunken brawl on a Saturday night, but now it's not safe for ordinary folk to walk the streets after dark, especially in the poorer areas.

"When I look round Holgate, I can't believe how it's gone downhill over the last few years. It used to be a respectable neighbourhood, but now it's getting really rough. So many immigrants have taken over the bigger houses, with a family in practically every room. There are even squatters in number sixty up the road from me.

"And as for the High Street - the shops are not worth visiting these days. There are so many turned into supermarkets and half of them sell a load of foreign rubbish. Whatever happened to the family greengrocer like poor Billy, or the butcher or baker?"

"Or candlestick maker, Nan?" Donnie grinned at her cheekily and she pretended to give him a box on the ear.

"You may take the mickey out of your old grandmother, but life was a lot better in the old days, I can tell you. We may have all been poor, but people were a lot friendlier and there was a kinder spirit about. Now everyone seems to be out for what they can get. It's all 'live now, pay later'".

Nan sighed as she remembered the camaraderie of the Blitz, and then told herself not to be so soft. No one in their right minds would want those days back again!

As 1961 passed into the following year, Joan and her children gradually became accustomed to life without Harry. Mandy's GCE results were quite respectable and she achieved six good passes. Her days were filled with the secretarial course she was studying in the sixth form and she was heavily involved once more in the drama group. Nan knew that she still grieved for her father, but at least she seemed happy at school and was looking forward to embarking on a worthwhile career afterwards.

"I think she wants to find something in London. Like most girls of her age, she thinks it will be glamorous working in town with all the shops. Never mind the travelling every day! Still I daresay there's a lot more opportunities up West. It would be nice if she could get a secretarial position somewhere to do with the theatre. Combine her hobby with her job so to speak."

Joan looked wistfully at Nan. "I was talking to her English teacher at the open evening. She said Mandy's got real talent as an actress, should apply to one of the drama schools and train properly, which would cost a fortune. It would be another three years I'd have to support her and it's such an uncertain profession. But if she really wanted to do it, we'd manage somehow."

Nan rolled out pastry for the meat pie she was making for the lodgers' dinner. Eva had been joined by Alison, who was a student nurse at the Holgate hospital. She was a quiet, gentle girl who had lost both parents during the war and had been raised by an elderly aunt. The latter had recently died and Alison was now alone in the world. She had rented out her aunt's house while she did her training and had been glad to move into a family home as a lodger.

"So what does Mandy say about it - does she want to go to one of these stage schools?"

"She says not. Told me that she doesn't think she's got enough determination - it's such a competitive business, you've got to be really dedicated to succeed. I think she's probably right. You know Mandy - she's a gentle, unassuming soul, and I can't see her pushing herself enough. So I expect she'll join an amateur group when she leaves school and if she can get a secretarial job in that line of business, I think she'll be quite happy."

"What about Donnie, how's he getting on with his lessons these days?"

"Oh, he does his best, you know that. But he'll never set the world on fire. He's no scholar, let's face it. I'm worried about his chest again; he's had one cough after another this winter. This dratted smog doesn't help - I wish the whole country could become a smokeless zone, like they made the City a few years ago. Of course, he's off school so often, that doesn't help with his studies."

"Never mind, love. He's a good boy compared with the way some of these youngsters carry on these days. All their protest marches and more money than they know what to do with - they seem to spend a fortune on their pop records and weird clothes and make-up. At least Donnie's a kind-hearted lad and still happy to spend time at home with his family. Not like so many, hanging round street corners."

"I know, Mum. It's just I wish he still had Harry to guide him. Although of course Adam's wonderful with him." She smiled as she thought of the two heads bent over the model car they were building together. "In fact Adam's wonderful with all of us. Considering he's a confirmed bachelor, it's amazing the way he's fitted in."

"I never heard him say he's a confirmed bachelor". Nan spoke sharply, without thinking, and Joan looked at her in surprise.

"Well he's fifty-five isn't he? I shouldn't think he's likely to get married now. Let's face it, he never socialises much. He's a bit of a homebody, I've always thought. I can't imagine him meeting anyone and settling down - can you?"

"Who knows? Just because he's in his fifties doesn't mean he's not interested in a relationship with someone - if the right person came along that is." She deftly trimmed the excess pastry off the pie dish and tossed it outside for the birds.

"You sound as though you're matchmaking, Mum. Who have you found to pair Adam off with? Someone from your evening class is it?" Joan chuckled as Nan shook her head and told her not to be so daft, but it was obvious that she had hit a nerve. Knowing how her mother loved to sort out all her nearest and dearest to her own satisfaction, Joan was quite convinced that Nan had plans for Adam's future, even if he didn't know it.

In fact, as the months passed, Nan was becoming rather depressed whenever she thought of Adam. Their meetings became rarer as he spent most of his spare time with Joan and her children. Nan was grateful that he was such a help to them all but couldn't help feeling neglected by his absence. A heavy summer cold pulled her down even further, and she was glad to accept Irene's invitation to spend a week on the farm recuperating.

When she returned and rang to ask how Joan was getting on, Mandy answered the phone. "Mum's not here, Nan. She and Adam have gone to a concert at the Festival Hall. Someone in the staff room had a couple of spare tickets apparently so they decided to go on the spur of the moment. I think it's Tchaikovsky and you know how Mum likes his stuff."

"Alright, pet. Just as long as you're all alright. Tell

your Mum I hope she had a nice evening. It'll do her good to get out for a change." Nan felt absurdly deflated as she sat down with a cup of tea, before going upstairs to unpack her bag. She was glad that Joan was having a night out, of course she was, but in the old days it would have been her that Adam would have taken. Berating herself for being such a misery, she tried to shake off her ill-feeling, but it was an uphill task.

As the summer passed, Nan found herself entering a period of general depression and gloom. She went through all the usual motions of running the house, tending the allotment, writing to the various grandchildren and going to her evening classes, but all the spirit seemed to have gone out of her life. She missed Harry, she missed Billy, but most of all, she missed Adam. Whenever she saw Mandy, who often called in on her way home from school for a cold drink and a chat, she was forever talking about the excursions that they had enjoyed in Adam's car at weekends.

"He's so lovely, Nan. He never minds giving me a lift home from the pictures if I've gone with one of my friends - you know how Mum worries about me being out at night on my own. He even takes Donnie to the school football matches on the weekend. Mum says she doesn't know how we'd manage without him. And he's really good with her as well. Makes her laugh when she's had a bad day at work - she's brightened up a lot lately."

"That's good, pet. I'm glad it's working out for you all."

Nan decided to stop moping and feeling left out and invited them all round the following Sunday for a roast. It was a hot July day and Mandy suggested they should eat in the back garden. There was a lot of to'ing and fro'ing, carrying table and chairs outside and then all the crockery and cutlery, but it made a pleasant change to eat al fresco, and listening to them all laughing and joking, Nan felt a lot better. What an old crosspatch she had been, grudging her own daughter a little pleasure in her life after so much heartache.

When Adam accompanied her indoors to collect the bowls of dessert he smiled as he put an arm round her shoulder. "It seems ages since we've had the chance of a chat, Nan. I've missed our evenings together. What say we have a meal one night soon?"

"That would be lovely, Adam. Come round next week and I'll do your favourite casserole."

"No, you're going to have a night off. I'll pick you up and we'll go out to that nice little restaurant in Hampstead that you liked. How does that sound?"

"Oh, that'll be a real treat! I shall look forward to it."

The next day, on a sudden impulse, Nan called into the hairdresser and made an appointment to have her hair cut and permed. Then she got on the bus to Wood Green and splashed out on a smart sleeveless dress in a pale blue silk. Browsing round Boots, she picked up a new lipstick in one of the very pale pink shades that were so popular and, after trying various testers, bought herself a new perfume.

On the day she was meeting Adam, she went off to the hairdresser and then had a long, lazy bath before getting herself dressed and made up. Looking in the full-length mirror inside her wardrobe door she was rather scared at the amazing difference she saw in the woman before her. The short curly hair completely transformed her face, and the straight, simple dress made the most of her shapely figure. When she heard Adam's familiar call from downstairs, she hastily picked up her short white gloves and clutch bag that matched her high heeled sandals and hastened down to greet him.

"Why, Nan, you look wonderful! What have you done to your hair? It looks so different!" He took her by the shoulders and turned her slowly round to observe the transformation from all angles. "What brought all this about?"

Blushing and laughing, she said, "Can't a woman get her hair done and buy a new frock without all this fuss?"

"When she looks as good as you, she deserves a fuss! Now Madame, your carriage awaits. Strictly speaking it should be a Rolls, but I'm afraid you'll have to make do with the Mini!"

It was a lovely evening. The little Italian restaurant was as charming as Nan remembered from their previous visit. Adam was at his most amusing, full of stories about a recent student 'Bob Hop' at his school and how the latest dance craze, 'The Twist', even had some of the younger members of staff on the floor.

When they had finished their exotic ice cream dessert and were preparing to enjoy their coffee and liqueur, he became serious and, leaning towards her confidentially across the table, said, "I had an ulterior motive for asking you out tonight, Nan. There's something very important I want to ask you."

Nan swallowed and her heart began to pound uncomfortably. Struggling to appear quite collected, she said, "Ask away, love, I won't bite you know".

"Nan, I've really missed our chats recently. I've always been able to talk to you and hopefully you'll appreciate how I feel about things. We've known each other a long time now, and I like to think we've reached an understanding?"

"Yes, I'd say that's true, Adam." Nan gazed into his

serious eyes, and wondered if he recognised in hers the depths of her feelings for him.

"We've talked before about relationships and age, haven't we? We've always agreed that age isn't important if two people share a closeness - have attitudes and interests in common, that's what we said, didn't we?"

"Yes, we did." Nan waited for him to continue, hardly daring to catch her breath in anticipation of his next words.

"Well, the thing is, you and I haven't seen much of each other lately because I've been spending so much time with Joan and the children. Since I've moved to Muswell Hill I've begun to feel like a real member of the family, not just a lodger."

"Oh, Adam, we've always thought of you as one of the family, practically from the first day you walked through the door!" Nan smiled lovingly at him, thinking what a short time ago that seemed, rather than ten years.

"Yes, you all made me welcome, right from the start, but this is something different, Nan. Oh dear, I don't quite know how to say it!" He bit his lip with a half-smile on his face and she longed to reach across and kiss him, but she knew that first move had to come from him. So she said quietly, "Just say it, Adam. You know you can say anything to me."

"Of course I can. Right, here goes. The truth is, Nan, my feelings towards Joan have changed. Helping her come to terms with Harry's death, and obviously sharing the house with her, and all the daily problems concerning the children and other domestic things - we've developed a new closeness.

"To put it plainly, Nan, I've suddenly realised I've fallen in love with her and I intend asking her to marry me. I know there's thirteen years between us, but that really doesn't seem to matter. We've got so much in common - even more so now that we work together - and I really do care about the children. I think they like me and of course I'd never try to take Harry's place with them, but we all seem to get on well together.

"So, Nan, I'm asking do you think I stand any chance with her?"

The candle in the Chianti bottle sputtered a little in a sudden draught from the open window beside the table, which brought with it the heady fragrance of the honeysuckle climbing the wall outside. The romantic accordion music continued to play 'Moon River' above the chatter of the other diners. Nan was locked into a moment of disbelief and a physical pain that actually caused her to give a little gasp and her fingers tightened convulsively round the stem of her liqueur glass, spilling the dregs of Cointreau on the gaily checked tablecloth.

Adam swiftly reached across and mopped at the stain with his napkin, laughing as he did so. "I thought you'd be surprised, but I didn't realise it would be quite such a shock, Nan. Is the thought of having me as a son-in-law so appalling?"

"No, no of course not... I'm sorry about the mess, so clumsy of me." She managed a faint, apologetic smile at the waiter who had silently materialised to deal efficiently with the minor crisis. "Not a problem at all, Signora. Would the Signora please accept another liqueur with the compliments of the management?"

"Thank you, yes." Nan had never before felt the need of a stiff drink to calm the trembling in her limbs and settle her churning stomach, as she did at this moment. Normally she would have been horribly embarrassed at this small social gaffe, but on this occasion was thankful for the brief respite before the need to continue the conversation with Adam.

So when they were settled again with fresh drinks and refilled coffee cups and he relaxed back in his chair and looked at in her in silent query, she had been able to gather herself together enough to attempt the appropriate words and manner.

"I won't pretend this isn't a surprise, Adam. I know how much you've become a part of Joan's family, but it never occurred to me that you might intend anything more than a close friendship. Naturally I can't answer for Joan's feelings. It is only fourteen months since Harry's death, but I know she thinks very highly of you, as do the children. Beyond that, I'm afraid I've no idea. You'll just have to ask her."

"Which is precisely what I intend to do, as soon as the opportunity arises. But if I'm lucky enough for her to agree, you would be quite happy about it, Nan? I promise you I care for her a great deal and I'd spend the rest of my life trying to make her happy. She has confided in me about all that old business with Oliver and the fact that Mandy was his child so I know she's had a lot of heartbreak in her life. I really want to make all that up to her, if she'll let me."

Every word was like a physical blow, and Nan longed to put her hands over her ears and beg him to stop. But somehow she managed to keep a half-smile in place and let him continue with this recitation of his dreams and plans for the future.

"You know I still own the old family house back in Canada, and it's been leased out all the years I've been in England. I thought perhaps we might take a trip over there after we're married and decide what to do about it. I'd like Joan to see my home and it would be interesting for her to visit the place where she was born, don't you think?"

"Yes, yes, I'm sure it would. Adam, I'm sorry to cut the evening short, but I do have the beginnings of a blinding headache. I've probably been stupid and drunk too much! But I think I'd better get home to bed and sleep it off, if you don't mind."

"Of course, Nan. I'm afraid I've been babbling on and been a real bore. It's just that I can always talk to you about my feelings, as I can nobody else. I don't know where I'd be without you, Nan" He smiled the 'David' smile and patted her hand. The hard lump of emotion that was constricting her chest threatened to dissolve in a wave of tears as the irony of his words underlined the agony of her trampled dreams and lost love.

Somehow she got to her feet, murmured thanks to the waiter who draped her white crocheted shawl about her shoulders and almost ran along the street to Adam's car, while he settled the bill. Unseeing, she bumped into a group of noisy youngsters who were listening to the latest Beatles hit on a transistor radio, and sprawling across the entire pavement.

She stumbled sideways into the gutter and one of them shouted after her, "Watch it, Grandma! You wanna take a drop more water with it next time!" His mates all guffawed loudly and Nan felt a scarlet wave of humiliation wash over her. This was the final indignity underlining the terrible mortification of this heartbreaking evening.

She made a solemn, unspoken vow in that instant, that she would never reveal to another soul the fact that she had fallen in love with, and hoped for marriage to, a man twelve years her junior. A man that she had physically desired and had been deluded enough to believe could desire her in return - the man who was now intending to marry her own daughter.

She could almost taste the bile of self-loathing at the recognition of her pathetic delusions. And when she allowed herself to admit that she was actually experiencing a feeling of hatred towards her own daughter, Nan plumbed an abyss of despair that night, more soul-destroying than any she had experienced throughout her gruelling life.

The weeks that followed were the most refined torture for her. She waited on a knife-edge of suspense for the repercussions throughout the family when Adam made his declaration to Joan. She desperately hoped that Joan would reject him, and despised herself for that hope. He would be heartbroken and Joan would never be able to regard him in the same light again. The happy household at Muswell Hill would be disrupted and everyone would suffer because of it.

At last the moment came. On a Sunday morning as Nan shelled a bowl of peas from the allotment, the sound of laughter and voices rang through number thirty and Adam appeared hand in hand with Joan, Mandy and Donnie wreathed in smiles behind them. "Well, I've done it, Nan! I've asked her and she's been brave enough to take me on." They both beamed at her radiantly and Nan thought that Joan had lost ten years overnight, and Adam looked like an excited schoolboy.

"Isn't it fab, Nan? Mum and Adam are getting married!" Donnie was hopping from one foot to another in excitement and Mandy was glowing as she gazed at her mother, who was suddenly transformed in her eyes to an object of mature romance.

"Well, this is a surprise. I don't know what to say." Nan bustled about, emptying the colander of peas into a saucepan and making a great business of washing and drying her hands, desperately delaying the moment when she would have to meet Joan's eyes.

"It's alright, Mum, you don't have to pretend." Joan came up behind her and put her arm round her shoulders. Nan stiffened in total panic. How had she given herself away to Joan? Had her feelings for Adam been so blatant? She closed her eyes briefly, engulfed with embarrassment, and then heard Joan's next words as from a great distance.

"You don't have to say you're surprised. Adam has told me that he confided in you that he was going to ask me. Said he needed your blessing to give him courage!" She kissed her mother's cheek. "Mum, I'm so happy! I can't believe it's happening. I'm just so lucky to find someone like Adam."

"Hey, if you carry on like that, I'll start believing you and become insufferably conceited!" He came round to Nan's other side; they put their heads close to hers and she was the centre of a ring of affection, while the two children rushed upstairs to tell Eva and Alison.

Nan swallowed hard and made one of the most difficult speeches of her life. "I'm so glad for you both. I know you're making a wise decision and it's wonderful that you'll be a complete family again, Joanie. Children need a father, even at Mandy's age, and they've known you so long, Adam, I'm sure you'll all get along just fine.

"Now, I think I've got a bottle of sherry in the front room, so we can all have a celebratory drink." Thankful for any excuse to get away from their loving embrace and joyful faces, she hurried out of the room.

"Poor Mum. She hates breaking down - always has to be the strong one - but she's so happy, she was having a job not to cry. I expect she's having a little weep on her own now." Joan put both arms round Adam's neck. "To tell you the truth, I keep wanting to have a good howl. I can't remember being this happy for years. I want to pinch myself all the time to make sure I'm not dreaming."

"You're happy! Oh my darling girl, I never knew it was possible to feel so utterly euphoric. I know I'm so much older than you, but at the moment I feel about Mandy's age! I want to shout it from the rooftops, 'Joan is going to be my wife!'"

"Oh, Adam, I do love you so much!" Joan pulled his head down and their mouths met in a long, passionate kiss. This physical relationship was so new to them both, they were each bewildered by its overwhelming effect.

Adam had never had any close contact with a woman since the death of his fiancée at the end of the war - he had thought that any capacity for passion had been shrivelled for ever by the terrible grief he had felt at Lucille's death. Joan's relationship with Harry had been a loving one but, over the last few years, making love had become simply a pleasant and increasingly rare habit. They were more loving companions than passionate lovers.

Now Joan and Adam were both surprised by the force of the sexual desires that were sweeping through them and secretly delighted that in spite of their more mature years (particularly in Adam's case) this marriage promised to be exciting and fulfilling in every sense.

This was one reason why they decided there was no point in wasting time before setting a date for the wedding. "We both want to get on with our new life together and make the most of the years ahead," Joan told Nan on the phone a few days after the announcement of their engagement.

"Adam's taking me into town on Saturday to buy an engagement ring. I told him it's not necessary, but he's insistent that we follow tradition in every way. So we think we might have a winter wedding, just after Christmas. What d'you think, Mum"

"That sounds wonderful, Joanie. Oh, I'm sorry, I've got to go. There's someone at the street door. Probably the insurance man. I'll talk to you later, love." Nan put down the phone, shaking and ashamed at lying to her daughter. But for a moment her heart had rebelled against listening to all the happy plans with which Joan was obviously going to regale her.

For God's sake pull yourself together, woman! You have got to put your own feelings on one side. Start behaving like a caring mother, instead of some lovesick teenager. Nan was constantly having such conversations inside her head these days; it was the only way she seemed able to control herself with the rest of the family.

The wedding date was eventually fixed for New Year's Eve. Joan would have been content with a quiet registry office ceremony, but Adam was eager to have it in church. "Of course we don't want to have a big fuss - we're neither of us in the first flush of youth, are we? So I thought I'd get a nice suit and Mandy is going to be my bridesmaid. Donnie will give me away. I'm so glad that Robert and Irene and all the kids are going to be there. I know it's always a problem getting away from the farm, but Robert says their new stockman is very reliable. It's a pity we can't contact Rita - it would be lovely to see her again, wouldn't it, Mum?"

"Yes, there have been so few get-togethers with her over the years. Still, she seems happy enough."

"We're having the reception at the restaurant in Ally Pally. They've got a room for small private functions, so we can use that for a sit-down meal. After all it's only the family and one or two friends of ours from the staff at school." Joan chattered on enthusiastically about all their plans and Nan managed to make the right responses with what felt like a fixed smile on her face. Nowadays, it was only when she was alone in her bed that she could let down her guard and allow her despair and loneliness to shake her body with bitter sobs.

One subject that she could feel genuinely pleased about was Mandy's progress. At the end of the summer term her school career had finished in a blaze of glory when she played the lead in 'Romeo and Juliet' with the school drama group. Praise was heaped on her performance from all sides and it gave her just the extra confidence she needed as she set about finding her first job.

She had applied for a number in London but in the end decided to work for a secretarial agency doing temporary work until she found exactly the right position. When she visited Nan a few days before she was due to start she was bubbling with excitement and it soon transpired that this was not solely at the prospect of a new career.

"Nan, it's so thrilling. Paul Marriott has asked me out to the pictures! You remember him, don't you? He was Romeo in the play."

"Oh, yes, ever so good I thought he was. Very nice looking boy as well."

"Isn't he gorgeous? I can't believe he wants to go out with me. All the girls really fancied him. They thought I was so lucky having all those romantic scenes with him on stage! I didn't expect to see him again after the end of term, but he rang me at home. I don't know what I'm going to wear, Nan. I'm so nervous!"

"You'll be fine, sweetheart. Here," Nan extracted some notes from her well-worn purse, "Buy yourself a nice top or whatever you want. Nothing like some new clothes to give you a bit of confidence."

"Oh, Nan, you are an angel!" She practically strangled her grandmother in an exuberant hug and then proceeded to dance round the kitchen.

Nan watched her with a loving smile, thinking how fast the years had flown since Mandy was a baby in the bassinet out in the garden. A symbol of hope for the future she had been, when they all celebrated the end of the war. Now she was grown up and off on her first date. Suddenly Nan felt inexplicably sad and, for the first time she could remember, incredibly old and tired.

Fortunately all the family were so wrapped up in their own plans that no one noticed Nan was quieter and more introverted than normal. But then the golden bubble of happiness that surrounded Joan and her daughter was burst with a sudden near-tragedy that brought them all up short.

It was October and the first frosts had started. The afternoon had been extremely cold and one of the familiar London smogs had descended. Nan had spent the day tidying the beds on the allotment. The last tomatoes had been picked so she had made a bonfire of all their foliage together with that from the runner beans. By the time she reached home she was aching in every muscle and looking forward to a hot bath before starting on the lodgers' dinner.

Walking along Holfield Terrace she had been thankful it was such familiar territory. Talk about not seeing your hand in front of your face! The impenetrable gloom sat well with Nan's own depression as she closed the front door behind her and thankfully switched on the light.

Even now, years after electricity had been installed, she would fleetingly think what an improvement it was on the old days - groping for matches and carefully igniting the fragile gas mantles, so easily fractured by a clumsy movement.

She had just removed her ancient gardening coat and bent to poke the kitchen fire into a warmer blaze when the phone rang in the passage.

"Mum! Mum, it's me!" Joan's voice, high with panic vibrated in Nan's ear.

"What is it, Joan? Is something wrong?"

"Oh, Mum, I'm at the hospital. It's Donnie. He's had a dreadful asthma attack. They say he's really bad, Mum!"

"Alright, lovie. Don't worry, I'll come straight over. I'll ring for a taxi. But it may take a while in this dratted smog."

"Don't bother with the taxi, Mum. Adam's already on his way to collect you. Oh, I am scared, Mum. Donnie looks so white and frail - they've got an oxygen mask on him all the time and his breathing sounds dreadful!"

"Try not to get in a state, Joanie. Have you told Mandy?"

"Yes, I rang the company where she's working at the moment and she's coming straight to the hospital. But all the trains from London are running late in this weather."

Nan murmured a few more soothing words before replacing the receiver. Then methodically, as in any crisis, she did the practical things that needed doing. A quick wash and change into clean clothes. A note for Alison and Eva with instructions as to the cooking of the shepherd's pie waiting in the fridge, along with the apple tart for dessert. As Adam still had not arrived, striving to calm her churning stomach, she laid the dinner table and went round the house drawing the curtains. Then, hearing the car pulling up outside, she quickly picked up her coat, scarf and bag and hurried out of the front door.

For once the prospect of being alone with Adam in the dark intimacy of his little car did not bring the sense of discomfort it would normally have done. Now Nan was a mother and grandmother to the exclusion of any more personal feelings.

Concentrating on the difficult journey through the murky streets, with the blurry splashes of streetlights the only points of reference, Adam gave Nan a brief account of the afternoon's events.

"Apparently Donnie really wanted to watch a football match that his school were playing in. He's had a shocking cough and cold this last week, and I know Joan was worried about him. She forbade him to go to the match - insisted he must come straight home after school. But typically he thought he'd get away with it. Joan and I don't usually get in from work ourselves till nearly six on a Wednesday - there's a staff meeting we both attend. He thought he'd be home before us and we'd be none the wiser.

"Anyway, the match was abandoned half-way through because of the weather and he set out to walk home. Thought he'd take a short cut through the park, somehow missed his way in the smog and managed to walk straight into the duck pond! Of course he was soaked through and by the time he did get home he was in a terrible state.

"We arrived at the same time and Joan saw right away that he was in for a bad attack of asthma. Insisted we take him straight to casualty. Lucky she did. The journey took ages and by the time we got there he could hardly breathe and was practically unconscious."

"Poor little lad! Still he's had these bad attacks before, hasn't he? I'm sure they'll be able to sort him out alright." Nan determinedly kept her voice calm and optimistic, trying to believe in the sentiments she was expressing.

"I hope you're right, Nan, but he certainly does look bad. Worse than I've ever seen him". Adam's voice was very serious and sent a shiver of apprehension through her body. As if sensing the distress she was enduring, he briefly relinquished the steering wheel with one hand and squeezed her cold fingers comfortingly. Nan longed to drop the barriers and burst into tears and feel his arms about her, as she knew they would be, but on his part for all the wrong reasons. So she swallowed hard and groped in her bag for a handkerchief as an excuse to remove her hand from his.

The next days at the hospital were a terrible nightmare for all of them. Donnie lay comatose for much of the time, attended by grave-faced doctors and bustling, kindly nurses. He was in a cubicle on his own and Joan and Adam, Nan and Mandy sat with him, by turns. Poor Mandy seemed to grow up before Nan's eyes during that terrible time.

She had recently changed her hairstyle, cutting off the long pony-tail in favour of a wispy, urchin cut that emphasised her heart-shaped face. The old National Health glasses had been exchanged for a pair of smart new ones with fashionable upswept frames. She was still painfully thin, but was learning to disguise the shortcomings of her figure with clever dressing. Her lunch times were spent happily browsing through the big shops in London, and in the weeks since she had left school, Nan had detected a more mature outlook.

Now experiencing the sudden life and death tragedy that had turned her world upside down, with the sight of her adored younger brother struggling before her eyes, she seemed to lose the last heedlessness of childhood and became a young woman.

Donnie was battling double pneumonia and his

naturally fragile constitution seemed to have little strength left to fight it. Nan, sitting through the long night hours, staring at his waxy face and listening to his gasping breaths, sent up one silent prayer after another on his behalf.

"Harry, lad, if you're up there somewhere, do your best for your boy. He's such a lovely, happy creature, with not a mean bone in his body. He doesn't deserve to die, with all his life ahead of him.

"I know I've been a wicked woman these last months, grudging my own daughter her new happiness, but if you'll spare him, Lord, I promise I'll try and be truly happy for them and never think of Adam in that way again. Only, please don't take him away from us yet..."

It was the next night that the crisis was finally reached, and in the early hours of the morning Donnie turned the corner and started on the road to recovery. A sobbing Mandy was wrapped in her grandmother's arms while Adam held Joan, after the doctor had come out to the waiting room and broken the glad news to them all.

"Oh, Nan, I can't believe he's really going to be alright. I was so scared he was going to die!" Mandy buried her face against Nan's comfortable bosom and listened to the familiar voice crooning reassuring sounds, as she gently stroked the young girl's hair.

The whole family was very subdued in the aftermath of Donnie's brush with death. The winter weather was very severe and Joan became paranoid about her son venturing outside at all. Eventually, Adam persuaded her to have a long discussion with the consultant at the hospital when Donnie went for his check-up.

"Tell him all your fears and ask him how best to deal

with them. What are Donnie's options? Find out exactly what he can and can't do. I know you want to wrap him in cotton wool, darling, but he's a lively twelve-year-old boy who naturally wants to join his mates in all their activities. If the doctor says there are some things he musn't do, then fair enough - you'll have to make Donnie toe the line. But maybe you're being over-cautious after the recent scare."

Joan clung to the man who had become such a rock in the last weeks and knew that he was, as usual, making a lot of sense. But neither of them could have envisaged what far-reaching consequences that hospital consultation was to have on their future life together.

Now that the crisis about Donnie was over, Mandy was once again revelling in her new, adult lifestyle. Her wages were not over-generous, and by the time she had bought her season ticket on the train, and allowed herself money for lunch in a cheap café, there was not a lot remaining. So she had decided to collect a grown-up wardrobe mainly by the means of one of the popular mail-order catalogues.

Being a sensible girl, she never committed herself to repayments higher than her budget could handle. Gradually she purchased some nice skirts and tops; a winter suit with a reversible three quarter length coat – 'so I've got two for the price of one, Nan'; two sets of accessories, with the shoes, bag and gloves all carefully matched; and a bright yellow mac that made the greyest winter morning seem cheerful.

Looking through her granddaughter's latest purchases Nan rejoiced to see the bright eyes and happy smile. Mandy was glowing and obviously enjoying life at the moment.

"So how's that boyfriend of yours, Paul, is it?"

"Oh, we only see each other once a week, Nan. You

know he stayed on in the sixth form to finish off his 'A' levels. He's hoping to go to a polytechnic next year and study engineering. He's working really hard at the moment so he doesn't have much time for yours truly!"

"Well, you never know, love, you might meet someone else now you're out in the big wide world!"

"Oh no, Nan. I'm really keen on Paul. He's so special." She gazed into the fire with a dreamy smile and Nan suddenly wished with all her heart that she could protect this innocent granddaughter from all the sadness and disillusion of growing older. How sure she was of her first youthful passion and how little she knew of the real world and all its pain.

"So, d'you reckon this Paul feels the same way about you then? I know you made a lovely couple as Romeo and Juliet, but real life's a bit different, pet."

"I realise that, Nan. But we aren't stupid. We are both serious about each other and one day hope to be together. But we know that's a long way off. Paul will have to get his engineering qualifications and then find a job. But we're quite happy to wait and it'll be worth it in the end, won't it?"

"'Course it will, love. If you're sure of each other, waiting can only be a good thing in the long run - a real test of your feelings, being apart while he's away, studying."

"I'm determined to get on with my career as well. The agency is sending me to work for a new company that's just opening offices in London. They're Australian and now they want a European base. Apparently they're employing temps to start with, but anyone who does well may be offered a permanent job. The pay would be good and I should think it will be very interesting helping to set up an office right from the beginning. I'm really looking forward to it. If I work there permanently I should be able to start saving a bit - in readiness for my bottom drawer!"

"That's the spirit, love. You set your sights on a goal and work for it. No one got anywhere without ambition. You never know, you might be off on your travels 'down-under' with your new boss!"

But it was not Mandy who was destined to set off on her travels. Instead, Joan and Adam dropped their bombshell on the family two weeks before Christmas. All the wedding plans had now been organised and Nan was trying to fulfill the vow she had made by Donnie's hospital bed. She had gone shopping with Joan for her wedding clothes and even insisted on buying her a pretty blue lace negligée for her trousseau.

The cars, flowers, cake and photographer were booked and now they were all praying that the awful weather that had much of the country snowbound – 'worst since 1881' Nan read in her paper - would not cause problems for Irene and her family travelling up from Cornwall.

Nan had been wrapping her Christmas gifts when Joan and Adam let themselves into number thirty.

"Alright, Mum, it's only us. Goodness, it's icy out there."

"Hello, you two, you're a nice surprise. I'll just clear this lot off the table and then I'll make you a hot drink. Poke up the fire a bit, Adam."

"We've got something important we want to discuss with you, Mum. We haven't mentioned it to anyone else except the children, yet." Joan took off her coat and sat opposite Nan, with a look on her face that was hard to read. It was a mixture of anxiety, determination and...excitement. Adam said nothing, but drew his chair close to Joan's and took her hand in his.

"Right, you'd better tell me all about it, then." Nan

clasped her hands tightly with a premonition that she was going to have to brace herself for the revelation that was coming.

"You know we had a long chat about Donnie at the hospital recently, and they said that his health will always be delicate. His lungs have taken a real battering over the years and he'll never be robust. It seems that living in what they call the Thames basin doesn't help. The weather is so often damp and misty. What he really needs is a more bracing climate."

"So you're going to move then? Not thinking of joining Irene in Cornwall, are you? It would make a lot of sense, I suppose."

"No, Nan, it's a bit more drastic than that." Adam looked seriously at her, and as usual a tiny voice reminded her of his similarity to her beloved David. The gentle voice, the sincere eyes, full of warmth and honesty. "You see I've just recently had a letter from my solicitors in Canada, reminding me that the lease on my old family home is due for renewal. The tenants who have been living in it are moving out and the solicitors will be looking for new people to move in.

"I've been thinking for some time that I'd like Joan to visit my old home and now the news about Donnie's health has crystallised the issue. You know yourself how clear and pure the air is in Canada and I'm sure Donnie would settle down very well there. He could finish his education and maybe train for something in the timber business as a career. He likes carpentry at school - has a real flair for working with wood - and as you know, my family made their money from timber, so I know something about it."

"But obviously it's a very big step, Mum. Well you know that yourself from when you went out as a young bride." Joan smiled at Nan, as her mother's eyes grew distant with memories of those far-off days.

"But of course the other important consideration is Mandy". Adam nodded at Nan. "I'm sure you know how happy she is in her new job with this Australian company. She has high hopes that they'll take her on as permanent staff."

"Not to mention her feelings about young Paul. I know it's probably just calf love, but at the moment she thinks the sun shines out of him." Joan sighed and bit her lip, worriedly.

"One part of me is really thrilled at the idea of going off to Canada - it would be a wonderful start to our new life together for Adam and me. But it probably wouldn't have occurred to us, if it weren't for this business about Donnie's health. That makes it seem like fate, almost.

"But now I feel torn between the two children. Donnie is really excited about going, but Mandy was horrified when we told her about it. She'll be eighteen next year - she's a young woman with her own life to lead - but I can't bear the thought of leaving her behind, alone in some little bed-sit.

"It'll be bad enough to be parted from her and all of the rest of you, let alone wondering if she's safe and eating properly!" Joan gave a half-laugh and half-sob, and Adam pulled her against his shoulder in a comforting hug.

Nan turned her eyes away from them and used the excuse of making some tea in the scullery to give herself time to control her emotions.

She had been struggling so hard over the last weeks to forget her own feelings for Adam and banish forever the fantasy she had briefly entertained of a life shared with him. She had striven to think of him as a dear friend and a future son-in-law, but it was a terrible strain every time they met within the family. Like Joan, her emotions were now tearing her apart.

In one way it would be a relief not to see them together as man and wife in the future. But the thought of her much-loved daughter and grandson living so far away and no longer a part of her daily life was a terrible wrench. It would probably be years before they all met again. In order to be free of the emotional turmoil that she was experiencing over Adam, it seemed she must also lose two of the people she loved most in the world.

Then Joan's dilemma about Miranda came into her mind and she knew at once what she must say, for the good of all her family.

"It's a very big step, Joanie, of course it is. And I can see how torn you are about the two children. But in the end you don't really have a choice, do you? If it's for the good of Donnie's health, you've got to go. As for Mandy, don't fret about her. You know I've always kept one room spare upstairs for family to visit, and what better use for it than this? Mandy can lodge with me and I think you can trust me to see she comes to no harm, can't you?"

"Oh, Mum, you are wonderful! That would be the perfect solution. Mandy adores you and she's always thought of number thirty as a second home. It will be such a relief to know she's got you to keep an eye on her. Thank you so much for making it easier for me. Where would I be without you?" She flung her arms round Nan, half laughing and half crying. Nan patted her back, swallowing her own emotion, knowing all at once just how hard a sacrifice it would be, when she finally waved her Joanie goodbye.

It had always been a favourite saying of hers - 'The

biggest gift you can give your children is the freedom to leave you without feeling guilty' - and that was never truer than when she stood on the dock and watched the liner pulling away from the shore in the first week of 1963.

The whole family had been borne along on a wave of excited activity once the decision had been made that Joan, Adam and Donnie should leave. As well as the wedding, they now had to pack up the belongings in the house at Muswell Hill. Some items were sold, some crated to be sent out to Canada and others stored in the loft at number thirty. Nan was most anxious that Mandy should feel really at home in the big bedroom at the front of the house, so she had it redecorated to suit the young girl's personal taste. Mandy's own furniture would be installed of course, including her pretty kidney-shaped, glass-topped dressing table with new skirts to match the pink flowered curtains. Nan bought her a pink candlewick bed cover and a cream carpet, so the overall effect was charming and feminine.

The wedding on New Year's Eve went off without a hitch, although the reception afterwards turned into a farewell party for family and friends. Nan had steeled herself to watch her daughter walking down the aisle to marry the man that she herself loved so deeply. Joan had looked elegant and pretty in a short, cream brocade dress with a straight skirt and long sleeves. Over it was a matching coat that was trimmed with cherry velvet to match her pillbox hat, and a small muff to which she had pinned a spray of Christmas roses mixed with holly berries.

Behind her paced Miranda, a delightful vision in a dress and jacket of cherry velvet that echoed her mother's outfit. A cream pillbox topped her elfin face and she carried a posy of bronze and cream chrysanthemums. Donnie, in his first suit with long trousers, marched proudly beside his mother as he led her to stand beside Adam.

Nan wiped her eyes surreptitiously as the choir sang 'Love Divine' and then returned the comforting squeeze that Irene gave her hand. Of course Irene believed that Nan was simply experiencing the emotions of any bride's mother - she could never begin to guess the seething turmoil of longing and regret that Nan was determinedly subduing within her trembling body.

The bridal couple had spent a couple of days in London as a brief honeymoon and Nan had endeavoured to keep herself occupied with all the last-minute packing she had undertaken to carry out for Joan. Donnie was in such an over-excited state, he was enough to wear her out all by himself. But then the last day had come and the whole family had gone to see the ship weigh anchor. As the faces of Joan, Adam and Donnie became smaller and smaller, Nan finally ceased her struggle to hold back the tears and wept unashamedly in the arms of her granddaughter, who was sobbing as if her heart would break.

"Come on, lovie, it's done now. They're gone and we must make the best of it. We're all going to miss them, but the world's getting smaller all the time and before you know it, you'll be going to visit them for a holiday. I know your Mum doesn't like the thought of flying, but I expect you'd love it.

"Now let's go home and get on with our own lives, eh? You've got your new job and I expect Paul will be longing to see you tonight and hear how you're doing. So no more tears, there's a brave girl. It's just you and me, and I daresay we'll rub along fine together, won't we?"

"Oh, yes, Nan. I'll love being at number thirty with you. If anyone could make it more bearable, losing Mum and Donnie, it's you. I don't think I could have borne it otherwise." Miranda mopped her eyes and gave her grandmother a watery smile, and they turned towards Irene and Robert's Land-Rover arm in arm.

PART IV : 1963-1965

Mandy adored working for Sanders Pty. right from the beginning. When her position there was made permanent, she was overjoyed. She had never met any Australians before and was enchanted by the informal, friendly, but hard-working attitude of Daniel Woodley from their first meeting. Although conventionally dressed in a dark business suit, shirt and tie, there was a restless energy about him that conveyed a sense of one used to wide open spaces and nature in the raw.

He had put her through the usual shorthand and typing tests and asked about her experience. She found the Australian accent fascinating and sensed at once an enormous enthusiasm for his work.

"The company is totally owned by Mr Clement Sanders. It's his baby and he built it all up himself. He has fingers in a great many pies, I can tell you. He's the original self-made man. His first real pile came from opals I believe, and that was back in the thirties. Like a lot of other fast thinkers, he made a fortune during the war. He wasn't afraid to take chances and somehow everything he touched turned to gold. Now he has investments in all kinds of business - land, oil, minerals, hotels, nightclubs, you name it and he's probably got money in it. He's the original entrepreneur, our Mr Sanders."

"So has he never done any business in England before?"

"Only indirectly, I think. He's concentrated mainly on

the Asian markets. But he's recently taken over a company that manufactures fruit machines - one-armed bandits that is - and he's decided to set up an operation for that in Europe.

"He's also got investments in some European hotel chains and I think he's decided to concentrate over here for the foreseeable future. Once this office is organised as a headquarters, he'll be coming over himself to look around and diversify his investments even more. He's got a nose for any new venture that's going to make money. He's amazing, believe me."

"What's he like, as a person? Do you get on well together?"

Daniel was relaxed and chatty, leaning back in his chair, jacket off, tie loosened and quite unlike any of the other business men she had worked for as a 'temp', so that Mandy felt quite comfortable asking him questions about his boss.

"We get on fine, so long as I give him one hundred per cent commitment to the job. He pays very generously, but he expects his pound of flesh, I can tell you. He's a really down-to-earth bloke, no side at all in spite of the fact that he must be a multi-millionaire now. I guess it's because he started out as an ordinary working class feller himself."

"Is he married, with a family?"

"No, there's no Mrs Sanders. Never has been as far as I know. He often says he's got no one to leave his fortune to, but reckons he's probably got a fair share of unacknowledged heirs around the world!"

Mandy looked blank for a moment and Daniel laughed. "You're a bit of an innocent, sweetheart, aren't you? I mean that Clement may not be married, but he's certainly no slouch in the ladies' department. Sown quite a few wild oats in his time - even now he always has some gorgeous female on his arm when he's out socialising."

"Oh, I see." Mandy blushed and felt a little stupid at her own naivety. But Daniel smiled kindly at her and changed the subject, asking her to bring in the catalogues of office furniture she had been acquiring.

"We're going to really have to get our fingers out over the next few days, honey. Got to sort out all the furnishings for the whole office now the decorators are finished and the carpets are down. These hired bits and pieces have done the job temporarily but when Clement arrives he'll expect top quality surroundings with up-to-date equipment and every luxury."

Mandy thoroughly enjoyed planning and ordering the furnishings for the office suites. No expense was spared and, as well as a comfortable room for Daniel and a smaller, but equally smart one for herself, they also furnished a reception area with desks for other office staff they would be employing and of course a lavish separate suite for Mr Sanders himself.

"It's really gorgeous, Nan. A huge desk, with a chair behind it that I could lose myself in, as well as some big couches and armchairs for visitors. There's a lovely, glass-topped coffee table and a big bookcase that has a central section that swings round and has a drinks bar hidden behind it! And he's got a separate washroom all to himself!"

"Sounds like something out of the films." Nan was fascinated to hear the details of the new world that Mandy was entering. At least it was taking her mind off missing her mother and brother. They had actually phoned from Canada when the ship had docked and now Joan was writing every week with excited descriptions of their new life.

As she waxed lyrical over the spectacular scenery with its vast forests and the thundering glories of Niagara Falls, it was a bitter cup for Nan to drink. If only things had been different, she would have been the one revelling in the wonders of the Canadian countryside and looking over the beautiful family home within sound of the falls, which had been Adam's, and indeed David's, birthplace.

'We're staying in a hotel nearby at the moment, as Adam wants to completely redecorate the whole place to suit us both, before we move in. So I'm having a wonderful time choosing wallpapers and carpets and generally spending a fortune. But as you know, that's not a problem for Adam, who's being his usual generous self.' Nan put down Joan's letter and tried to swallow the lump of angry bitterness that seemed to sit physically above her heart. Just be glad for them, be generous, be a mother, she told herself.

Mandy remained full of enthusiasm about the new job and was gaining in confidence almost daily. Her excellent salary as a permanent member of staff was enabling her to enlarge her modest wardrobe considerably. She was experimenting with make-up and acquiring a slightly more sophisticated polish. So much so that young Paul was finding the change a little intimidating.

On one of their Saturday night dates they had been to see 'Billy Liar' at the local cinema and he seemed very quiet and withdrawn. After the film they stopped at the coffee bar in the high street as usual. Mandy had been chattering on for a while about the new office equipment when she realised that she was getting little response.

"Is something the matter, Paul? You've been ever so quiet this evening. Is school getting you down? How are the 'A' level studies?"

"Hard work, and pretty boring, if you must know.

Nothing like as glamorous as working in a posh London business, earning a fortune while you're spending another one on office furniture!"

"Paul! I thought you'd be pleased I'm getting on so well. And I'm not earning a fortune, anyway."

"Well the amount of clothes you're always buying it seems like it. You're wearing a new coat for a start."

"I haven't bought that many new things, and besides I've got to look smart now I'm working in London. I have to meet different business contacts when Daniel has meetings. Sometimes I have to sit in with them and take notes, so it goes with the job."

"Well, it's all very nice for you I suppose, but frankly I'm a bit sick of hearing about your precious Daniel and the wonderful electric golfball typewriter he's bought you. And how come you call him 'Daniel'? If he's your boss, why don't you call him Mister Woodley?"

"I do when we've got business meetings, but he's Australian and I told you, they're much more informal than us. He's really nice, Paul, with a great sense of humour. You'd like him if you met him."

"Fat chance of that happening. We don't exactly move in the same circles, do we?"

Paul moodily swirled the remains of his milkshake round with his straw, and looking across at his rather petulant face, Mandy couldn't help feeling a little impatient. In his jeans and windcheater, he did look incredibly young and boyish. One part of her ached to kiss him and bring a smile back to his adorable, pouting mouth, but the new, more mature self wished he'd grow up a bit.

"I'm really sorry if I've been going on too much about work. Of course it must be uninteresting for you. It's just that it's all so new and exciting for me. I can't believe how much I'm doing and how they trust me to do it on my own, even though I'm so young and inexperienced. I suppose it's because they're an Australian company. If it was an English firm, I'd be working my way up very slowly."

Paul moved closer to her along the banquette seat they were sharing and shyly put his arm round her shoulders. Although satisfactorily passionate when they were ensconced in a dark shop doorway, or sharing the couch in the front room at number thirty, he was reluctant to demonstrate his feelings for her in public.

"I'm sorry, Mandy. Of course I'm really pleased it's going so well for you. It's just all such a slog at school at the moment, and then there'll be the polytechnic, if I'm lucky, before I can even start earning proper money. And here's you swanning around with all these high-flying business types in a different world. I suppose I'm scared you'll get fed up with just coming out once a week to the pictures with me. It's not very exciting for you, is it?"

"Don't be daft! As long as we're together I don't care where we spend our evenings. I know how hard you're working and it'll all be worth it in the end. Please don't be down." She smiled and snuggled close to him, and gave him a swift but meaningful kiss on the lips. Paul blushed, but his arm tightened about her and feeling very worldly-wise and womanly, she knew that he needed this reassurance.

By June the office was operating smoothly with three new girls working under Mandy's supervision as a switchboard/receptionist, copy typist and accounts clerk. Daniel was very cock-a-hoop because he had landed a hugely successful contract with a large brewery to install Sanders fruit machines in their pubs throughout the country. He breezed into Mandy's office one morning waving a letter in great excitement.

"This is it, Mandy! A letter to say the boss will be arriving on an extended visit next week. We're to book him into a suite at the Dorchester and he may look for a permanent penthouse flat when he gets here.

"Boy, things will start cooking with gas now. When Clement arrives, the office will be a real hive of activity, believe me!"

"Oh, Daniel, I think I'm going to be terrified of him. I've never met a millionaire before and I'm bound to make a mess of things. Suppose I can't do my shorthand fast enough for him. Suppose I read it back wrongly!" She gazed up at Daniel with a look of total panic in her expressive eyes and he swooped to give her a smacking kiss on the cheek.

"Stop worrying, honey. You'll do just fine. You're the perfect little English girl, you're quiet and efficient and you're also extremely pretty. You can't fail with old Clement, trust me!"

Blushing and laughing, Mandy acknowledged that it was the kiss more than the compliment that had set her pulses racing. Daniel was undeniably handsome, being tall and muscular. His vivid blue eyes were usually twinkling with good humour and his reddish gold hair was crisp and curly. Much of his working life had been spent outdoors and he was very keen on swimming, having been a lifeguard for a while on Bondi beach, which had left him with a healthy tan. He seemed unaware of his own good looks, but his casual charm made him a guaranteed lady-killer.

She was aware from various phone calls he received that he had several girlfriends he took out and about to theatres, restaurants and clubs, and she imagined they often accompanied him back to his flat in Earls Court. She knew that he meant nothing by the kiss or his extravagant compliments and 'honeys' but it was hard not to be attracted by his foreign exuberance and lighthearted approach to life.

The next few days were rather fraught as all the staff geared themselves up for the arrival of the big boss himself. Mandy had scoured the filing cabinets repeatedly making sure she could lay her hands at a moment's notice on any contract or figure he might wish to examine. Daniel had stocked the office bar with all the necessary liquor to suit Mr Sanders' taste. The hotel suite was booked, and on the day of his arrival, Mandy decided to buy some flowers to decorate his desk and coffee table.

She arrived a little earlier than usual to give herself plenty of time for last-minute arrangements and went straight through to the executive suite to put the flowers in water. Opening the door, she was astounded to find the room already occupied.

"Oh, I didn't expect to find anyone in here." She hesitated in the doorway, staring at the stocky figure that sat behind the large desk, which was now spread with a variety of documents.

He was a man in his late sixties with a fine head of thick grey hair. His face was deeply weathered, speaking of a life spent much in the open air, but his square-fingered hands were beautifully manicured and conveyed that his labouring days were many years behind him. The dark jacket of his expensive suit was flung carelessly across the coffee table, along with a cream silk tie. The matching shirt had been opened at the neck and the sleeves rolled up. On the breast pocket the embroidered monogram CS would have told Mandy his identity if she had not already guessed.

"Well, now. You must be Miranda, if Dan's description

is accurate. Quite an early bird, aren't you? Anxious to impress the big boss, were you? Very inconsiderate of me to beat you to it!" He smiled conspiratorially at her, but she was aware that although his lips curved, his eyes remained coldly assessing her.

"Good morning, Mr Sanders. I thought some flowers might be welcoming when you arrived. We weren't expecting you till after lunch."

"Dan will tell you, I like to keep people on their toes and do the unexpected. I caught the flight yesterday and arrived late last night. Now you're here, you can rustle me up some coffee - black, no sugar - O.K.?"

"Certainly, Mr Sanders". She hesitated awkwardly, wondering whether to leave the flowers or not and he nodded at the large crystal bowl that she had chosen with Daniel to ornament the coffee table. "The flowers will look fine in that. And make sure that fresh ones are brought in every few days. It was a good idea, Miranda." He nodded dismissively and bent over his papers again.

When she returned with a tray bearing a fine china cup and saucer and a small plate with some biscuits, he was deep in conversation on the phone. He gestured for her to place the contents of the tray on his desk and carried on talking. As she bent close to him, she caught a wave of sharp, expensive cologne from his smooth-shaven face. His voice sounded quick and authoritative and he was exactly what she might have expected him to be. Walking silently across the deep pile cream carpet and closing the door quietly behind her, Mandy had a premonition that her enjoyable, hardworking but light-hearted days with Daniel were definitely in the past.

Her surmise was correct. Mr Sanders brought a whirlwind of high-powered business activity in his wake and the office staff were all swept along with it. He was constantly setting up meetings, exploring various opportunities for future investments in all sorts of fields. Any that he felt worthwhile, Daniel would have to examine in fine detail, and then decisions would be taken. Mandy was always relieved if the meetings took place outside the office. When Mr Sanders left in his hired Jaguar Mark X, the whole place became more relaxed.

When meetings took place in his suite, Mandy would sit on tenterhooks waiting for the intercom to buzz as he requested some file or other document, or told her to bring in refreshments for his visitors. She dreaded having to sit in on the meetings and take notes, in case her shorthand let her down and she would be found inefficient. Mr Sanders obviously expected total excellence from all his staff, and paying such good salaries was prepared to demand it at all hours. Many an evening Mandy was about to cover her typewriter and put on her coat when he would buzz without apology and expect her to take shorthand that had to be typed back before she left.

When she mentioned this to Daniel, he grinned and gave her a hug. "That's the boss for you. He eats and breathes work, and figures if he pays good money, we should all be available to do the same. But don't worry, Mandy, you're doing just great. This company is really expanding in Europe and before long we'll be getting much bigger premises, and you're going right to the top with it. No worries!"

As the weeks passed, Mandy found she was gradually relaxing enough to enjoy the pace of the busy office life and the challenges it brought with it. Slowly her confidence in her own ability increased, and although she was still very wary when around Mr Sanders, he did not terrify her as much as in those first weeks. He rarely spoke to her on any subject other than business, but she would find him watching her occasionally with a slightly quizzical expression on his face. Once he actually showed his satisfaction with her work in a more personal way.

He had spent a couple of days in Paris, investigating a large chain of continental hotels in which he planned to invest, and on his return stopped by her desk on the way to his own office. "Everything alright while I've been away, Mandy? No major crisis?"

"Everything's fine, Sir. I've left all your messages in a folder and starred the most urgent ones. I've sorted your mail into that requiring immediate attention and others, and there's a file of the copies of letters I've answered on your behalf, as you instructed."

"Fine. You're a good girl, and I'm pleased with your work. Here's a little something for you from the Duty Free." He tossed a gift-wrapped package down in front of her and with a nod, walked away before she could thank him properly.

Amazed, she unwrapped the pretty box and found it contained a large bottle of Carven's 'Ma Griffe' perfume. When she showed it delightedly to Dan a little later he nodded and smiled at her.

"That's typical of the boss, honey. Very generous and thoughtful when you least expect it, but he'll always demand absolute loyalty in return. A great bloke to have as a mate, when he wants to be a mate, but he never really forgets he pays your wages, and a nasty piece of work if he's ever crossed. I know, 'cos I've seen him in action with some of his business rivals. Ruthless is his middle name!"

In September Mr Sanders went back to Australia. He was very pleased with the progress he had made with his European operations and knew that Daniel would handle matters in his absence for the next few months.

"But I shall be back after Christmas, Mandy, and then we'll really make things start to hum. Various deals I've been negotiating will be finalised then and I shall look for larger premises. I'll take on more staff and you'll be in charge of them, in addition to your duties as Daniel's secretary. But when I'm here myself, you'll work for me direct. I may think of buying a home as an English base next year. I have a fancy to put down a few roots in the Old Country"

"Did your family come from England originally, Sir?" Mandy was feeling more relaxed than usual in his company. They had finished work after a very busy day, and when he had signed all her neatly typed letters in the leather bound signature book, he had seemed in the mood for more personal chat.

He walked across to the bookcase that also contained the hidden bar and poured himself a glass of whisky, and to her surprise gestured to the row of bottles. "Join me in a glass. You've earned it today. What'll you have? How about a Martini? One of those won't hurt you."

"Why, thank you, Mr Sanders. That would be very nice." So, she sat back in the big armchair beside the coffee table, instead of her usual upright one where she took shorthand at his desk, and he relaxed opposite her. And it did not seem odd to ask him a personal question about his ancestry.

He swirled the amber spirit round in the heavy crystal tumbler silently and then looked at her with a little smile. "I suppose most Poms would say that all us Aussies have

English ancestry, wouldn't they? Assume that we still have marks of the ball and chains around our ankles from the convict ships, right?"

"Oh, I didn't mean that..." Mandy blushed, but he gave one of his rare, barking laughs. "It's alright, my dear, I'm teasing you. As it happens I am English-born, and not Australian. You may have noticed my accent isn't as marked as Dan's. But I've lived 'down under' for a great many years, so I think of myself as more Australian than anything else. If truth be told, I've lived in a number of countries in the past. I suppose you could say I'm a citizen of the world."

"It must be wonderful to have travelled to so many places. I've never been out of England. In fact the farthest I've ever travelled is my aunt's farm in Cornwall!"

"Well, there's no reason why you shouldn't see something of the world with the Sanders company. Perhaps you can start by accompanying Dan when he goes over to Paris in the new year. He'll be backwards and forwards to meetings quite a lot, and it might be useful to have you along sometimes. I'll mention it to him."

Miranda went home quite starry-eyed that night to Nan, with the news that she would be having a trip abroad and would also be taking on new responsibilities in the new year.

"That's wonderful, love. You've done ever so well there. I'm really proud of you. You'll have to write and tell your mum all about it."

Christmas that year was quiet at number thirty and seemed rather strange, with the absence of Joan, Donnie and Adam. They phoned on Christmas morning but Nan was concerned that Mandy must be missing them all very much. Although Alison had gone to stay with friends, Eva was cheerful company, and the three of them played cards, watched the Queen's speech on TV and went for a walk through Ally Pally in the afternoon to recover from their big meal. In the evening Mandy was invited over to Paul's house where his family were having a party.

He had just finished his first term studying at the polytechnic and Mandy was so thrilled to have him back in Holgate. They had written every week during their separation and both had plenty to say. He was full of his new friends and fellow students and was very busy with lectures. Mandy felt it was easier to tell him about all the events of office life, now that he had new and interesting experiences of his own to relate. Their reunion had been ecstatic when he returned a few days before Christmas and they had been out together every evening.

"But after Boxing Day I've got to get down to some serious studying, Mandy. I've quite a bit to do during the vacation, so that I'm up to date for the beginning of the new term. There's so much to take in and it's a constant pressure. You know me, I'm not exactly brilliant - one of the world's 'plodders', I'm afraid!"

"Don't put yourself down, Paul. You must be pretty brainy to have got accepted for the engineering course at all! There's no way I'd ever have managed it!"

"No, but you're doing fantastically well at your job. That was a great Christmas bonus you got and it sounds as though you're going to have loads of people working for you next year. A really high-powered career woman, I've got!" Mandy laughed, but secretly she was tempted to agree with him. Apart from missing the family in Canada, life was very good at the moment.

The pattern continued through 1964. She accompanied Daniel to a number of business meetings in Paris and around Britain. Most of the time it was quite demanding with endless meetings at which she had to concentrate very hard on her note-taking, so by the end of the day she was glad to have dinner and go off to bed.

Sometimes she would eat with Daniel, but quite often he would be wined and dined by business contacts. At first she had felt very hesitant and shy eating alone in the hotel restaurants, but gradually became accustomed to the experience and grew more confident. She was also delighted that her schoolgirl French had stayed with her, and quite impressed Daniel at times when she was able to converse in it.

They continued to enjoy a happy working relationship. She revelled in his irrepressible Australian humour and he took pleasure in helping her gradually acquire a more sophisticated veneer and a professional secretarial polish. When they had been to meetings outside London, he would take her home to Holgate in his cherished MG sports car, and she had been able to introduce him to Nan.

As expected, they had hit it off immediately, and Nan had promptly invited him to stay for dinner. "He's a really nice young man, lovie. I'm so glad you brought him to meet me. Now I can picture him when you're talking about the office. Very good-looking too. Does he have a girlfriend? I should think they'd be queuing up!"

"They probably are, Nan. He's got a little black book and I believe he goes through them in rotation! But from the way he talks, I don't think there's anyone special. I can't see him settling down for ages. I think Mr Sanders has a very high opinion of him, and Dan knows it! I daresay he sees himself becoming a millionaire before he's much older. When Mr Sanders retires, I expect Dan'll be running the whole organisation."

"So this Mr Sanders, hasn't he got any family to pass it all on to then? Seems a shame to have built up such a successful business and no-one to inherit it."

"Well, Dan reckons he's a bit cagey about his past. A self-made man who's probably cut a few corners where the law's concerned."

"How did Dan come to work for him in the first place?"

"Apparently his mother had known Mr Sanders years ago, before he made his money. Her family worked on a sheep station and Mr Sanders was a shearer travelling round the area. It's hard to imagine now with his posh suits and hand-made shirts! Anyway, years later, she and Dan were living in Sydney - I think she split up with his father when Dan was quite small - and she was working in a bar. Mr Sanders was drinking in there and they recognised each other. Dan was just looking for a job, hadn't had much of an education, and Mr Sanders offered to give him a chance. Dan obviously impressed him and gradually progressed. I think they get on really well together, but Dan's always careful to remember who's the boss!"

In the summer they were ready to move into their larger premises in Central London and Mr Sanders came over for the opening. This time he was staying for an indefinite period and let it be known he planned to hunt for a permanent home. Mandy was working for him full-time now and Dan's secretarial work was handled by one of the other clerical staff. Mandy supervised them all and she was installed in a very grand office, opening directly off Clement Sanders' own suite. She missed her close contact with Dan; he was often away on extended trips chasing up contacts, sometimes on the Continent or in Scandinavia. Mr Sanders was planning to open a company that would run tourist cruises along the fjords. "He's nothing if not varied in his interests," Mandy laughed to Nan.

Although so busy at work, her free time tended to hang rather heavily these days. Paul was studying hard in Bristol and there was little likelihood of seeing him in the long vacation as he was planning to work abroad on some student labour scheme. When they did meet for a rare weekend visit, Mandy was aware of an increasing rift between them.

"Well it's hardly surprising, love. You do lead very different lives, don't you? Once he's finished studying and got a job things'll be better, I expect." Nan smiled sympathetically, watching as her granddaughter carefully wound her damp hair round rollers, in front of the kitchen mirror. Casually dressed in tight yellow three-quarter length pants with a printed yellow and chocolate shirt tucked into the waist, she was a slim, charming figure. Hard to believe that she was turned nineteen already. Where did all the years go, Nan asked herself.

Just then the phone rang and a familiar voice asked for Mandy. "Hiya, honey. There's a crisis on back here. I know it's Sunday afternoon, but the boss could do with you to make some notes at an unexpected meeting. This Norwegian contact has just shown up, and it looks like a deal that's been simmering is about to go through. Can you be ready if I send a cab to pick you up in half an hour? I'll shout you dinner afterwards, that's a promise."

"That's fine. I'll just dry my hair and get changed."

"Good girl. The boss'll see you right, you can bet on it".

Truthfully, Mandy was glad to have her rather empty

Sunday afternoon interrupted and quickly brushed out her hair so that it lay smoothly behind her ears and donned a pink linen shift dress with a smart jacket, whose stand-away neckline prettily accentuated her heart-shaped face. White medium-heeled pointed shoes and a matching box-shaped straw bag finished off the outfit, and watching her hurry out to the waiting taxi, Nan felt her usual wave of pride.

The meeting went smoothly and then Mandy typed up the minutes while Mr Sanders whisked his guest away for an early dinner. She had copies ready on his desk when he returned, and he patted her approvingly on the shoulder after briefly scanning them.

"Excellent work, Mandy. I'm taking Mr Erikson to the airport myself, but no doubt Dan will put you in a cab. I appreciate you interrupting your Sunday for me."

"I've promised her dinner as a reward, boss. Then I'll drive her back to Holgate myself."

"Holgate - that's north London, isn't it? Do you live with your family there?" Obviously very mellow and pleased with himself after finalising this lucrative Scandinavian contract, Clement Sanders actually showed some interest in the personal life of his secretary - a rarity on his part.

"I live with my grandmother. My mother and brother live in Canada, with my stepfather."

"No desire to fly the nest and get a place of your own, then? Most youngsters of your age can't wait to become independent."

"Oh, I'm quite happy with Nan. She has two other lodgers and we all get on well together." Mr Sanders nodded, unspeaking, his mind already obviously elsewhere. As soon as he left, Dan locked up and the two of them went off to a nearby French restaurant that was a favourite of his.

The hours sped by and as usual were full of laughter as Dan regaled her with stories of his misspent youth in the outback and the scrapes he had survived with various girlfriends. He and two mates had spent a wild year backpacking round Europe and their adventures were truly hair-raising to someone of Mandy's sheltered background.

As they had seen so little of each other in recent months, they found a special pleasure in each other's company. When they finally left the restaurant it was quite late, and Mandy wondered where the time had gone.

Walking along to the car, Dan casually draped his arm about her shoulders, and not for the first time she was aware of a frisson of sexual excitement at the physical contact. He was uncharacteristically silent on the drive home, and when they drew up outside number thirty, said quite seriously, "I've really enjoyed tonight, Mandy. I've missed you over the last months while I've been travelling. I didn't realise how much until this evening."

"I've had a lovely time, Dan. Thank you for taking me out to dinner."

"Would it be O.K. if we did it again soon? Maybe a show or a film, after work? How would you feel about it?"

Their glances locked and Mandy knew that they had reached some unlooked-for watershed in their relationship. Dan had a new expression in his eyes and she could feel her pulses racing. All thoughts of Paul had fled, and she heard herself saying rather breathlessly, "I'd really like to go out with you again, Dan."

"Great. I'll speak to you tomorrow when we've both got our office diaries. Now you'd better go inside. Your Nan will be wondering what's happened to you - and if you carry on looking at me with those gorgeous eyes, I might just do something she wouldn't approve of!" They both laughed, but Mandy was blushing and experiencing a delicious excitement. She was quite sure that whatever he had in mind - approved by Nan or not - would be extremely agreeable as far as she was concerned.

If Mandy felt any guilt about Paul over the coming months, this was alleviated by the knowledge that he was gradually losing interest himself in their relationship. His letters grew shorter and further apart. He had become involved in various societies at the polytechnic and was very keen on the Campaign for Nuclear Disarmament. They were forever organising rallies and marches and the name of Laura Gordon cropped up increasingly, as she was the main force behind all these activities.

Reading about his enthusiasm and admiration for this fellow student, Mandy felt very frivolous in comparison. She had set out to be honest over her outings with Dan, and described various films and shows they visited. But Paul never referred to the matter in his letters, and she became more and more convinced that he was gradually losing enthusiasm for their youthful plans of a future together.

Nan was very aware of the change in Mandy's relationships and worried accordingly. Paul had always been very sober and reliable as an escort, and Nan had instinctively felt he was totally trustworthy. With Dan she was more apprehensive. She found him very likeable and utterly charming, but he was obviously very experienced in his relationships with women and at twenty-nine was ten years older than Mandy. The latter was becoming more besotted with every date they had and was swept off her feet by all the attention he was giving her.

Things were fairly quiet in the office as Mr Sanders was taking time out to inspect a number of country properties he was considering as a permanent English base.

"I reckon he's wasting his time. He's not the type to enjoy the country life for long. He'll probably end up with a penthouse in Mayfair, if you ask me." Dan grinned as he leaned against her desk, watching as she efficiently opened and sorted the day's mail.

"D'you fancy seeing a film tonight? I thought maybe we could have a look at 'Goldfinger', or if you prefer something a bit more girly, how about 'Mary Poppins'? If you can get away on time, we can have dinner at the Spaghetti House first? What d'you say?"

Agreeing happily, Mandy made a mental note to ring Nan and warn her she would be out for dinner. As she went about her duties in the office she felt as though she were floating several inches above the cream carpet. Dan was out at meetings for most of the day, but when he returned in the afternoon, he came straight into her office.

"How's my favourite girl, then? Been slaving away all day like a dutiful secretary, have you? Here's a reward." From behind his back he produced a bunch of long-stemmed crimson roses.

"Oh, Dan, they're so beautiful! Thank you very much." As she stood up and took them from him, he leant forward and placed his hands on either side of her waist. His warm breath fanned her cheek and a faint tang of after-shave mingled with the perfume of the roses as he murmured huskily, "Mandy, it's you that are so beautiful. I don't know what you've done, but I can't get you out of my head. Every time I'm away from the office, I'm counting the minutes until I can get back here with you. It's no line, I promise. I don't know what's hit me. You've taken over my life, d'you know that?"

Mandy wasn't sure exactly how it happened, but somehow she had swayed forward and then his mouth had come down hard on her own. The strong hands were pulling her tightly against him, and she was aware that her fingers were reaching up of their own volition to lock behind his neck and then softly explore the red-gold curls that clung tightly to his skull.

The embrace was what they had both been secretly wanting and expecting for weeks now, and it was exactly as earth-shattering as she might have anticipated. They both laughed shakily as they eventually drew apart and then of course the intercom buzzed and Mandy automatically reached for it.

As she discussed a forthcoming appointment that needed to be rescheduled for Mr Sanders, she was conscious of Dan's hands stroking her shoulders and neck and his breath tickling her ear as he leaned close to her back, whilst she struggled to retain a tone of cool efficiency in her voice.

After that their whole relationship entered a new and increasingly intense phase. Their mutual physical attraction was escalating all the time and Mandy had the sense of being out of control and whirled along to an inevitable conclusion. Dan never attempted to pressure her into a situation that was against her will, but the truth was simply that she ached for him as much as he desired her.

She wondered when she was at home if Nan suspected what was happening, and almost expected that some half-veiled warning would be forthcoming. Nan had always been very open and natural with her grandchildren in her attitude towards sex, just as she had been with her own daughters. She made no secret of the fact that she had been pregnant before her marriage, simply pointing out what a disaster that had turned out to be.

But Nan said nothing. Not through a sense of tact, but because she had other things on her mind. Indeed Mandy had noticed that she had been quieter than usual, looking very pale and drawn. When she had questioned her grandmother, Nan characteristically made light of it.

"Oh, I'm alright, lovie. Just a bit tired that's all. I've not been sleeping too well lately and now the nights are drawing in and winter's almost on us, I suppose I'm feeling the cold getting to my old bones. I'm not as young as I was, and it's no good pretending I am!"

"Perhaps you ought to have a break, Nan. Why don't you go and stay with Auntie Irene for a week? Cornwall should be a bit milder than up here and you know you love the farm. It would set you up for the winter."

"I'll see, pet. Don't fuss. Your old Nan's fine."

But she was not fine, not fine at all. In fact she was beginning to seriously wonder if she was having some sort of breakdown. Over the last few weeks, it seemed that whenever she went out of the house, she had the sense of being watched. At first she told herself not to be so stupid, but it happened time and again. She had never been a fanciful woman, prided herself on her down-to-earth practicality, but the feeling of eyes following her as she walked through the streets was increasingly frightening.

In early November she was actually thinking of consulting her doctor or the police. Sometimes she was sure that she was definitely being followed, but other times she convinced herself it was all in her mind. Now her life was really being affected by this fear that had come out of nowhere. She was afraid to go to work on the allotment, because the afternoons were getting darker and sometimes she was the only person there. When the lodgers and Mandy were out at nights, she was finding herself jumping at every little sound in number thirty.

If the television was on, she kept turning down the sound to check that there was no movement in the rooms above. Often she would peer out of the windows from behind the curtains and was sure that a shadowy figure was standing in the porch of the house opposite, which was untenanted at present. Then she would see a parked car that appeared to have a solitary occupant, but in the darkness she might have been deceived - perhaps the car was empty.

Her nerves became tauter with every passing day, and any unexpected sound would make her jump violently. Mandy's suggestion that she pay a visit to Cornwall was appearing more and more attractive, and the thought of a long sensible heart-to-heart with the most practical of her daughters seemed very inviting. When Mandy mentioned that she and Dan had to go on a business trip to Paris, and might extend it to include a weekend break, Nan made up her mind.

"I think I will have a few days away myself when you get back, Mandy. I'll give your Auntie Irene a ring and ask if I can go down. I'll give this place a good clean through and stock up the cupboards while you're away so you'll be able to manage alright while I'm gone."

"That's good, Nan. You are looking definitely under the weather these days."

"Not like you, sweetheart. I've never seen you look so pretty. You and Dan are really getting on well together, aren't you?"

"Oh yes, Nan. He's a wonderful person. We have such fun and he really bothers about me. Always takes care of me, you know? Opens doors for me, helps me out of the car, all the little things. He makes me feel, sort of…cherished, I suppose. Does that sound daft?"

"No, lovie. I know just what you mean. That was how I felt with David..." Nan sighed as her eyes turned towards the familiar silver-framed photograph of herself and David on the mantelpiece.

How long ago that magical time had been, but his memory was sharp and poignant still. The deeply disturbing interlude with her mistaken feelings over Adam had only re-awakened all the old longing that she had managed to subdue in the years since David's death. So now she was able to smile in sympathy at her granddaughter and hope with all her heart that this love affair would have a happier ending than her own.

Mandy packed for her trip in a flurry of anticipation. They would have two days of business and then a whole weekend to themselves before returning on the Monday morning straight to the office. Clement Sanders had called in once or twice, but seemed preoccupied. Dan was of the opinion that he was planning yet another business coup.

"He usually gets a bit secretive when he's got a new idea in the pipeline; likes to get it all sorted out before he drops a bombshell on the rest of us. The bigger the success, the more uncommunicative he is beforehand. Won't give anything away until he's positive he can make it work. That's the boss all over."

"Did you tell him we're staying in Paris for the weekend? Will he mind?"

"I didn't mention it. But it's nothing to do with him, is it? So long as we do our jobs properly and get the business out of the way first, it's up to us how we spend our free time, honey." He slid an arm round her waist and pulled her against him. The lean hardness of his body pressed against her own soft curves, and as usual her pulses raced. Both of them sensed that this weekend would finally see the inevitable result of the heady physical attraction that was magnetising them towards each other.

Nan was glad to sit down on the Saturday evening and put her feet up. She had just finished the end-of-season clear up on the allotment, weeding and hoeing and leaving it tidy for the winter months. She had enjoyed a long hot soak in the bath and then had a chat to Irene on the phone. It was arranged that she would travel down by train to Cornwall the following Wednesday.

On the way back from the allotment she had experienced more strongly than ever the sensation of being followed. When she had turned the corner of Holgate Terrace she could have sworn there was the sound of footsteps following but she had resisted the urge to break into an awkward run. By the time she reached number thirty she had been gasping for breath and was shaking badly. As she stepped down to the basement door, she had glanced behind her and saw a male figure standing halfway along the street.

His coat collar was turned up against the raw November cold, and a trilby hat was pulled low over his eyes. Not unusual garb at this time of year, but why did she have the impression that he wished to conceal his identity? She had stumbled down the area steps and fumbled hurriedly to turn the key in the lock. Once inside, she had, unusually, put the chain on the door. But now, warm and relaxed from her bath, a bowl of home-made soup inside her, a new library book awaiting her enjoyment, Nan was able to laugh at her panic.

Getting old and fanciful, that's your trouble, Nan Stuart. Should know better. Never mind, a few days with Irene and the children, and you'll be back to normal. Then it'll be time to start planning Christmas, I shouldn't wonder. Daresay Mandy will want to be with Dan this year. Perhaps he'd like to come here for the day. Wish our Rita would get in touch - be lovely to see her for a change. Supposing she could come with all her brood - what a crowd we'd be then!

Nan allowed her thoughts to drift idly towards her various grandchildren and her cherished dream of finally getting them all together at number thirty for a 'proper family Christmas'. The warmth of the fire was very soporific and she knew that her book was gradually slipping down her lap as her head nodded forward onto her chest.

The sharp ring of the doorbell abruptly shattered her pleasant reverie and she jerked upwards as her heart pounded in shock. "Whoever can that be now? Perhaps one of the lodgers forgot their key. Right scatterbrains the pair of them." She muttered out loud to calm herself as she belted her pink candlewick dressing gown more tightly round her and made her way along the passage to the front door.

Some residual feeling of anxiety made her leave the chain in position so that she opened the door only far enough to look at the person waiting outside. He said nothing for a moment and she simply stared at the male figure that she recognised as the one who had been lurking at the end of the street earlier that afternoon.

"What d'you want? Who are you?" Nan's voice came out huskily as she attempted to quell the panic that his shape had inspired. It had a terrible familiarity that triggered a rising dread that was knotting her stomach.

There was a strange sense of inevitability that prepared her for the sound of his voice before he actually said a word.

"Hello, Nan. Long time no see, girl. Talk about a bad penny."

"Is it really you?" This must be one of the nightmares that over the years had still plagued her. But the sharp chill of the autumn evening cutting through to her body that was shivering already from shock convinced her that this was painfully real.

"As ever was, Nan. Well, aren't you going to invite me inside? Extend the hospitality of number thirty, just as you did all those years ago?" He chuckled mirthlessly, and without a word she undid the chain and stepped aside to let him into the passage. Needing no further invitation, he walked casually through to the kitchen and stood before the fire, looking curiously round him.

Nan remained rooted in the doorway, one hand clutching the handle for support, since her knees threatened to give way at any moment. He looked back at her with an amused smile, as he tossed his trilby hat on to a chair and followed it with his smart black overcoat. They stared silently at each other, assessing what the years had done, mutually recalling the details of their long-ago last meeting.

"Charlie Stuart, the devil from my past. Or are you just his evil ghost come to haunt me?" Nan's words hissed between them as all the pent-up betrayal and bitterness that she had nourished for forty-three years surged through her body in a storm of emotion.

"No ghost, Nan. Large as life, that's me. If either one of us looks like a ghost at the moment, I reckon it's you. Been a bit of a shock, have I? Why do I get the feeling you're not overjoyed to see me? After all these years, a husband might expect a warmer welcome from his long-lost wife." He laughed again. But the eyes were cold and Nan knew that he was taking great pleasure in deliberately pushing her into a declaration of her hatred.

With a supreme effort at self-control she took a deep breath and sat down on an upright chair beside the table. Clenching her fists in her dressing gown pockets, she managed to steady her voice as she asked levelly, "What have you come back for, Charlie? We both know that any marital bond between us was broken when you abandoned me with your daughters all those years ago in Canada. Left us to starve in the backwoods for all you knew. I seem to remember you even took the last pennies of my housekeeping money from the old tea caddy. Come to rob me again have you? Although you don't look exactly down on your uppers this time."

And it was true. His grey suit was finely tailored and the white shirt and dark tie were good quality. His polished black shoes were of soft leather and he generally exuded an air of well-being. She noticed a gold signet ring on his finger and a solid gold watch beneath his cuff. Along with a smell of the November night air, he had brought into the room a headier fragrance that Nan recognised as an expensive cologne for men.

His weather-beaten face was very lined with a slight puffiness - the legacy of many years of rich food and alcohol. But his head still bore a thick mass of curls, even though now an iron grey, instead of the glossy black she remembered from his youth. His figure was stockier than she recalled - he had always been wiry as a young man - but he was very upright in his stance and unbowed by his seventy years.

Unbidden in her mind, there rose a picture of the last time she had seen him. He had rushed out of their farm cottage near Niagara Falls, in his hand an old bag stuffed with a few personal belongings. He was desperately fleeing from the law and there had been a sweaty stench of fear that rose from his old labouring clothes. The police had wanted him for smuggling across the border to America. It was moonshine whisky that he had manufactured in an illicit still in the old shack in the woods. He was also on the run from some of his poker-playing cronies to whom he owed large sums for gambling losses.

"No, I'm far from down on my uppers, Nan. Just the opposite, in fact." His voice broke into her memories, and she saw him looking about the kitchen with a slight sneer on his mouth. "Mind you, it doesn't look as though a lot's changed at good old number thirty. One or two concessions to the modern world, I suppose. See you've finally got electricity, television as well. And central heating, my word!" He strolled to the scullery. "What's this, a washing machine and a fridge - whatever happened to the old meat safe?

"And let's have a look at you, Nan. You must be, what, seventy isn't it this year? Not many grey hairs yet, but a few wrinkles of course. Still kept your slim figure by the looks of it under that robe. Yes, all in all, you don't look bad at all, girl." He sat down in the chair across the table from her with a patronising smile, and Nan felt a mad impulse to pick up the poker from the grate and smash it across his face.

"Alright, Charlie. You've had your fun. Now tell me what you're doing here really. I know it's not out of concern for me or your family, that's one thing I'd bet my life on."

"Well, Nan, it's hard to say really. I suppose if I'm honest it's mainly curiosity." He nodded at her and she realised that for once that was exactly what he was being - honest.

"All these years I've rarely been back to Blighty. Just occasional trips, but as you can see, I've prospered. Oh yes, I've had my share of bad times - got into more scrapes than enough. Done a couple of stretches inside, lived rough at times, even thought my last hour had come once or twice, but Charlie Stuart always bounced back. Eventually my luck turned and Dame Fortune really smiled on yours truly. Now I've made my pile and I'm enjoying it. I can sit back and let the world go by now. Life's been good the last years and I've started to take stock, Nan.

"I suppose I miss the need to drive myself these days. I've got more money than I could ever spend in my remaining years. There don't seem to be any risks left to take, except in business and they're only paper risks, Nan. Even gambling has lost its edge, now I can afford to lose!

"So I suddenly found myself driving through north London a couple of months ago and I had a fancy to look round Holgate again - the scene of my misspent youth, you might say. I strolled through Ally Pally and thought of all the rolling about we did late at night in the grass. You were a wild little thing then, girl! Looking back, I can't imagine how Emily Fisher's daughter came to lose her virginity with so little struggle!"

Nan's hand raised itself of its own volition in a clenched fist and he caught it effortlessly before she could strike him as she had intended. His fingers were still strong, and a strange electricity crackled between them as they gazed steadily at each other for a moment, the sound of Nan's harsh breathing filling the room.

"So age hasn't taken your temper then, Nan? I remember you had a wicked tongue on you when you were roused, but I don't recall you ever raising your hand to me." He shook his head in mock reproof, and let her go.

"So, as I was saying, I had a fancy to look round the old places and when I saw from the phone book that you were still living here, my curiosity got the better of me. It might surprise you to know I've been keeping an eye on you the last few weeks, girl. Thought I'd see what you were up to."

"So it was you all the time? I don't suppose it bothers you that I've been terrified to think that someone's been following me about? Lucky for you I never called the police." She glared at him, thinking that this was yet another cause for her continued animosity towards him.

"Well, so you were getting scared, eh? No need, girl. I never planned to do you any harm. I might even do you a bit of good if the fancy takes me. Daresay you could do with a few extra quid in the bank, eh? Play your cards right, Nan, and I might be persuaded to be generous!"

"I wouldn't touch a penny of your filthy money. Probably all ill-gotten gains the lot of it! I don't need anything from you. The time when you should have been supporting me and your daughters, you never gave us a second thought, did you? Left us alone struggling to make ends meet for all the years they were growing up. When I think how I worked all hours God sent just to put food in their mouths and clothes on their backs! You've no idea, have you, you swine?"

"My daughters, yes." Unmoved by her tirade, he leaned back and stared at her thoughtfully. "So what's become of the little darlings? All three safely and respectably married and bringing up a mob of grandchildren for us, are they?"

Not answering for a moment, Nan realised that perhaps this was the crux of Charlie's return. Maybe, finally, a sense of mortality was turning his thoughts to his progeny and a desire to make some sort of commitment to their future. With a bitter sense of triumph, Nan thought perhaps a small revenge might be possible at last.

"Yes, they are all happy and safe with families of their own. But if you think I'm going to put you in touch with them, you must be mad. They all know the truth of how you treated us back in Canada and they have nothing but contempt for you. You never wanted to be a part of their lives and they won't want you back at this late date, that I do know. Oh, and just for the record, you had four daughters, not three!"

He stared at her in silence for a moment, a puzzled frown aging his face. "What d'you mean, four? You weren't pregnant when I left, surely? As I recall, you'd been denying me the pleasures of the marital bed for quite a while, ever since that dozy cow of a sister of yours let you know I was smuggling moonshine. If you were in the club, girl, it wasn't mine, that I'd swear!"

"No, Charlie, I wasn't pregnant, thank God. Your fourth daughter wasn't mine at all. But as it turned out, I brought her up along with ours. In fact she believed I was her mother until she was married with a child of her own."

"What are you talking about, woman? Whose child was it? I don't recall that any of the floozies in Welland could have been pregnant when I left. I'd had my hands too full with that sex-mad sister of yours to leave any bastards behind me."

She could see that at last she had rattled his composure, and it was obvious that this quest for knowledge about his descendants was really important to him.

Smiling bitterly, Nan delivered her coup de grace. "You said it yourself, Charlie. Your other daughter's mother was that 'sex-mad sister' of mine, as you're pleased to remember her. She came back to Canada when you abandoned her, as you did us. She suffered God knows what torments to find her way back to me, and she gave birth on the floor of the shack where your baby was probably conceived. I delivered her myself, and I promised her as she breathed her last that I would care for the child like my own. So that was your fourth daughter, Charlie. Satisfied?"

The silence between them lengthened. He had paled beneath his tan and she could see that she had finally managed to shock him out of his smug composure.

"I had no idea she'd come back to you. I thought she'd survive alright. She always seemed tough as old boots, Ruby. I'm sorry, Nan." Just for a second, she heard a faint echo of the young Charlie she had fallen in love with so long ago. The hesitant vulnerability that lurked deep beneath his streetwise instinct for putting himself first in order to survive at all costs. Then he sighed deeply and drew himself upright.

"Well, too late for remorse now, eh? Tell me about the grandchildren, Nan. Are there any boys I can leave my money to, eh? Someone I can groom to take over my business perhaps? Be nice to get to know them all in my last years." He nodded affably and Nan once again felt the rage coursing through her limbs.

"As it happens, you have twelve grandchildren. Six boys and six girls. Joan has two, Irene has four, Rita has five and Mavis, that's Ruby's daughter, has one. But that is all the information you'll get from me on the subject. Suffice it to say that two of those grandchildren live abroad, and none of the others would give you the time of day. So don't bother to try and trace them. It would be a waste of time and your precious money. We've survived without you all this while, so you can go back to obscurity and the past where you belong.

"All these years I've believed you were probably dead, and as far as your family's concerned, dead is how you'll remain. You don't deserve the comfort of their love in your old age, since you never gave them the benefit of yours when they needed it the most. So you can leave now, and I pray to God I never set eyes on you again!"

She rose and looked down at him seated across the table, and their eyes locked in a silent battle of wills. Then he slowly stood up. "Yes, I can imagine they've all been nurtured with tales of my evil misdoings and learnt to worship Saint Nan who never had a wicked thought in her entire life. I don't suppose there would be much point in my contacting them after all.

"I'll think about it though, and believe me, if I choose to upset their staid little lives and perhaps offer them a more exciting future, then I'll certainly find a way to reach them. You'll not stop me, Nan, so don't flatter yourself!"

He picked up his hat and coat and took another slow look round the kitchen. "You never had a ha'p'orth of ambition did you? Quite content to live your humdrum little life in the same drab surroundings. Now you're exactly the sad, embittered old woman I might have expected, Nan.

"What a wasted life! When I think how lovely you were when I first knew you! If only you had dared to reach for something beyond safe domesticity, Nan. What a life we might have led together all these years!"

For an instant she read emotions of real regret and lost love in his eyes, and the voice almost sounded on the edge of breaking down, but then he turned and walked swiftly out of the room.

She heard hasty footsteps along the passage and the

sharp snap of the front door closing. He was gone, and Nan wished from the bottom of her heart that he had not returned from her past to rock the safe security of her existence.

In a different world Mandy gazed through the hotel window at the lights of the Parisian boulevards spread out below. Behind her she could hear Dan whistling in the shower as he got ready to take her out for dinner. This was their third night in Paris and Holgate seemed on another planet. Mandy had phoned her grandmother the evening before to check that all was well and given her the number of the hotel in case of emergency.

She wondered briefly how seriously Nan would view the change in her own relationship with Dan. Knowing what a realist she was, Mandy suspected that Nan would not have been at all surprised by the fact that they were sharing a bed. Possibly her mother might view things a little differently, Mandy mused with a wry smile.

Although Joan had been technically unfaithful to Harry, her affair with Oliver had taken place when she believed her husband had been killed in the war. She had always brought up Mandy quite strictly to believe that nice girls did not have sex until they had a wedding ring on their finger. Mandy had listened to her condemning the permissive society of the sixties, which they were always reading about in the papers, so it was hard for Mandy not to feel a sense of guilt as she turned and looked at her own reflection in the mirror.

She was wearing an exquisite frothy pink lace negligée over a matching bra and pants set that Dan had laughingly bought that afternoon for her in the fabulous Galeries Lafayette department store. It had made her feel incredibly wicked and rather excitingly like a kept woman, but with her scrubbed face, at the moment devoid of make-up, she had to admit she looked more like a little girl dressing up in her mother's clothes.

Dan appeared behind her, wrapped only in a bath towel, his hair still damp and smelling delightfully of soap. He wrapped his arms about her and smiled over her shoulder at their reflections.

"What a gorgeous couple we make! Made for each other, that's us." He turned her towards him and cupping her face in his hands asked tenderly, "Happy, sweetheart? No regrets?"

"Oh, Dan, of course not. I must admit I do feel a bit guilty when I think how my mother would react if she knew, but it's my life and I think I'm entitled to live it the way I choose. Besides, she's hardly likely to find out, so far away in Canada, is she? It might be different if she was still back in Holgate. I'm afraid she'd only have to look me in the eye and I'd blush and she'd guess right away!"

"Don't feel guilty, honey. What we do is our business - we love each other, we're happy, and since we're both free and over the age of consent, I don't see we're harming anyone, do you?

"Besides," his fingers slowly undid the satin ribbon fastening her negligée, and slipped it gently off her shoulders, letting it drop to the floor. "I have every intention of making an honest woman of you in the not too distant future. How about we get married on your twentieth birthday in April?"

"Is this a proposal?" Mandy gasped as his lips traced a path downwards from the hollow between her throat and collar bone and his fingers kept pace, moving down her spine between the lace-covered hook of her bra fastening and the waistband of her pants.

"It's about as formal as you'll get, sweetheart. Us rough colonials don't go in much for bended knees. Although if you really want me to..."He sank down before her, burying his head against the smooth skin of her flat stomach, so that she shivered with pleasure and entwined her fingers in his auburn curls. She knew then that this was a golden moment she would remember as long as she lived - the instant when the rest of her life was mapped out before her.

That whole weekend was total magic. In later years whenever Mandy heard an accordion playing, or smelt a Gauloise cigarette, she would immediately be transported to that time of carefree happiness. She and Dan were utterly caught up in the wonder of discovering each other in their knew-found closeness. They did all the usual tourist activities and revelled in the sheer glory of being young, in love and in the most romantic city in the world.

They climbed to the top of Notre Dame and traced the silvery path of the Seine below them, where the night before they had dined on a Bateau Mouche festooned in coloured lights. They strolled, entwined, through the Tuileries Gardens, past the Louvre and along the Champs Elysées, resting at a pavement café and sipping hot chocolate in the crisp November sunshine. Dan snapped her beside the Tomb of the Unknown Warrior under the Arc de Triomphe, and she persuaded a passer-by to snap them both at the foot of the Eiffel Tower.

They strolled beside the river, fascinated by the bookstalls and pavement artists, then visited the Place du Tertre in Montmartre, where a student quickly sketched them for the price of a few francs. "I'm going to have this framed and put on my desk back in the office. What d'you reckon the boss will say?" Dan laughed as they made their way up the steps of Sacre Coeur and gazed at the rooftops of the city spread out below them.

"Will he mind about us, d'you think? Does he suspect already?" Mandy wondered, and Dan shook his head. "Not him. He just sees us as two employees he pays a very good salary and who he probably imagines eat, sleep and breathe work, like him.

"Besides, he knows I've always been a bit of a wild bloke and played the field in the past. I used to make him laugh with stories of my terrible antics and he'd tell me a few of his own youthful escapades. I'm sure he sees you as a very prim and proper little English girl just barely out of the classroom. It would never occur to him that we might get together." He lifted her hand and gently nibbled the base of her thumb and then tucked it warmly in his pocket.

"So will he be happy for us, then?" Mandy leaned her head on his shoulder and dreamily listened to the street musician playing 'La Vie En Rose' on his accordion behind them.

"I expect he'll be quite happy as long as we continue to do our jobs with the efficiency he expects from all his staff. I don't suppose he'll like it when you leave to have a brood of my babies and he has to find a new secretary!" They laughed at the thought of so much ahead of them - their whole lives to look forward to - and Mandy knew that she would probably never match the exquisite, carefree joy of that period ever again.

When they returned to the office, it was to find a sheaf of memoranda from Clement Sanders, including a message that he was off to Australia for the next month or so to deal with various business matters that needed his personal attention. So the news of their altered relationship remained a secret for a while longer.

Nan seemed rather distracted and quieter than usual, even after her visit to Cornwall. Although she was not as edgy as she had been, Mandy was convinced she had something on her mind, but she resisted all efforts to discuss it. However, with the advent of Christmas on the horizon she seemed to come out of her preoccupation a little. Dan had been invited to spend the holiday with them, and as Alison was going home to her family, Nan said he would be able to sleep in her room. "And don't you dare laugh, or come creeping down to me in the night", Mandy instructed Dan. "I'm sure Nan guessed we shared a room in Paris, but there's no point in making an issue out of it. She'd feel awkward, and also as she's supposed to keep an eye on me for Mum, I expect she'd feel guilty at not doing her job properly. She knows Mum wouldn't approve!"

"No worries. Let's keep the family sweet. After all, I want them to agree to our getting married next year, so I need to create a good impression, don't I?" He grinned engagingly as he sat on the corner of her desk, while she sorted the post.

"I'm really looking forward to this Christmas at your Nan's. It's ages since I had one with a family round me. Not since I was a nipper, I suppose."

"How long ago did your mother die? Was it very awful at the time?" Mandy looked at him sympathetically. He rarely spoke of his family history, and she was eager to know more about it.

"I was back-packing round Europe and she caught a really bad strain of flu. She never looked after herself properly and it turned to pneumonia. By the time I got home, she was dead and buried."

"That must have been terrible for you. What about your father? When did you last have any contact with him?"

"I reckon I was about four when he decided to go walkabout. I can't really remember him at all. Just vague recollections of the blues he used to have with Mum". He fell silent and his face wore an uncharacteristically vulnerable expression. Mandy could see that the emotional scars left by his parents' broken marriage had gone very deep. "The old bloke never contacted us again. Mum said he probably drunk himself to death or died in a pub brawl. Said he was no loss to either of us. Worked her fingers to the bone to look after me, she did. We never starved, but some of the places we lived in were pretty rough, I can tell you. When she bumped into the boss one night at the bar where she worked, it made a big difference, that's for sure."

"Well you're going to have a proper English family Christmas this year to make up for all the rotten ones you've had on your own." Mandy slid an arm round his neck and pressed her cheek against his. Although he was ten years older than her, sometimes she felt he was just like a little boy that she wanted to mother.

It was a wonderful holiday for all of them. Dan set out to captivate Nan with his irrepressible humour and cheerful nature. He arrived at number thirty on Christmas Eve loaded down with gifts and items to supplement Nan's larder. She was overwhelmed at his generosity and was very touched by the huge bouquet of chrysanthemums and roses that he gave her as a special token of his gratitude for her hospitality.

When they sat round the tree on Christmas morning, opening all their gifts, she was almost speechless when she opened the slim blue velvet box containing a delicate gold watch, which was from Dan and Mandy.

"It's too much, both of you, really it is! I've never had anything like this before in my life." Nan was lost for words as she carefully fastened it round her thin wrist and admired the detail of the fine-linked strap.

"You deserve it, Nan. We wanted you to have something really special. It's to say thank you from Dan for making him part of the family, and from me as well. You've taken such good care of me since Mum went to Canada and it's helped so much when I've really missed her and Donnie." Mandy gave her grandmother a warm hug, and they both simultaneously swallowed a lump in their throat.

The most exciting moment for Mandy came when she opened the tiny box that Dan handed her. Inside, nestling on a bed of cream satin, was an exquisite solitaire diamond ring.

"Oh, Dan, it's so beautiful! I can't believe it - you've chosen exactly the sort of engagement ring I've always imagined wearing!"

"Two great minds, love! Told you we think alike didn't I? Shows we're meant for each other!" Laughing he took her hand in his and carefully slid the ring onto her third finger. "If it doesn't feel right, we can easily get it altered."

"It's absolutely perfect! Look, Nan, isn't it wonderful?"

Nan agreed, and privately wondered how Joan was going to react to the news that her daughter had got engaged on Christmas Day. Of course her own letters, as well as Mandy's, had not hidden the deepening relationship between the young couple, but Joan had seemed to have reservations when she wrote back. It was only natural, thought Nan. Being so many miles away, knowing that Mandy was not yet twenty, Joan was bound to feel protective towards her much-loved daughter. But Nan herself felt quite content with the match.

She realised that Dan had certainly sown a few wild oats in the past, but she was convinced that he was committed to his relationship with Mandy and obviously adored her. When the thought fleetingly crossed Nan's mind that at some point he might want to take his wife back to his homeland and make a life for them both in Australia, she swiftly pushed it away. Cross that bridge when we come to it, she admonished herself firmly.

The beginning of 1965 was overshadowed for the whole country by the death of Winston Churchill. To Nan's and Joan's generations, who had lived through the horrors of the war, he would always be a symbol of everything that was strong and courageous about the British spirit. The whole populace mourned as they watched the solemn pageantry of his funeral on television.

In the occasional letters that Nan received from Mavis or her daughter, Joanne, there was news of the war currently being fought in Vietnam. Nan was thankful that Joanne had no brothers who might have to decide whether or not to burn their draft cards. Joanne herself was nearly eighteen and looking forward to entering university. From her letters, Nan gathered that she was more excited about the social life than bothering about any academic achievements.

Mavis was most anxious that she should mix with the type of girls 'who come from good families', which might be interpreted as 'girls whose families are rich enough to make sure their brothers would be an excellent match for Joanne'. But that was typical of the old Mavis that Nan remembered so well from years gone by. I don't suppose she's likely to change now, thought Nan ruefully.

Clement Sanders remained in Australia as the weeks passed. Dan and Mandy had broached the subject of fixing a wedding date several times. He had originally wanted it on her twentieth birthday in April, but Joan was determined that was far too soon. She felt it should be a year later, when Miranda came of age. Of course the young couple felt that was far too long a wait, and were now pressing for the coming September.

Nan wrote to Joan advising that it would probably be as well to agree. "I'm sure they're really serious about each other, and although Mandy is very young, she's always had an old head on her shoulders. The responsibilities of her job have helped her mature even more. As for Dan, he's ten years older than her, and obviously knows what he's doing. I'm sure if you could meet him face to face, your mind would be set at rest." Nan hoped that Joan would see sense and not unnecessarily alienate the young people by withholding her consent. In the event, the whole issue was taken out of their hands by the inexorable hand of fate.

It was in May that tragedy struck. Dan was in Denmark for a fortnight when Clement Sanders returned to London. As usual, Mandy was working long hours while he caught up with items of business that had piled up in his absence. She had completed an enormous pile of letters and taken them in the signature book through to his office for him to read and sign.

"Thanks, Mandy. You've knocked off that lot pretty smartly. While I'm signing them, I want you to take this contract and witness my signature, would you? It's a new deal I've struck with the Scandinavian company who run our fjord tours. They're adding some more boats to the line. Just put your signature and address under mine, thanks." Mandy complied and then took all the mail back to her own desk to put the letters in the envelopes and leave out for the office junior to collect. By the time she had finished, her employer was coming out of his office. She thought he looked unusually strained and there was a hesitancy about his manner as he paused beside her desk.

"I'm leaving myself now, Mandy. If you like, I can give you a lift. I'm visiting someone in north London tonight and I see that you live in Holgate. So you might as well come in the car with me. Strange, all the time you've been working for me, I never knew where you lived." He gave her a vague smile, and Mandy was puzzled.

It was so rare for him to make any sort of personal contact that she didn't find it at all odd that he had only just realised where she lived! Maybe he's mellowing as he gets older, she thought, quickly accepting his offer. A trip in the Jaguar was infinitely preferable to strap-hanging in the tube, that was certain. As the chauffeur negotiated the evening rush hour, Mr Sanders seemed determined to pursue his sudden interest in Mandy as a person outside his employment. He asked about her education, where she had acquired her secretarial training, and what other companies she had worked for prior to his own.

"Holgate is quite a journey for you. D'you take the bus to Wood Green and then get the tube? I used to know it years ago, but I imagine it's changed over the years. Are you still living with your family?"

"Yes, I live with my grandmother - she has two other lodgers as well. My mother remarried and went to live in Canada, so Nan took me in. She's lovely - we get on really well together."

"I see." He was silent, gazing out of the window at the passing traffic. Mandy was content to relax in the comfortable leather upholstery and think how she would regale Nan with the story of living like 'the other half' for a change.

When they reached the outskirts of Holgate, Clement Sanders slid open the partition dividing the interior of the car and gave the chauffeur instructions for reaching Mandy's street.

"You must have a good memory, Sir, if you can recall the actual road. Did you live in the area yourself?"

"For a short time, back in the dim and distant past. But I knew some people in Holfield Terrace, so I can still find my way there."

"Oh, I wonder if my grandmother would know them. She's lived there all her life."

"Who knows? Stranger things have happened." He turned away and his voice became somewhat vague, as though he had no further interest in pursuing the matter. Mandy fell silent, in deference to the change in his mood. So typical of him, she thought. When the car drew up outside number thirty, as she reached to open the door, a ray of evening sunlight glittered on her ring.

The sight seemed to return her employer from his reverie and he said in a more jovial tone. "I see you've acquired a ring while I've been away. Does that mean you're engaged now?"

"Yes, it happened at Christmas actually."

"Well, congratulations. I sincerely trust I won't be losing your services in the near future. I value you very highly, my dear." He smiled at her, and for once the warmth did seem to reach his eyes.

"Oh, no, we shan't be getting married for a while. I'm only just twenty, and although we'd like to get married this summer, I don't believe my mother is too keen. I think the earliest will be September. Probably if she has her way, I'll have to wait till I'm of age!"

"So I shan't have to look for a new secretary just yet. Glad to hear it. Goodnight, Mandy, see you tomorrow." He nodded and sat back in his corner, unfolding his evening paper as he did so.

"Goodnight, Sir. Thank you for the lift." Mandy got out, with a quick wave to George, the chauffeur, who cheerfully touched his cap and closed the door after her. Neither of them noticed that as the car drove off, Clement Sanders was looking out of the back window and watching till Mandy disappeared from view down the area steps.

Over the next few days, she felt unlike her usual self. It didn't help matters being exceptionally busy at work. Clement Sanders was always a demanding boss, and whenever he returned from a prolonged absence the workload was enormous. Usually Mandy enjoyed the challenge, but now it almost seemed too much. Nan eyed her with increasing concern each evening when she returned, white-faced and exhausted, much later than her normal time.

"He's working you into the ground, that man. He may pay you good wages, but it's not fair to expect so much of you. When your Dan gets back, I hope he'll tell him so!" Nan clucked disapprovingly as she removed the dinner plates from the table, Mandy's barely touched.

"Don't fuss, Nan. It's just a question of catching up with the backlog, that's all. We're nearly there now, and I like to keep busy. Besides, Dan is coming home on Friday and we'll have a nice weekend relaxing together. If this good weather keeps up, we'll probably go down to the coast for the day. Some sea air will do me the world of good."

She had left the office a little early on the night that

Dan returned. Even her employer had noticed that she was looking pale and tired and came into her room in the late afternoon. "We seem to have finally caught up with everything now, Mandy. You've done well the last few days, so I suggest you take an early mark. Have a long weekend and put your feet up. You deserve it."

"Thanks, Mr Sanders, it will be nice to miss the rush hour. When Dan comes in, he'll see I've left all his memo's and messages on his desk." She gathered her handbag and jacket and thankfully left the office behind her. She was counting the hours till Dan returned, and hoped that he might come over to see her later. It would probably depend how long the boss kept him talking business, she thought.

In the event, business was one subject that barely entered the conversation. To his surprise, after a few brief words about Dan's trip, his employer gestured to an armchair and said in a serious tone, "Sit down there, Dan. I've something I want to discuss with you. It's about young Mandy."

"Mandy?" Dan grinned at him, as he accepted the can of Fosters that his boss handed him from the bar fridge. "She's told you then? I thought she was going to leave it to me to break the news. Still, that's girls for you, can't keep anything to themselves, can they?"

"Told me what?" He sat down opposite the younger man, a tumbler of scotch in one hand.

"About the engagement. That's what you meant, isn't it?" Dan smiled proudly, as he waited for the expected congratulations.

"She told me she's engaged, yes. Well, actually I noticed her ring and asked her about it. But what have you got to do with it?" He narrowed his eyes, and leaned forward intently, as he awaited the answer.

"She didn't tell you I'm the lucky bloke? Mandy's engaged to me. Isn't it fantastic?"

The silence was almost palpable as Clement Sanders gazed across the coffee table, his expression unreadable. Then very deliberately he swallowed his drink in one gulp and placed the heavy crystal glass down before him.

"No, Dan, you can't be engaged to Mandy. It's quite impossible. Listen to me, and you'll understand why marriage between the two of you is out of the question."

Mandy had almost given up hope of Dan arriving that evening. It was gone nine o'clock, and she had thought his flight from Denmark might have been delayed. Or, more likely, he was held up by Mr Sanders, she thought. She expected him to ring at any moment with words of apology, and plans for meeting the next morning. But then, just as she was deciding to have a bath and go to bed, there was the sound of a car door slamming and Dan clattering down the area steps to the front door.

Her tiredness forgotten, Mandy flung it open and hurled herself into his arms. "Oh, Dan, I've missed you so much. It's been ages - seems much longer than two weeks since you left." As she lifted her mouth to his, she was startled when he didn't respond. Instead of the passionate kiss she expected, he simply pulled her tightly against him, in an embrace so fierce she thought her ribs would crack, and then he silently buried his face against her hair.

"Darling, you're squeezing me to death!" She gasped laughingly, and then grasped his hand. "Come inside and see Nan. No doubt she'll tactfully make herself scarce and then we can say hello properly on the couch!"

But he shook his head, no answering smile on his face. "I really need to talk to you, Mandy. Get your things and come out to the car. We'll go for a drive. There's something we have to discuss..." He turned away, and with an odd sensation of fear, Mandy thought for the first time since she had known him, Dan looked all of his thirty years and more.

Sensing that now was not the moment for questions, she called out to Nan, "Dan's here, Nan, we're just going for a drive", and grabbing her bag and jacket from the hallstand, followed him up the steps to the car. He opened the door, settled her into the passenger seat and then got in himself. Without a word, he started the engine and accelerated away.

The silence lengthened between them as he negotiated the streets of Holgate and then reached the North Circular Road, where he cruised along in the deepening twilight. At last Mandy could bear the tense atmosphere no longer.

"Dan, talk to me, please. What's happened? I've never seen you like this before. What's gone wrong?"

"I don't know how to explain, Mandy. It's just that I suppose I've had time to consider while I've been away and, well - there's no easy way to say this - I don't think we should go ahead with the wedding. We have to break off our engagement."

Mandy gaped at him in amazement. Of all the words she expected to hear, these were the last. "But what's happened to change your mind? Is it someone else? Have you met somebody, is that it?" Her voice faded into almost a whimper, as the pain of visualising him with another woman twisted her physically inside like a knife.

"God, no! It's nothing like that. It's just that I've realised how different our backgrounds are. I'm a lot older than you - you're so young and sweet - and I suppose I just don't think it would work. I'm not good enough for you,

Mandy, you deserve someone a lot better than me."

He shook his head and his voice broke. To Mandy's horror, she saw in the lights of an oncoming car that tears were rolling slowly down his cheeks.

She leaned over and put her head on his shoulder. "Oh, darling, stop talking like this, you're scaring me. Of course you're good enough for me - we're perfect for each other, right? That's what we've always said, haven't we? How lucky we are to have found each other - born on opposite sides of the world, and somehow we've managed to get together? If that's not fate, what is?"

Dan groaned and squeezed her hand. "Oh, Mandy if only you knew!"

"I know that I love you and you love me, and that's all that matters. You do love me, don't you? That hasn't changed has it?" She waited for his answer, in a silence that seemed to last a lifetime, before he said, softly, "Yes, I do love you, sweetheart. That hasn't changed, and it never will."

"Then everything else is nonsense. You're suffering from engagement nerves, that's all. Well, I've got something to tell you which will make you realise how stupid all your doubts are." She sat back, smiling radiantly at him. The road was quiet now, as he had turned off the dual carriageway, driving aimlessly while they talked, and he glanced sideways at her. This conversation was not going the way he had planned, and for the moment he was at a loss.

She looked so adorably young and vulnerable in the dimness of the car's interior. Her face, bare of make-up, hair that she had recently allowed to grow longer, brushed back into a youthful ponytail. How could he tell her the truth and wreck her world?

"I've been longing to phone you in Denmark, but I wanted to wait and tell you face to face. I'd thought we could have a day at the coast and I planned to take a picnic with champagne and tell you at just the right romantic moment, but I can't bear to wait any longer. Dan, I'm pregnant. We're going to have a baby. Isn't it wonderful?"

The shock of her announcement, on top of the previous devastating news he had already received that evening was too much for Dan. Unable to credit what he was hearing, he turned his eyes away from the road, to see the joy and excitement dancing in hers.

Desperately searching for the right words, trying to make sense of tragedy heaped on tragedy, Dan was only vaguely aware of the sudden glare of headlights swinging round the bend ahead. A split second too late he realised that his inattention had allowed his MG to drift towards the centre of the narrowing road. With his final conscious thought, a voice in his head screamed that this was the best solution. Then the impact of the lorry meeting the sports car and turning it over and over blotted out all reality.

It was midnight when the phone rang at number thirty and roused Nan from a fitful doze. She had gone to bed, but never slept properly while Mandy was still out. She always left the landing light on, and if she woke and found it switched off, she knew her granddaughter was safely home, and could settle to an untroubled sleep. Now, as she hurried downstairs wrapping her dressing gown round her, she registered the fact that the light was still on, and an awful premonition of disaster gripped her before she lifted the receiver.

Willing herself to remain calm, she listened to the words of the sympathetic policewoman who was phoning from the hospital casualty department. Mandy's bag had been found in the car and they had seen her address in the front of her diary. Nan shakily wrote down the details of the hospital and said she would be on her way immediately. She was given no information, other than the fact that her granddaughter was seriously injured.

As she put down the phone and strove to control the wave of giddiness that threatened to overcome her, she was thankfully aware of Eva's strong arm around her shoulders. "I heard the phone, Nan. Is it Mandy?"

"Yes, she's been badly hurt in a car crash. I've got to get to the hospital straight away." Nan looked round vaguely, totally at a loss. Each of her seventy-one years sat heavily on her shoulders at that moment.

"You go and dress, Nan. I'll call a cab and then you must have a hot drink while you're waiting for it." Eva helped her back to her bedroom, then ran downstairs again to phone. Nan managed to find her clothes and then sank down on her bed, as the effort of dressing seemed to use up her slender resources. Eva soon returned with a cup of hot, sweet tea.

"Drink this, Nan. I'll get some clothes on myself and come with you. I'll wake Alison and she can be ready to take any message when we get to the hospital. Once you find out how Mandy is, you'll want to phone her mother and your other daughter, Irene, won't you?"

"Yes, yes, I will." Nan gradually pulled herself together as the tea, laced with a little brandy, did its work and the initial shock receded a little. "Bless you, Eva. You are a treasure." She grasped the young woman's hand and essayed a faint smile.

"Maybe I can finally repay a little of your kindness to me, yes?" Eva squeezed her fingers and then went to dress.

They were both ready when the cab appeared, and a shocked Alison waved them off. "Just ring me as soon as you know anything, Nan, and I'll do whatever you want in the way of phoning round. Don't worry, I'll cope with everything this end."

"Thanks, Alison. You're both such good girls." Nan fleetingly recalled how it had been Billy or Harry in the past that had always been there for her in an emergency, now it was the younger generation that she was coming to rely on. Where had all the years gone, she wondered in passing. Anything to stop herself from dwelling on the frightening reality of what might be awaiting her in the emergency ward at the hospital.

When they arrived the sister in charge redirected them to the intensive care unit, and Nan, with mounting dread, knew that Mandy's condition must be very bad indeed. A sympathetic nurse met them and took them into a small waiting room. "The doctor's in there at the moment, but you can see her when he's finished. I'll get you a cup of tea while you're waiting." The minutes dragged like hours, but at last a tousle-haired young man in a white coat entered the room.

"Are you Miranda's grandmother? I'm afraid this has been a nasty shock for you." He sat down beside her and looked seriously into her face. "I have to be honest, her condition is critical at the moment. We're trying to stabilise her but she's lost a lot of blood as well as sustaining a nasty head wound and multiple cuts and grazes from flying glass. When the lorry hit the car it rolled over several times we think, so she took an awful battering. Several cracked ribs and a fractured wrist."

He shook his head, and then said quietly, "But I'm afraid the worst problem is the fact that she was pregnant.

Of course she lost the baby, and haemorrhaged very badly. We operated as soon as she arrived, but there was quite a bit of internal damage. I'm afraid that it's not likely that she could ever have another child. I'm so sorry."

"Pregnant! I'd no idea. I did notice she'd looked a bit under the weather, but she's been working very hard..." Nan pulled herself up. "What about Dan, the driver? They were engaged you see."

"I'm terribly sorry. There was nothing we could do for him. His injuries were...extensive. He would have died instantly at the moment of the crash."

"Oh my poor little Mandy. Whatever will she do?" Nan's voice broke and she buried her face in her hands. Eva put her arms round her and looked at the doctor. "May we see her granddaughter now, doctor?"

"Yes, of course. You can sit beside her, but she's still unconscious. She won't be round from the anaesthetic for a while, apart from anything else." Nan could hear the unspoken words 'that's if she recovers consciousness at all'. With a head injury they really had no idea what would happen, she supposed.

It was heartbreaking to sit beside the still form, hooked up to various frightening-looking machines and dials. Tubes and wires seemed to lead off from every exposed part of her body, and her head was swathed in bandages. Her ashen face was horribly patterned with scarlet abrasions and already discolouring with purple and yellow bruises, which would get worse over the next few hours. The silence was broken by the bleeping and sighing of the various items of life-monitoring equipment and Nan sat with her eyes rivetted on Mandy, trying to will some of her life-force into the young girl.

She was aware of a sense of *déjà vu* and realised it

was the same sort of vigil that she and Harry had spent beside Joan, years ago in Cornwall. But at the back of her mind was the thought that if she did survive, the poor child would have to face the terrible loss of her fiancé, as well as the baby that she would have loved. Add to that the prospect of a childless future and Nan could see that Mandy's life would look bleak indeed, should she recover enough to face it.

Eva tiptoed away at one point to phone Alison and ask her to contact Irene, and request that she in turn contact Joan in Canada. Presumably she would want to fly back to her daughter's side at once.

But even that consolation was to be denied Nan. For it seemed that young Donnie was suffering a bad recurrence of his asthma and had also been rushed into hospital, with the fear that pneumonia could follow. So poor Joan was torn between her two children. Knowing that Nan would not leave Mandy's side, she decided that her place lay with her son. But Irene would be on her way from Cornwall within the hour.

While the doctors were attending to Mandy, Nan allowed Eva to take her to the hospital canteen and force down a slice of toast, although it tasted like ashes in her mouth.

"Is there anyone else we should contact, Nan? What about Mandy's work? Her boss will wonder where she and Dan are. Shouldn't we contact him?"

"Oh, yes, of course. Ask Alison to ring, will you. The number's by the phone. Ask her to explain what's happened. Say we'll let him know about Mandy. Not that he'll be too concerned, I don't suppose. She gives the impression that he's rather a cold fish. But no doubt he will be upset about Dan. Was an old friend of his mother, I believe. I don't know if there is any other family. I don't think so. Perhaps Mr Sanders will know. I suppose there will have to be arrangements made - the funeral and everything..."

Nan's voice faded and she groped in her bag for a handkerchief, hearing the laughter of that happy lad who always had a cheeky grin and a big hug for her. She looked down at her gold wristwatch through a mist of tears, as she recalled Christmas morning such a few short months ago. The poor young couple who had everything to live for, and now this!

The day dragged on and Nan continued her vigil. Irene arrived and took over from Eva. Mandy's condition remained unchanged and each time the doctors paid her a visit, to Nan's fevered imagination their faces seemed even graver. In the late afternoon she sent Irene home to number thirty to collect some fresh clothes and an overnight bag. She was determined to stay at the hospital, and the staff wisely did not argue. There was a small room in the intensive care unit where she might sleep for a while and she would be on hand if any sudden change should occur in Mandy's condition.

After Irene went, Nan was asked to leave during yet another medical examination and sat down in the empty waiting room. She leaned her head back and closed her eyes. She was desperately tired, but her body felt wound up like a tightly coiled spring, and she could not imagine ever sleeping again. But she must have dozed for a few moments because she did not hear the door open or the approach of footsteps, so the familiar voice spoke almost in her ear without warning. "Nan, girl, wake up, it's me."

Slowly her eyelids lifted and she half believed it was a dream as she met the dark eyes boring into her own.

"Charlie, is it you?"

"Yes, girl, it's me." He sat heavily down on the seat beside her and she noticed unthinkingly how lined and exhausted his face had become. His shoulders had a defeated slump to them and there was a look of terrible pain in his expression.

"What are you doing here? Who asked you to come? You've no business in this place. We don't need you." She struggled to sit up straight and put some strength into her voice, but it lacked conviction. Even the old hatred of Charlie Stuart could not overcome the terrible knowledge that her granddaughter might be dying in the next room.

"You may not need me, Nan. But I need to be here. How is she? How's Mandy?"

"There's no change, they say. She hasn't recovered consciousness. The anaesthetic must have worn off by now, so the longer she lies there, the more likely it is that she's suffered brain damage. And she's in shock after losing so much blood of course. If she pulls through I think it will be a miracle. That's what I've been praying for all these hours." She shook her head and buried her face in her hands. Even Charlie's unwanted appearance seemed totally unimportant now.

But he was speaking, and in spite of herself, his words gradually registered. When the full import of what he was saying finally began to sink in, she sat up slowly and gazed at him in silent horror. "When your lodger rang, I had to come over. I couldn't take it in at first. Both Dan and Mandy. It's so terrible - after the shock of what he told me yesterday evening - it's too much to bear, Nan. When he said they were engaged, I knew it had all got to come out, but I didn't realise how he'd take it. When I explained they couldn't get married, he rushed out of the office like a madman. But I had to tell him, Nan, I couldn't let them go ahead, could I?"

"What are you talking about? Tell him what? Why couldn't they get married? You're not making any sense, Charlie. And what were you doing in his office, anyway? How did you come to speak to Alison?" Nan gazed at him, her voice rising in a sudden panic, as the questions poured out of her, but intuitively she knew that the answers would be the last devastating pieces in the tragic jigsaw that this day had uncovered.

"Haven't you guessed, Nan? I'm Clement Sanders. I had to change my name years ago when I came out of prison and wanted to make a new life for myself. I kept the same initials and became Clement Sanders."

"So all this time that Mandy's been working for you, you've known she's your granddaughter? So why did you come to see me last year? Pretending you knew nothing about the family and all the while she was seeing you every day!"

"No, no, it wasn't like that at all, girl!" He caught the fist that she had clenched in rage, and in spite of her struggle, held onto it while he spoke in a low soothing voice as he endeavoured to stave off the rising hysteria that threatened in her voice. "I had no idea who she was, on my life. I had only just decided to spread my business interests into Europe. For years I'd been building up an empire in the East and down under. But there were lots of opportunities over here and it seemed the time was right. Dan was doing well and I wanted to give him his head a bit, see how he'd cope on his own without me looking over his shoulder all the time. It was sheer coincidence that he looked for staff at the agency where Mandy worked.

"Even when I came over myself and met her, I had no

idea. I never enquired about her personal life - she was just a good secretary as far as I was concerned. The same with her relationship with Dan. They appeared to work well together, but I knew he had sown a lot of wild oats and she seemed a real young innocent. It never occurred to me for one moment they might get involved."

"So when did you realise your own granddaughter was your secretary?" Nan's voice was calmer now and she removed her hand from his.

"Very recently, as it happens. I asked her to witness a contract for me. When I saw her address I nearly had a heart attack, I can tell you. Then, looking at her, I could see you, and young Joanie of course. Even then I kept thinking it might not be true. I thought maybe she just lodged with you, but of course she told me she lived with her grandmother when I gave her a lift home one night."

"I heard all about it. Really thrilled she was, riding in the boss's Jaguar. Said it was how the other half lived. So why didn't you say anything to her? Weren't you going to tell her the truth?"

"I hadn't made up my mind. I guessed from what you said that none of the family had ever heard a good word about me from you. I wasn't sure there was a lot of point in opening up the past. This way I kept my eye on her and through her, the rest of the family. I did think I might get to know her a bit better, become more of a friend than an employer in time. It was such a shock, I hadn't really come to terms with it."

"You're breaking my heart, Charlie! Don't forget the reason your family haven't got a good word for you - it's the result of how you treated us in the past. If you'd really cared, really regretted what you did, how is it you never came in search of us when you first made a success of your life? Not that we'd have wanted your filthy money, but it would have showed you cared - that your conscience had finally surfaced after all these years!"

"Go on, Nan, spit out your bitterness and venom. No doubt I deserve it, and what I've got to tell you now won't make you think any the better of me. But you might as well know the whole truth. You can decide after that what to tell Mandy - if she survives, poor kid."

He closed his eyes for a moment and swallowed hard, and Nan caught a glimpse of the youthful, vulnerable Charlie who had appealed so much to her girlish heart. Then, staring straight ahead, hands clasped between his knees, he brought his tragic story to a close.

"When Dan came back to the office last night he told me that he and Mandy were getting married. I'd commented on her ring, but never asked who the chap was. I never thought for one moment I'd know him. When Dan told me the news I was astounded. It was like some terrible Greek tragedy unfolding in front of my eyes.

"I tried telling him that it wouldn't work - the difference in their ages and background - that kind of thing, but of course it was grasping at straws. When he realised I was seriously trying to persuade him to change his mind, naturally he got angry, with good reason. Lost his temper and told me his private life was none of my business. Was all set to resign and walk out then and there."

Charlie laughed, mirthlessly. "What a chip off the old block, eh. I don't think I've ever been so proud of him, Nan. But watching his face, as I told him the real reason why they couldn't marry, that was like a knife going through me, girl. I reckon I paid a bit for all my wrongdoing in that moment. Not that you'd believe it, I know."

"The real reason. What was the real reason, Charlie?"

Nan whispered, her pulse fluttering in her throat, which had suddenly become very dry.

"Dan was my son, Nan. I'd met his mother years ago when I was a shearer in the outback. Her old man was a bad lot - thought nothing of beating her black and blue when the fancy took him. Had a string of Abo women as his mistresses and led her a dog's life. I made her laugh and we had some good times together. Then I moved on to the next station and that was that. I had no idea that she got pregnant.

"Years later, after I'd made my pile and the business was expanding, I just walked into this cocktail bar in Sydney, where she was a waitress. We recognised each other at once and had a drink for old times' sake. Then she told me about Dan. Her old man had gone walkabout, although she let him believe that Dan was his, and she had brought him up on her own. And a good job she did. I expect you're thinking I make a habit of leaving my women to bring up my offspring, aren't you, girl?"

"Well it's no lie, is it, Charlie?" She sighed deeply as she looked at his bowed head and knew now the rest of the story before he recounted it.

"I explained to Dan that I was his father. Well, I'd always intended that, some day. I'd made a will already, leaving everything to him, but I wanted him to gradually take over the business from me on his own merits, not just because he was the boss's son.

"Then of course I had to tell him about Mandy. She had mentioned to him about the villain of a grandfather who had abandoned his family in the wilds of Canada, so he knew what I was talking about. But even then it didn't really sink in. I had to spell it out for him, poor devil. The reason they couldn't marry - that Mandy was his own niece."

"Half. She would be his half-niece. Dan was Joan's half brother."

"Alright, half-niece, but it was still too close a relationship for them to marry, wasn't it? Or should I have let them go ahead in blissful ignorance? Is that what you think?" Now Charlie's voice was rising, and Nan realised just how deeply he had been hit by all of this.

"I don't suppose you could have, Charlie. It would have been wrong to have kept it from them."

"'Course it would. Supposing they'd had kids. Who knows how they might have turned out. I said that to Dan. I suppose they might have gone ahead and made sure there weren't any children. But I still think it would have been wrong, wouldn't it, Nan?" He turned to her, his look begging her to tell him that he'd made the right decision.

"Yes, Charlie it would have been wrong. In fact the decision was already out of your hands. You see Mandy was pregnant with Dan's baby. But she lost it last night in the crash. That's why her life's hanging in the balance, I think. Even if she does live, she'll never be able to have children now."

"Oh, my God, Nan! I'm so sorry. So terribly sorry." Charlie put his head down and sobbed. Nan stared at him unmoving for a moment.

All through the years she had reflected on Charlie's wrongdoing, harbouring so much bitter resentment at his betrayal with her own sister. The privations she and the children had suffered because of his abandonment, followed by so many years of drudgery for her as she struggled to give the four girls a decent home - endlessly she would turn over the awful catalogue of his sins.

Although she was now in her seventies, the scars still

had not faded and the fires of loathing that she had stoked so assiduously in her soul burned just as brightly as when she had been a young mother in her twenties.

But looking at his bowed head and listening to his racking sobs, it all finally slipped into the oblivion of the past. It seemed that now Charlie Stuart was just beginning to pay the penance for all his wrongdoing, and to her own tired surprise she took no pleasure in witnessing his agony.

"It's too late for repentance now, Charlie. Too late for bearing malice as well, I'm finally realising. The past is past, and we can't unravel the twisted consequences - we just have to live with them and suffer for our own wrongdoing.

"When you left us alone in Canada and then had your careless fun with Dan's mother, it was all written in the fates, wasn't it? That these two lovely youngsters would pay the price for your sins. Sins! There's an old-fashioned word! I can just hear my old dad using it.

"There was a man who hated you, Charlie. With his dying breath he called you my nemesis and predicted that your descendants would bring me pain through all my life. Seems he was right, doesn't it?" She shook her head and closed her eyes, so bone-weary that it was all like some nightmare that she no longer had the energy to endure till its end. Charlie's sobs were the only sounds to break the silence for long minutes, and then the door opened and the young doctor stood before them.

"Mrs Stuart, good news at last. Miranda has just regained consciousness. Her condition seems to have stabilised and I think she's turned the corner."

The next days passed in a sort of daze for Nan. So many painful emotions were churning her up that physically she wondered how long she could keep herself going. Mandy was asleep for much of the time, and still heavily sedated to combat the pain and shock of her injuries. Her face was a dreadful sight as all the bruises and cuts changed it from deadly white to all shades of purple, blue and yellow. After a few days she was moved from the intensive care unit into a small private room - this Charlie insisted on organising.

He came each day to the hospital and would spend a little while at Mandy's bedside, mostly when she was asleep. Nan would sit watchfully by, ill at ease seeing them together. He ensured the room was filled with flowers and fruit, and when Mandy saw him and tried to talk to him, he always assumed his Clement Sanders persona. It was strange for Nan to hear him change in his voice and mannerisms. He became the wealthy businessman, used to ordering people about and used to having them obey. She found it hard to remember to call him Mr Sanders in front of Mandy, and treat him as an employer.

But he never stayed more than a few moments when Mandy woke up, just telling her he was glad to see she was making good progress and asking if she needed anything.

"It's kind of him bothering so much. I always thought he was a very unfeeling sort of man, never caring about his staff, but I really misjudged him, didn't I, Nan?"

Her voice was flat and expressionless and she lay perfectly still, propped up on her pillows, her arms stretched out on top of the hospital covers. She was wearing her own pink nightdress that Nan had brought in, and it seemed to drain every vestige of colour from her face. When the nursing staff brought her food, she would lethargically spoon up the mouthfuls, but showed no interest in the choice of menus, to which, being a private patient, she was entitled.

Sometimes Irene, Alison or Eva would visit as well as Nan, but Mandy's responses to all their conversational attempts were polite but disinterested. Nan dreaded as the days passed that she would speak of Dan. Charlie had arranged all the legal formalities and the funeral had taken place very quietly. Nan, Irene and Charlie had attended the brief service at the crematorium and seen the ashes scattered in the gardens there.

Nan had wept terribly as she remembered the lovely young man who might have been Mandy's husband and the father of her own great-grandchild. But then she remembered his birth relationship through Charlie, which would have made the situation so impossible - and she wept even more bitterly.

Mandy insisted after two weeks that Irene should return to Cornwall. "There's no point in your stopping up here away from your family, Auntie Irene. They must all miss you and I'm sure Uncle Robert is at his wit's end trying to run the farm and cope with all of them. I expect I'll be out of hospital soon, anyway, won't I, Nan?"

"'Course you will, pet. You get back to Cornwall and the farm, Irene. It's been lovely having you here, but your own family need you." She patted her daughter's arm gratefully, and Irene nodded. "Alright, Mum. I know you've got that nice Mr Sanders to turn to if you need anything. He must think the world of you, Mandy. He's been really good hasn't he?"

"Yes, but it's only what she deserves. He's always saying what a wonderful secretary she is." Nan found it very hard to go on with the pretence about Charlie. She had wondered very briefly the first time he had encountered Irene if there would be any flicker of recognition between them, but of course it never happened. The twins had been only a year when Charlie had gone out of their lives.

It had been unavoidable meeting him so often, sometimes being thrown together when they had to wait outside Mandy's room while the doctors were with her, that gradually Nan had given him brief details about the family. He seemed pleased that Joan and Irene had done well, and gently amused that Rita had inherited his own feckless streak. He was less interested in Mavis and Joanne, and Nan suspected that over the years his guilt had forced him to try and forget her betrayal with Ruby.

One afternoon as she sat knitting by Mandy's bed, the moment she had dreaded arrived. Without any preamble, her granddaughter said quietly, "Dan died in the accident, didn't he, Nan? And my baby as well?"

"Oh, lovie, I'm so sorry."

Nan reached out her hand towards her, but she smiled and shook her head. "It's alright, Nan. I've known since I first woke up, I think. I just haven't wanted to talk about it. I did feel it was my fault though - I'd just told him about the baby, as he was driving along. I think he was so surprised he took his attention away from the road and didn't see the lorry till it was too late. Silly of me, telling him something so important just going along in the car..." She bit her lip and Nan thought the tears would come, but she controlled herself and asked, "Did the doctor tell you about the baby, Nan? I suppose you were shocked?"

"Not me, lovie. Remember I was pregnant with your mum when I got married. It happens that way sometimes. It always has and always will. These may be the swinging sixties, but sex has been here for a lot longer than that, you know!"

"Oh, Nan, you are lovely! What would I do without

you?"

"You'd manage somehow, I daresay." She picked up her knitting and wondered how to ask if Dan had told Mandy about the enormous revelation that Charlie had made to him that night. Somehow she thought not, as the young girl had not shown any signs when talking to Charlie. But she had to know for sure.

"I don't suppose you can remember much of that evening, can you? The doctors were saying that when you've been in a crash you usually forget everything that happens just before and after it."

"No, I do remember, Nan. Dan had been talking rather oddly. I think being away had given him time to think about us and our future, and it had sort of scared him. He was saying maybe we shouldn't get married - the difference in our ages and backgrounds were important. Said he wasn't good enough for me..." She choked and Nan handed her a tissue.

"Of course I said he was being really stupid. That if we loved each other, that was all that mattered. Then I told him about the baby - and then I saw the lights of the lorry." There was a long silence and the pain in her eyes nearly broke Nan's heart.

When Mandy was given the news that she was about to be discharged from hospital, Nan asked Charlie to come and have a discussion with her in the hospital garden. It was high summer now and the flowerbeds were a riot of colour. They chose a seat beside a vivid display of marigolds and their smell in later years always reminded Nan of that moment.

"Mandy is coming home soon and she has got to try and get on with her life again. The only way is to put the past behind her. I've suggested that as soon as she's strong enough she goes on a long visit to Joan in Canada. The change of scene and being with her mum and brother will do her the world of good."

"Yes, that's a splendid idea, Nan. When she's ready to go, I'll book the flight for her. My expense, of course."

"Very well, Charlie. And that's where it stops."

"What do you mean 'stops', Nan?"

"You step back and bow out of her life. When she returns to London she will be much better working for someone else, with no daily reminders of Dan. She'll never forget him, of course she won't, but she's young and in time, God willing, she'll meet someone else. There's no reason for you to keep in touch after that. Give her a good reference and let her go."

Charlie looked at her in silence. For a moment she expected he would argue.

"She doesn't know anything about our relationship or Dan's, does she? He didn't tell her that night, did he?"

"No, she just thinks you're a very caring employer, and that's how it must stay, Charlie. In fact the best thing would be if you closed down your European interests and moved back to Australia permanently. But that's up to you of course.

"Circumstances have brought you back into our lives, but it can't do the rest of the family any good to know about it. For Mandy it would only add to all the heartache of the last few months. She's a sensitive girl and in a very emotional state at the moment, and I won't have you taking the risk of upsetting her further. If you sever all contact, there's no chance of the truth coming out.

"If you really care anything at all for her, it's the one thing that you can do to help her future happiness. Perhaps it's fate's way of paying you out for your past wrongdoing and giving you a chance to make some sort of retribution."

The silence was unbroken except for the humming bees collecting the pollen from the blazing yellow flower heads, and the distant sound of an ambulance's siren as it brought another casualty to the emergency department.

Then Charlie sighed heavily. "I know you're right, Nan. But it's hard, girl. Dan had come to mean a lot to me - the only family I thought to have in my old age. Now I've seen for a short time what my own family might have been like. I've been like a passer-by peering into a window, and I wish I could be part of it. But I know I can't rock everyone's boat now. As you say, it will be the price I'll have to go on paying.

"Don't worry, I'll say goodbye when she leaves this place and I expect I'll go back to Australia. If I send you my address, would you consider letting me know how you're all getting on, Nan? Would that be too much to ask?"

"Let me think it over, Charlie. But I'll probably decide against it. It will be better for everyone if we cut the ties and keep our distance, as you've done from us all these years."

She looked deep into his eyes and knew that, although the anger and bitterness had finally been purged from her memories, much as she wished it might be different, there was no way she could ever forgive the transgressions of his past.

Returning her gaze he recognised this, as he said quietly, "You're a hard woman, Nan Stuart".

"You should know, Charlie. It was a hard man that made me this way," said Nan.

EPILOGUE : SEPTEMBER 1966

For the first months after Mandy left hospital, it seemed that she would never recover any of her former positive outlook on life. She spent a month in Canada with Joan and her family and did her best to respond to all their loving kindness. If Joan had condemned her daughter for the passionate relationship with Dan that had ended in her pregnancy, she never voiced it. Indeed, the knowledge that her daughter would be unable to have any further children was enough to arouse her maternal sympathy to the exclusion of all other emotions.

Mandy was pleased to be with them all again - in particular she enjoyed young Donnie's company - but somehow she yearned to be back in Holgate and the safe familiarity of number thirty. Nan of course had missed her dreadfully and was eagerly preparing for her return in time for Christmas when she bumped into an old friend.

"Hello, Mrs Stuart, how are you keeping?" It was young Paul Marriott looking very smart in a business suit and with a new assurance about him.

"Paul! Well this is a surprise. We haven't seen you about for ages. What are you up to these days?"

"Well, I've finished at college and I'm working for an engineering company in the City. I like the people and hopefully there's a really good career opportunity with them."

"Well I am pleased for you, lad. I know how hard you worked at school and college, so you deserve to get on. Are you still living in Holgate with your mum and dad?"

"Yes, for the time being. It means commuting to London every day, but it's a chance to save a bit, then I'll maybe get a place of my own in a year or so.

"How's Mandy getting on? I heard about the accident - it was terrible her fiancé getting killed like that. I wanted to pay her a visit, but I wasn't sure if she'd feel like seeing me. We sort of drifted apart after I went away to college, but I was really sorry to hear what happened."

"That's nice of you, Paul. As a matter of fact she's been staying with her mother in Canada, but she's coming home next week. I'm really looking forward to it. I think physically she's recovered alright, but emotionally it's probably all left a lot of scars. Now she's got to try and pick up the pieces of her life. I suppose her first priority is to get a new job."

"D'you think it would be O.K. for me to call and see her soon? If she's at a loose end she might be interested in joining a local drama group that's just started up. I've been to a couple of meetings and it looks as though it'll be fun. She was great acting in the school plays, so maybe it would take her out of herself if she's feeling depressed still."

"Paul, I think you might be a life saver! Come round when you like next week and have a chat. Take it slowly and don't try and pressure her, she's very fragile at the moment, but I'm sure some young company will be the tonic she needs."

And so Mandy began the long road back to normality. It was a slow process at first, but Nan was relieved to see her gradually improving. She started work for her old temping agency in town, and would often travel on the same train as Paul.

After some initial persuasion she went along to the auditions his drama group was holding and was given a part in the next production. Once involved, she quickly became absorbed in the play, and Nan was relieved to see her laughing and talking enthusiastically with Paul when he gave her a lift in the secondhand Mini he had just acquired.

As the early months of 1966 passed it seemed that Mandy had really put the tragedy of Dan and the accident behind her. She no longer wore her engagement ring and her relationship with Paul was progressing slowly but surely into a more significant phase. The youthful infatuation of their schooldays had now become a loving and close friendship. It was obvious that Paul was devoted to Mandy and she had come to rely on his quiet strength. It was no surprise at all to Nan when they announced their engagement on Mandy's twenty-first birthday in April.

She had refused to have a big celebration, but had gone with Paul to see a show in London after dinner at a very smart restaurant. The ring he gave her was a small hoop of sapphires, nothing like as glamorous as Dan's offering but she was more than content with it.

"I feel so lucky to have found Paul again, Nan. He's such a kind, considerate person. He's far more serious than Dan, doesn't have his crazy sense of humour, but we do have fun together and I know he cares a lot about me."

"And what about you, lovie? Do you really love him? Are you quite sure?"

"Yes, Nan, I am. It's not the grand passion that I had with Dan, but I don't believe that ever happens more than once in a lifetime. I've told him about everything that happened between Dan and I. He knows I lost a baby and that the doctors say I won't be able to have another."

A look of pain crossed her face and her eyes filled with

tears. "Paul is so wonderful, Nan. He says it's me he loves. He's not bothered about children, but if we decide to have them in the future, we can always adopt. I'm so lucky to have found such an understanding person, aren't I, Nan?"

"Yes, Mandy, you are. But as long as you realise it, and do all you can to make him happy, then I reckon he'll be pretty lucky too."

So now it was a golden September afternoon and the whole family had assembled at Holgate church for the wedding. To Nan's delight, Rita and all her brood had been rounded up for the occasion and come to stop over at number thirty, sleeping on the floor where necessary! Joan, Adam and Donnie were on holiday from Canada and of course Irene, Robert and family were all up from Cornwall. Even Mavis and Joanne had made the trip from America, stopping at the Dorchester of course!

Watching as the photographer assembled them all around the bride and groom for the family groups, Nan was almost bursting with pride.

Mandy had all five of her female cousins as bridesmaids, in a 'rainbow' wedding. Joanne at nineteen was statuesque and confident in green, her auburn curls catching on fire in the sunshine. Rita's daughter Kate, aged eighteen, was paired with Irene's sixteen year old June, both pretty and slightly plump in pale lavender which set off their dark colouring. Rita's other two girls, Sally and Beth, aged fourteen and thirteen, were bubbling extroverts in pale lemon.

Rita herself was looking quite matronly these days, her generous curves bursting out of a brightly patterned summer dress whose mini skirt was highly fashionable, but not quite suited to her age or figure. Beaming placidly beside her, Matt had changed little from the shy young soldier that Nan remembered when Rita had first met him in the NAAFI. Their boys, Benjy and Luke, now twenty and nineteen, were both stocky young men whose ruddy complexions and muscular frames bore witness to their active life on the canal boats.

Irene and Robert were their usual well-dressed confident selves. His hair was thinning a little now and she too had put on a little weight, but her elegant cream dress and jacket with a tiny matching hat proclaimed her the comfortable, middle-class wife and mother that she would always be. Their twins, Christopher and Callum, now eighteen and just starting at university, were handsome boys, towering over their father, and were so identical even their parents had difficulty in distinguishing them. Their younger brother, Malcolm was a gangling thirteen-year-old, struggling with spots and not sure what to do with his arms and legs, ill at ease in his first grown-up suit.

All my children together for once, thought Nan happily. Even the sight of Mavis in her stunning yellow Chanel suit, diamonds at her ears and throat glittering in the sun, was unable to shake the mood of quiet contentment she experienced at seeing them gathered for this happy day.

Looking at Mandy brought a lump to Nan's throat, and seeing Joan also gazing fondly at her daughter, it was obvious they were thinking the same thoughts. Mandy was an ethereally beautiful bride in a simple, straight dress of wild silk. The long sleeves with their tiny buttons and the sweetheart neckline all emphasised her dainty figure and charming femininity. Her lace veil trailed behind her, falling from a circle of white rosebuds, matching those in her bouquet, mixed with freesias that echoed the colours of the bridesmaids' dresses.

Nan prayed that she would never lose the air of radiant happiness that surrounded her as she laughed up at her handsome bridegroom, in response to the photographer's instructions. If Paul had his way, Nan knew that her granddaughter's path would be strewn with rosebuds for the rest of her life.

As she was pulled forward to join the family group, she was the picture of the proud family matriarch. Still upright and slim in an elegant lavender suit, a picture hat, gloves, bag and shoes all in dove grey, she belied her seven eventful decades. Her skin was a little more lined, there was more grey in her hair, but her eyes still sparkled with life and the joy of living.

From the smoked glass windows of the large car standing unobtrusively in the corner of the car park opposite the church, a pair of dark eyes wistfully examined the family gathered together. Unaware of the spectator, they laughed and joked as they prepared to hurl their confetti over the young couple about to depart.

Strange to think that they were all his descendants, one way or another, all a product of that first encounter with Nan as she stepped off the tram back in 1918. Now he was an old and lonely man, surrounded by every comfort that money could buy, successful in the eyes of the business world. But he was reduced to watching his own family as a stranger, hidden from their view.

Nan had remained adamant that no good would come of their keeping in touch. But he made sure that a private enquiry agent had kept him informed of Mandy's progress and although he no longer had his own business interests in Europe, he had determined he would see his eldest grandchild on her wedding day. Now he sat back and watched as the whole family departed for the reception from which he was barred.

He did not blame Nan for her implacable and unforgiving attitude towards him. He had given her good cause. But if she believed that Charlie Stuart was bowing out of all their lives forever, then she was sadly mistaken. Some day, some how, their paths would cross again, the fates would ensure it. The old man nodded to himself with a sad smile, and then ordered his chauffeur to drive to the airport.

For today, Charlie Stuart would be unseen at the family feast, but when the time was right they would finally come face to face with the living spectre from their grandmother's past and she would be powerless to prevent it.